Learning to

Fearful Rancher

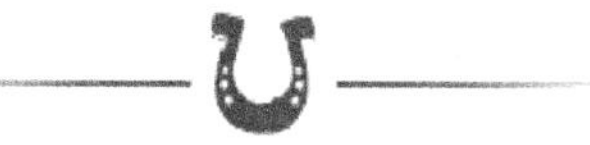

STAND-ALONE NOVEL

A Western Historical Romance Book

by

Ava Winters

Disclaimer & Copyright

Table of Contents

Let's connect!

Impact my upcoming stories!

My passionate readers influenced the core soul of the book you are holding in your hands! The title, the cover, the essence of the book as a whole was affected by them!

Their support on my publishing journey is paramount! I devote this book to them!

If you are not a member yet, join now! As an added BONUS, you will receive my Novella "**The Cowboys' Wounded Lady**":

FREE EXCLUSIVE GIFT
(available only to my subscribers)

Go to the link:
https://avawinters.com/novella-amazon

Letter from Ava Winters

"Here is a lifelong bookworm, a devoted teacher and a mother of two boys. I also make mean sandwiches."

If someone wanted to describe me in one sentence, that would be it. There has never been a greater joy in my life than spending time with children and seeing them grow up - all my children, including the 23 little 9-year-olds that I currently teach. And I have not known such bliss than that of reading a good book.

As a Western Historical Romance writer, my passion has always been reading and writing romance novels. The historical part came after my studies as a teacher - I was mesmerized by the stories I heard, so much that I wanted to visit every place I learned about. And so, I did, finding the love of my life along the way as I walked the paths of my characters.

Now, I'm a full-time elementary school teacher, a full-time mother of two wonderful boys and a full-time writer. Wondering how I manage all of them? I did too, at first, but then I realized it's because everything I do I love, and I have the chance to share it with all of you.

And I would love to see you again in this small adventure of mine!

Until next time,

Ava Winters

Prologue

New York City, New York, June 1885

"Tell us a story, Aunt Penny, pleease!"

Penny White tousled her five-year-old nephew's curly brown mop with a smile. "You'll have to ask your mama, Hamish. It is very nearly your bedtime, you know."

The little boy immediately transferred his attention to his mother who sat on the opposite side of the gently hissing coal stove, mending a torn dress sleeve. His big, ocean blue eyes begged her silently to say yes as the rain pattered on the shingle roof above and the drip-drip of leaks added their unique syncopated rhythm.

"Just a short one, Evie," Penny rallied to her nephew's cause.

Evie's soft gray eyes seemed tired in the light of the kerosene lamps as she looked up from the ripped seam she was restitching. Those beloved eyes seemed more tired than Penny could remember, to say nothing of the deepening dark circles beneath them. Her oldest sister's skin was sallow and haggard, and her black, wavy hair hung listlessly around her shoulders in ragged wisps. Evie barely managed a wan smile. Before she could answer, another voice filled the small room.

"I think I'd like to hear a story, too."

Penny turned her gaze to her middle sister, Sarah, who sat knitting a colorful sweater for Hamish from castoffs she had gleaned from the local mill. The clickety-clack of her needles tapped a ragged tattoo in time with the drips from the roof. Penny gave her middle sister a grateful blink. Sarah's smile blossomed, lighting up her pale face and soft blue eyes, even though her cheeks were just as hollow as Evie's, her mahogany brown hair just as lifeless.

"Come to think of it, so would I," Evie relented, giving the room a quick sweep with pained eyes. Penny knew what her sister was thinking as those gray eyes scanned the peeling wallpaper on the bare walls; the scuffed and worn floorboards; the shabby drapes that covered the tiny window; the wooden pails and chipped bowls that caught the rain from a roof that leaked like a sieve, no matter how many oil-soaked rags they stuffed into the myriad holes. A bundle of bedclothes lay stacked in the only truly dry corner, ready to be shaken out and snuggled into by four tired and shivering bodies.

Penny herself found it difficult to look at the interior of their attic home without feeling something close to despair. It was one of the reasons she loved to read and to make up her own stories. It was an escape. An escape that appealed to her very much in that moment.

As Hamish clapped excitedly and then snuggled up on his favorite aunt's lap, Sarah added another shovelful of coals to the stove and Penny closed her eyes. The old rocker she sat in creaked and sighed as she rocked slowly back and forth.

"Once upon a time, in a land far, far from here," she began, and then opened her eyes again to look into the expectant face of her young admirer, "there lived a prince named Hamish the Kind."

Hamish blinked rapidly. "Oh!" he exclaimed. "He has the same name as me!"

"Fancy that," Sarah said, giving Penny a wink.

"Did he live in a palace, Aunt Penny?" Hamish prodded.

"Oh, yes, but not any kind of palace you've ever heard of," Penny assured him. "Prince Hamish's palace was made entirely of living palm trees, waving slowly in a gentle, warm tropical wind. Prince Hamish had a huge hammock strung between the trunks of the trees and filled it with the biggest, softest, fluffiest down pillows you could ever imagine. At night he would lie on his back, floating on pillows and imagine he was sleeping on the clouds. Staring up at the inky black sky, he'd watch the stars playing hide-and-go-seek with each other behind the waving palm fronds."

The look on Hamish's face was all the evidence Penny needed to know that the real Hamish, the little boy living in a run-down tenement in Manhattan's Five Points slum, had already been transported away to the land of make believe she was weaving with her words. The ache in her heart made her eyes sting. If only she really could take him away from all the squalor and stench, the clamor and cold, to a place where they all could be safe and happy.

"Prince Hamish's beautiful mother and her two younger sisters lived in the palm palace with him. Night after night they would dance the hours away to beautiful music played by an orchestra of forest animals. Elephants blowing big silver trumpets, a chimpanzee on the grand piano, a great flock of flamingoes playing the strings with their long, pink legs. Prince Hamish and his family would dance till their feet could dance no more and their faces ached from smiling and laughing."

Penny looked down at Hamish. His head lay in the crook of her arm, his eyes closed, lashes fluttering fitfully. His breathing was deep and rhythmic.

"I'd say our little prince has already flown away to his palace," Sarah whispered, her mouth curved up in a tender smile.

"Perhaps we should join him in that castle in the sky," Evie said, laying down her mending with a sigh as she stretched out her back. "I know I could do with a hammock full of pillows."

Penny's heart broke. It wasn't fair that Evie and Sarah worked their fingers to the bone in Seamus Murphy's filthy, run-down sweatshop while she stayed at home all day. Keeping their tiny hovel as clean as she possibly could and taking care of Hamish were pursuits of leisure compared to the backbreaking, finger numbing, soul killing slavery that her sisters were subjected to.

"I can see in your eyes that today was an especially hard day," she said. "I wish you'd reconsider and let me work some of your shifts. Mr. Murphy won't know the difference. Then you can spend more time with Hamish, Evie. And the both of you could get some more rest. It's not human the way he treats you."

The look on Evie's face made Penny stop speaking abruptly. She had more to say but knew from experience that it would be better not to.

"That is exactly why I won't tolerate you setting foot in that place," Evie said grimly.

"You think Murphy won't notice, but he will," Sarah said softly. "He's already singled out Evie. Keeps trying to get her to be his mistress."

Penny stifled a gasp.

"And he's extra hard on Sarah," Evie added. "Says she smiles too much, so that must mean she doesn't have enough work to do. He's forever piling more onto her quota for the day. First it was ten coats, then twelve, now he's threatening to make her do fourteen a day."

Penny was horrified. She knew things were bad there, but these were things her sisters hadn't told her before.

"Oh, I'll show him a thing or two. Just let me take your place for one day, Evie!" she blurted out. Hamish stirred and mumbled into her shoulder. Penny quickly shushed him, running her hand over his messy curls.

"He'll eat you for breakfast, Penny," Evie said sadly. "Besides, that building gives me the horrors. It creaks and groans more than most of the workers in it. I wouldn't be able to live with my conscience if I allowed you to spend so much as a minute inside it. Please let it be, love. I need you to take care of Hamish. And, besides, there's your writing."

Penny huffed impatiently. "Writing? What writing?"

"Haven't you heard anything back from the publishers yet?" Sarah asked.

"Yes. I did. They turned me down. Again."

"I'm so sorry, dear." Evie stood up and went to place a commiserating hand on her youngest sister's shoulders. "It makes no sense. You write such beautiful stories for children."

Penny sighed. "Apparently the editors at *Our Little Men and Women* periodical don't think so." She paused as Hamish shifted in her arms, his mouth partly open, snoring softly. "Only you and Hamish appreciate my work. I may as well resign myself to that fact."

Evie knelt down on the floorboards beside the rickety rocking chair and gently stroked her son's cheek. "Papa would have said, 'Perseverance pays. Keep at it, Penny. Don't you give up.'"

"Yes," Sarah agreed, her voice wistful. "He would have. Just keep flooding them with stories, Penny. At some point they'll have to sit up and take notice of you."

"I'll think about it," Penny said, not wanting to brush off her sisters' heartfelt and sincere encouragement. The truth she couldn't bear to tell them was that she really was feeling rather hopeless about it and would just as soon give up and resign herself to becoming a seamstress or a kitchen maid than go on being disappointed by rejection after rejection.

A restless silence hovered between them for a moment before Penny spoke again.

"If you won't let me work at the shop, then how about I find some other work? I could clean houses, take in laundry. Even better, I could help mind some of the other children in our street."

Evie looked up at her sharply. "I've said all I'm going to say about this matter, Penelope Grace," she said sternly, despite the tiredness in her voice.

Penelope Grace. Evie only used Penny's full name when she was truly in earnest, which was the closest Penny had ever seen Evie come to anger. Even when Morris had absconded, hours before their hastily arranged wedding, leaving Evie with a growing babe in her womb and nowhere to turn.

Penny had decided to forgive her sister's charming and handsome, but horribly treacherous fiancé, but only because Evie expected it of her. At least she was under no obligation to like him. She turned her thoughts back to more deserving individuals.

Papa would have said ...

"I wish I could have known Papa and Mama," Penny said sadly as Evie slowly got up from her knees and moved over to where their bedding lay. Sarah proceeded to empty the buckets and bowls of rainwater into the street outside their only window. It was then that Penny realized the rain had stopped.

"I hope we have a fine day tomorrow." Sarah closed the window and stared out at the gloom through the mottled pane.

***

The next day was fine and sunny, as Sarah had hoped. Penny combed out her thick black hair, braided it expertly and wound the braid into a knot in the nape of her neck. The hairpins she stuck in it were rusty, but at least they did the trick: keeping her hair out of her way while she took care of Hamish and cleaned their home, such as it was.

After a meager breakfast of oatmeal and their traditionally lavish farewell to his mother and Aunt Sarah, Hamish lay obediently on his stomach, kicking his bare feet rhythmically on the floor. He was busily practicing his letters on the cracked slate Penny had managed to procure from Mr. O'Connor, the grocer in the next borough. The kindly old gentleman also supplied her with used chalk nubs, pencil stubs and the occasional half used notebook for her scribblings and Hamish's education.

Hamish, his curly brown head bobbing from side to side, lay muttering away to himself, sounding out the letters while the chalk scratched against the painted board. His voice sounded far more serious and graver than was usual for a five-year-old. Penny sat in the rocker—her favorite place to dream—and chewed absentmindedly on a pencil stub. She was supposed to be coming up with a new story, but all she could think of was her latest rejection letter.

How shall I ever convince them to accept my stories for publication? she wondered to herself. It didn't help that every publisher she had approached had told her they were looking for known talent. *It stands to reason that the only way to become known is to be published, so that just doesn't wash.* She'd never had the heart to tell anyone that. *Perhaps I should follow the route the Brontë sisters and Miss Austen took. Only, it feels like lying, to me, to pretend that my stories were written by a man.*

A sparrow landed on the windowsill, bobbing about and chirping agitatedly. The wind began to howl as a sudden, unexplained shadow dimmed the brightness of the sun. A baby cried in the room below, followed by a curse and a thump, which only made the poor thing cry harder. Hamish looked up from his slate. Penny gave him an encouraging smile. He went back to his letters.

I wonder if it's because I'm so young? Although young ladies are getting married at eighteen, so that surely can't be it.

Her thought was scarcely cold when a blood curdling scream rent the air. Penny almost upset the rocker as she tried to come upright. Hamish scrambled to his feet, looking fearful.

Another murder? Penny thought. *Oh, please, God, no. When will it end?*

The baby down below began wailing like a siren. Voices filled the street outside, some crying inconsolably, others shouting frantically. Hamish rushed to Penny's side, grabbing onto her skirts. She put an arm around him protectively, listening for some snippet of sensible language that would give her a clue as to what was going on. Going outside to see wasn't something she particularly relished doing in that moment.

A rap at the door made her jump, and Hamish gave a little whimper.

"Sit in the sleeping corner, Hamish, and don't move," Penny whispered in his ear. The little boy obeyed immediately, scurrying to the pile of blankets that would be hidden by the door when it opened.

The rap on the door came again. A man coughed—a little nervously, Penny thought. She took a deep breath and reached for the doorknob. As the heavy wooden barrier swung outward on loudly protesting hinges, she saw Mr. O'Connor standing there. His kind face was ashen beneath his salt-and-pepper whiskers, his hands clutched his battered old bowler in front of his chest. His pale blue eyes swam with tears.

"Mr. O'Connor?" Penny said, alarm coursing through her like hot lava. Why would the kindly grocer man be away from his store in the middle of the morning, looking at her with such a sad, stricken countenance?

"There's been an accident at Murphy's place, Penny, dear. The ... the whole building came down," he said, his voice quivering. He coughed again as Penny's heart began to thrash against her ribs like a wild animal.

"Evie? Sarah? Are they...? Do they need help?" There were little black spots in front of her eyes, and she couldn't see Mr. O'Connor's face clearly when he replied.

"I'm so sorry, dear. They ... they ..." He couldn't get the rest of the words out, but he didn't need to. His face and his eyes told Penny everything she needed to know. Everything she would rather not know. Everything she desperately wanted not to be true.

As if standing outside of herself, she heard a sob escape her throat. Her knees suddenly refused to hold her up.

Tottering backwards, she clapped her hand over her mouth to stop herself screaming as she sank to the floor, her mind a black whirlpool of confusion. Only one word came through clear as a bell, over and over. *No! No! No!*

"I'm so sorry, Penny. So, so sorry ..." Mr. O'Connor's words faded as he gripped her shoulders. Then her world went dark.

Chapter One

Four Horse, Arizona, July 1885

Hunter Blakely cringed and screwed his eyes shut as shards of morning light pierced his vision and made the throbbing in his head accelerate to a screaming crescendo of pain.

"No, Sally, please. Just keep them closed a little longer," he groaned, gripping his temples in a vain attempt to assuage the demon drink hammering at his brain.

"How much longer, Hunter?" Sally's voice, strident and demanding, brought on yet another wave of nauseating pain. Scrabbling under the bed for the bedpan, Hunter deposited the remainder of his dinner in it. He wiped his mouth on the sleeve of his shirt, only then realizing he still had all his clothes on.

"Just until ten o'clock, I reckon I'll be fine by ..."

Sally didn't let him finish. "It *is* ten o'clock, Hunter," she spelled out in clipped syllables. "What I meant is, how much longer is this ..." she hesitated, and Hunter looked up to see his cousin gesturing at his aching carcass strewn across the bed amongst a tangle of bedclothes. "No." Sally's voice hardened as she stepped over to Hunter's nightstand. "How much longer is *this* going to carry on for?" She held up an empty whiskey bottle, shaking it agitatedly for emphasis.

Hunter groaned and buried his face in his bedclothes. They reeked of alcohol and bile. He wanted Sally to go away. He wanted it all to go away. The ranch, the horses, the town, his ruthless, relentless memories. The memories most of all.

Alcohol was the only way he could find respite from them, even if only for a few short hours at a time.

"Hunter, for the love of Pete, look at me," Sally said. Her voice was a mixture of sadness, desperation and empathy. That only made it all the more difficult for him to look her in the eye. With effort—and a little shakily—he hoisted himself into a sitting position on the bed, staring blearily at the woman before him.

She was strong boned, and not very tall—standard ranching stock. Her mouse brown curls floated rebelliously about her face, refusing to be confined to any kind of hair clip or pins. Her face itself was round and childlike, despite her twenty-three years, with a—usually—cheery expression and a twinkle in her forest green eyes. Only, the cheery expression and the twinkle were conspicuously missing on that particular morning.

Come to think of it, they've been missing for a while, Hunter thought despondently to himself. He knew the reason. He was it. Ironically, that made him wish the empty bottle in her hand were a full one.

As she set the bottle back down with a loud *thunk* on the nightstand, Hunter's eyes were drawn to Sally's belly. He raised his aching eyebrows.

"Looks like that little tyke is about ready to bust out of there," he remarked, dimly aware that this wasn't necessarily the most appropriate time to be talking about the imminent birth of his cousin's first child.

"Yeah," Sally agreed, placing her hands on her hips, the way she always did when she had made up her mind about something and wasn't about to have it changed. "This little tyke is coming in a matter of days and that means I won't be around to help you or Maisie much longer."

Maisie.

He'd heard a baby crying earlier, as if it were a faraway echo from another land, another time. The leaden weight of guilt added to the discomfort in his stomach.

"Give me another week, Sally, please." Hunter didn't like the pleading sound in his own voice, but his head hurt too much to concentrate on being manly and authoritative.

Sally waddled over to the bed and plopped herself down beside him, letting out her breath in a long, despairing sigh as she leaned back on her outstretched arms. For a few moments she shifted about as if trying to find a comfortable position.

"You know I love you like a brother, Hunter," she huffed. "I ain't forgotten the years we grew up together as kids and how your folks loved me just like I was their own, but now I've got me my own family to care for. I got to put my baby first. For nigh on eight months, I've lived here at Blakely Stud Ranch, taking care of y'all, cleaning up Maisie's messes. And yours."

Hunter grimaced and looked away. It was embarrassing. Only Sally knew how deep he'd been looking into the bottle lately, and he knew she would keep it that way, but the shame he felt went deeper than his concern over who knew about it. He knew about it. Sally knew about it. That was more than bad enough.

Sally was still speaking. "It's time for you to pull yourself together. You're an all-fired mess, Hunt, and you know it."

Yes, he did. And he felt powerless to change that fact. But Sally was right. He knew she couldn't hang around much longer taking care of him and ... He bit his lip. How was he ever going to manage taking care of a little eight-month-old baby girl?

A sudden anger flared up in his pain-saturated, alcohol-blunted mind. It was all so wrong. It wasn't supposed to be like this. Amy shouldn't have gotten sick, much less died. If she had just gotten better; if he had just called the doctor in time; if they hadn't lived so far from any kind of professional medical care.

The doctor had said one of the reasons for the fever was because the baby was too big, and Amy's hips had been too narrow. Another was that she had been too young. Yet another that she'd been in labor too long. They said it wasn't his fault, but Hunter couldn't bring himself to lay the blame for his beloved wife's death at the feet of an unchangeable circumstance. All he knew for sure was that Amy would not have been in that position if not for him.

"Hunter? Did you hear me, or are you wool gathering?"

He shook his head, attempting to dispel the dark clouds of sadness that seemed to suck him down into a deep well of numbness as soon as the alcohol drained from his brain. "Sorry, Sal, did you say something?"

"I asked you if you'd ever done enquiries about getting someone in to help."

"Ah."

She'd asked him that a few times, and every time he'd told her the same answer. Nobody wanted to live out on his ranch, one of the furthest ranches from town. Besides, there were no housekeepers or nurses available in Four Horse.

The few single women who lived there were the regular kind of small-town girl who wanted to be part of every hoedown and county fair and Saturday afternoon gossip gathering on the boardwalk of Granville and Sons General Store. Living out on the range with a hermetic, grieving widower would seriously damage their chances of being part of many events like that.

Besides, they all still had designs to marry, and living with a single father, alone, out on a ranch in the middle of nowhere was sure to be a blot on their calling card.

"As the good book says, 'Flee even the appearance of unrighteousness,'" the reverend of their small chapel had reminded him with a sympathetic pat on the shoulder. He hadn't told the reverend that the actual "appearance of unrighteousness" he was fleeing was the chance that someone might see him drinking and promptly inform the whole town.

"Well?" Sally prodded impatiently.

"Well, what?"

"Hunter Blakely! By all the gods and little fishes, would you quit beating the devil about the stump!"

"Oh, getting help. I told you more times than I can count, that dog ain't going to hunt."

Sally sighed and lay back on the bed, her hands clasped awkwardly over the bulge of her midriff.

"How about if you get married?"

Those softly spoken words hit Hunter harder than any piercing sunrays from between the drapes or any screeching rooster crow outside his window.

"Married," he said flatly, his throat constricting.

"Yes. Get married. Get hitched. Tie the knot.

"I heard you loud and clear the first time," he said shortly. "And you'd best do yourself a favor and chase that idea clear out of your mind."

"Amy would have wanted you to be happy, I'm sure she ..."

"Don't you go telling me what Amy would have wanted!" He couldn't stop the dormant anger, always just simmering below the surface, from pouring heat into his face and his words. Dang it. How did Sally always manage to hit a nerve like that?

Sally struggled up onto her elbows to look him in the face. "I loved her too, you know," she said, that sad desperation in her voice again. "Maybe you've misremembered that I was her maid of honor, but I ain't forgot. She was just as much my sister as you're my brother."

Hunter heaved himself up from the bed, intent on marching indignantly over to his dresser. All he could manage was a foot-dragging shuffle. But he did reach the jug and bowl set upon it and proceeded to wash his face. The water was cool and cleansing. It distracted him from the tornado of emotion that threatened to rip him apart.

"Hunter," Sally's voice was as unrelenting as his regrets. "I hate to have to be the one to say this to ya, but don't you think you owe it to Pa to get ahold of yourself before the ranch falls to pieces around your ears?"

Hunter gripped the towel in his fists and pressed it his face. He wanted to yell at her to get the heck out and leave him be, but he loved her too much, even though he hated that she was right. It wasn't only Sally who viewed him as a brother, he himself often forgot that they were cousins at all.

He could remember the nights when they'd sat up for hours under a fort made of chairs and quilts, reading penny dreadfuls by lantern light. Hunter's parents had forbidden them from reading the questionable literature, but Hunter had managed to find some soiled ones dumped behind the general store and smuggled them home in his jacket.

He and Sally would laugh hysterically at the dramatic tales of doomed romance, their hands over their mouths to keep from making too much noise and waking his parents. Sally was also the one who had turned out to be a bottomless mine of priceless advice when it came to courting Amy.

Amy.

Her easy laugh seemed to float all around him the way her blonde hair used to float around her heart-shaped face whenever they went horse riding alone in the hills. If only he could have one more glimpse of those vivacious blue eyes that always seemed to be able to say, with one glance, what more than a thousand words could hope to express.

Oh, Amy. I'm so sorry. I miss you so much. His throat hurt and his chest ached with a pain that had nothing to do with the aftereffects of too much drinking, but no tears came.

"Hunter?" Her voice was gentler now. He couldn't ignore her, much less chase her away, as much as he wanted to wallow in his misery alone.

"What do ya want me to say, Sally?" he sighed, lowering the towel to the dresser and staring over the top of the mirror at the wallpaper beyond. It was a striped design, soft jade green and white, with curly, fern-like fronds in a dark olive-green winding around and between the stripes. Amy had picked it out from a catalogue, and he'd paid through the nose to have it delivered to their far-flung town. Not that he'd even noticed the cost. It had been his wedding gift to her.

"I don't know," Sally said, the honesty in her voice taking the last little bit of wind out of his sails. "I guess I just want to know that you and Maisie'll be all right when I have to go home to Four Horse."

"You want me to get someone in before you go, is that it?" As much as the thought repulsed him, he was beginning to think it was the only way.

"That would be a good start."

Hunter turned to face her again, half sitting on the dresser top. "I reckon I can do that. Now all we got to do is figure out where to get ahold of such a someone."

"How about we order you a mail order bride?" Sally said, her face deadpan. That, coupled with how quickly she'd said it, alerted Hunter's suspicions.

"Mail order bride!" he blurted out. "Have you gone right off your nut, Sal?"

Sally shrugged, looking a little too innocent for Hunter's liking. He'd seen that look on her face before. It was the one she wore when she was up to something, and she usually had everything planned down to the wire before she got to looking like that.

"I swear, Sally Mae Blakely Morgan, if you go messing about in my affairs, I'll ..." Hunter huffed out the last of his breath without completing his threat.

"You'll what, Mr. Blakely?" Sally prodded, a tiny glimmer of her usual tongue in cheek good humor shining through.

There wasn't any punishment Hunter could think of that was an onerous enough payment for meddling in his business, but he also knew his threats against Sally would be idle ones. They always were. And anyway, what was the worst she could do? Match him up with some poor girl who would soon find out he wasn't going to love her like a man ought to love a woman?

Like he had loved Amy.

Any woman subjected to that would be gone in a matter of weeks, no doubt. Let Sally do whatever tickled her fancy. There was only one woman for him, and she was dancing with the angels.

Amy.

"Well, if you ain't fixing to tell me what you'll do to me for doing you the favor of your life, then I reckon I'll just go ahead and get shed of my chores for the day. Matt'll be back later to help me pack our things. I cain't wait till later than tomorrow to leave." Sally laboriously rose from the bed and smoothed down her blue cotton house dress.

Her voice and posture cut such a figure of determination that Hunter coughed. "Now you mind what I said, Sal. No answering mail order bride ads, pretending to be me."

Sally turned back to face him. The twinkle was back in her eye. "As if I'd ever think of doing a thing like that."

"Yeah, well, I wouldn't put it past ya, so just don't even start thinking about it. I'll make good on my word and go into town just as soon as I'm cleaned up. Reckon I'll check with Mr. Rhimes, the blacksmith. As I recall, his daughter Ellie was looking for cleaning and childminding work."

"Ellie? Spinster Ellie?"

"What's it matter what she is? If she can clean my house and mind my child, she can have the job, and your mind can rest at ease. Just don't be answering any mail order bride ads."

Sally stood regarding him silently for a few moments, her head cocked to one side, the glimmer of a smile playing about her lips and eyes.

"Sally, promise you won't."

"Will that set your mind at ease, brother?"

"It surely will."

"All right, I promise."

Her smile blossomed across her face. Hunter sighed an inward sigh of relief. He might have just diverted a major disaster.

His mind drifted to his freshly acquired task. He wasn't too all fired keen on getting Ellie Rhimes in. She was a notoriously pessimistic soul, known to complain about everything. When the sun was out, it was too hot, and when it rained it was too wet. Still, he'd never heard anyone accuse her of being a chatterbox, which would suit him right down to the ground. He wasn't looking for conversation or company, simply a housemaid and a nurse.

"Wait here. I'll throw together a prairie oyster for you," Sally said and disappeared from the room.

Hunter almost gagged at the thought of the homemade hangover remedy, but his temples briskly reminded him that he had imbibed far more whiskey the night before than his brain could comfortably handle.

"I'd rather just go get the hair of the dog," he muttered to himself when he was sure Sally was out of earshot.

***

It was a couple of hours later, with his mouth still burning from hot sauce and the lingering sensation of a whole, raw egg yolk sliding down his gullet, that Hunter set out for Four Horse.

Considering how all-fired nasty that stuff is, a body would have figured it would work faster, he thought morosely to himself as the slightest bounce of the buggy on the wagon track sent fresh spasms of pain through his skull. By the time he had reached town, though, the midday sunlight wasn't quite as sharp on his eyes, and the fog in his head had begun to clear a little.

He let Billy, his most dependable old buggy horse, have his head as he ambled down the one and only, largely deserted, street of Four Horse between the sun bleached, wind chafed clapboard and adobe buildings toward Mr. Rhimes's smithy shop. He was in no hurry.

Serves me right for letting her die, the thought drifted through his mind along with the growing aversion he felt to procuring Ellie Rhimes's help.

As he reached the shop, the metallic clang of iron being forged into a usable shape became louder and clearer, partly resurrecting his throbbing headache. Hunter almost turned the buggy around, but the knowledge that he was not capable of taking care of Maisie himself—nor could he reconcile himself to sending her to live with Sally in town—kept him fixed on his purpose.

"Howdy do, Mr. Rhimes!" he called out over the din of hammering.

The swarthy old man set down his hammer, lifted the horseshoe from the anvil with a pair of tongs and dumped it into a bucket of cold water at his feet. The metal hissed, sending up clouds of steam.

Mr. Rhimes turned to face Hunter, his white whiskered face beaded and streaked with sweat. His thick leather apron was scarred with burn marks and soot, his shirt sleeves rolled up to reveal hairy arms so powerful they looked like they belonged on the body of a seven-hundred-pound grizzly, not a seventy-year-old man.

"It's a fine day to ya, Hunter, my boy," he boomed happily, his face creasing into a heartfelt grin. "One of your prize stallions thrown a hoof iron, then?"

"Ah, no, not today, sir," Hunter replied, his mouth feeling dry. "I was wondering if, ah, if Ellie was still, ah, looking for a housemaid position?"

"Well, bless your heart, my boy!" Mr. Rhimes exclaimed, his grin as warm as ever. "If you're offering, you're but a day late. Just yesterday she got herself a dandy old placement over yonder in Big Bug. Governessing for some rich folks who took a fancy to country living. She sure was happy to get away from this *one*-horse town!" He slapped his leg, letting out a singular guffaw at his own joke. "Heaven knows how long those foolish Easterners'll last out in a mining settlement, but there it is. There's just no telling folks these days."

Hunter nodded, trying to sort out the mixture of relief and angst in his mind. He also vaguely wondered if Ellie had been adopted by Mr. Rhimes. They were worlds apart in temperament.

"Well, I reckon I'd best keep looking, then," he said, lifting his hat in farewell.

"You might want to take a dander at the Miller place. Last I heard, Holly's mama was fixing to get her gainfully employed." Mr. Rhimes winked.

Hunter gave him a pained smile. There was no way he would survive Holly Miller and her endless prattling. And what if, heaven forbid, she should come across him seeking solace in a bottle of Old Farm Pure Rye? That thought made him remember that his stock of whiskey was depleted.

“Well, thank you, Mr. Rhimes. I’ll be sure to look into it,” Hunter said, intending to do the exact opposite. “You have a nice day, now, and send my regards to Mrs. Rhimes.”

“I surely will, thank you, son.”

Hunter turned Billy’s head toward the Lucky Horseshoe Saloon as the sound of clanging metal resumed. He hoped Ned, the town’s barkeep, wouldn’t ask too many questions. He was running out of excuses for his frequent whiskey purchases. One could only claim to be making so many poultices for foot rot or drenches for colic before folks started wondering if there was an outbreak of multiple horse diseases on his stud ranch. And people in Four Horse tended to wonder out loud.

Whatever happened, Sally must not find out. He was already trying to figure out what he would say to her about not having secured a nurse for Maisie in her place.

I’ll just keep a couple bottles handy. Only use ‘em if I cain’t sleep at all, he promised himself. He truly, desperately wanted to keep that promise. For his own sake as well as Maisie’s and Sally’s.

And for the sake of Amy’s memory. A memory he ached to hold onto for ever and ever, yet a memory that cut him so deep that it drove him to seek relief in the bottom of a bottle.

As fervently as he desired to keep that promise, Hunter feared he would not be strong enough. As desperately as he wanted things to get better, he could only see them getting worse. Hopelessness was becoming his most frequent bedfellow, and he didn’t know how to chase it away.

Chapter Two

New York City, New York, June 1885

Nobody could tell Penny what exactly had happened. Seamus Murphy had disappeared without a trace, his ramshackle wooden sweatshop now nothing more than a tangled mass of splintered, rotten wood, shattered glass, and the remains of sewing machines, broken beyond repair.

Some said the building had collapsed because of the rain and the fact that the Five Points slum sat squarely on the site of an old, spring-fed lake that someone had filled up. Others said it was because Murphy was a miserly old skinflint who never spent a dime on the upkeep of his building. Still others said it was a combination of both.

All Penny knew was that, in the blink of an eye, without any warning, her beloved sisters had been cruelly ripped from her life. As desperate as their circumstances had been, there had never been a shortage of love and laughter. Now she was left alone. No family, no income, no prospects. No hope.

That would have been bearable, to some extent, if not for the damning guilt and crippling loss that rolled over her in waves every waking hour since that horrible day when Mr. O'Connor had brought her the news. Since then, too, the growing realization that she was now solely responsible for Hamish weighed ever heavier on her mind.

Lying curled up on the pile of bedding in the corner of the room, Penny listened to the drops of rainwater falling on the bare floorboards. The blankets she lay on were damp and smelled musty. She knew she should be putting out pails and bowls to catch the rain, but her arms and legs weren't responding to her thoughts. Probably because her thoughts kept drifting.

Penny, love, I don't know what I'd do without you, you know that?

It was Evie's voice, echoing in the room around her.

One day you're going to be a famous author of children's stories, and people will be lining up for you to sign their books.

That was Sarah. Dear, sunshiny Sarah, who always seemed to have a smile ready, no matter how long her day had been, or how many times Mr. Murphy had pinched her arms for not finishing enough coats in a day.

I'm so happy you're here to teach Hamish. I'm sure he'll have as good an education under your watchful eye as any rich boy in one of those private schools in the city.

She'd always wondered what inspired Evie to have so much faith in her.

"Aunt Penny?"

Penny lay motionless. She'd heard her nephew, but she couldn't bring herself to respond. What was left for them? She had no job, very little money saved, and no relatives she knew of who could take them in. Would they end up in the poor house?

She shivered, realizing that the fire had gone out in the coal stove. Turning her head to see if there was still coal in the box, she noticed that the floor lay strewn with Hamish's homemade toys and writing materials. Penny closed her eyes. She didn't want to look at any of it. It was easier to lie staring at the water-stained rafters and hanker after what she couldn't bring with her from the past.

"Aunt Penny?"

His voice was more insistent now. The thud of little feet on the damp, squeaking floorboards vibrated through her body. Cold, desperate fingers gripped her shoulder and shook her.

"Aunt Penny! Wake up! I'm hungry!" His last word ended in a sob, and she felt a hot tear drop down onto her cheek. In a flash, her eyes brought the world around her back into focus.

"Well, isn't there still some of the stew Mrs. Madison brought? You can have my share." She couldn't bear to look into his eyes.

"I finished your share yesterday," Hamish whined, sniveling.

Penny blinked. "What day is it today?"

"I don't know," Hamish wailed. "I'm hungry! Can we get some food, please, Aunt Penny?"

Something inside of Penny snapped, and she sat up, wondering how long she'd lain there. She looked around. There were dishes on the lean-to sideboard, but they were all empty except for crumbs. A rat scurried across the worn wooden surface and twitched its whiskers at her before vanishing down the back. Up on the shelf where they kept their dry goods, the jars had all been taken down. The oatmeal jar lay on its side on the floor below, empty.

"Did you do that, Hamish?" she asked.

"Do what?" Hamish rubbed a grimy sleeve across his nose and eyes.

"Did you eat the last of the oatmeal?"

"Yeah. This morning. I was hungry."

Hot shame washed over Penny's whole body.

"How long have I been lying here, Hamish?"

He shrugged, his eyes troubled. "I don't know. Days and days and days."

Penny knew Hamish had a propensity to exaggerate, as most five-year-olds did, but the awful truth began to dawn on her that this time his exaggerations might not be far wrong. She buried her face in her hands as a pang of guilt shot through her chest.

I'm so sorry. I'm so sorry, Evie. I'm so sorry, God. I've neglected my own flesh and blood.

"Aunt Penny?"

Her head snapped up.

"Hamish, your Aunt Penny has not done right by you. We're going right now to Mr. O'Connor's, and we're going to get some greens and soup bones and make a big old pot of soup. How does that sound?"

She had to force herself to speak in a cheery tone. All she wanted to do was lie face down on those musty, damp blankets and cry. But Hamish needed her.

"I'm hungry now," Hamish said sadly. "Soup takes so long."

"We'll see if Mr. O'Connor has some of yesterday's bread for us, okay?"

That seemed to bring Hamish some comfort. He nodded. "Okay."

Penny stood and sniffed. What was that sour odor? Her cheeks flushed with embarrassment as she realized it was herself she was smelling. She couldn't remember when last she'd washed.

"I'll need to get washed up first, Hamish. Do you need to get washed up?"

The little boy nodded his grimy, sorrowful head.

"Can you take care of that yourself?"

Another nod. "We only have cold water, now. No fire," he added with a little shiver.

"Then we'll have to be right quick about it, won't we?" Penny said with another desperate attempt at cheeriness. "Let's see who can get done the quickest."

That helped to not only distract Hamish from the cold water, but also herself from her dark thoughts and abject hopelessness. For the first time in days, she put aside her fears of what would become of her and her nephew. Instead, she focused on something small and simple and immediate. Getting washed up and getting some food in their bellies.

Moments later they were washed up and shivering but laughing through their chattering teeth as they hurried down to Mr. O'Connor's grocery store. The rain had slowed to a fine drizzle, and a watery afternoon sun peeped shyly though the clouds when they stepped into the interior of the store.

"Matter of fact, I do have some bread from yesterday I was going to give to the poor house, but I surely can spare some for the two of you," Mr. Connor said with a fatherly smile when Penny explained her plan.

"Could I pay for the greens and the soup bones when I find some work?" she asked, wishing she didn't have to beg.

Mr. O' Connor scratched his whiskers. "No, I think I have a better idea. One of the delivery lads took ill this morning and went home early. Why don't you chickadees do his afternoon rounds for him, and in return, you can take all the greens and soup bones your wee heart's desire."

Penny's wee heart swelled with gratitude as tears pricked her eyes.

"What do you think, Hamish?" she asked, looking down at her nephew. "You think we can do some deliveries for Mr. O'Connor?"

"Oh yes! I can run real fast, Mr. O'Connor," Hamish declared, squaring his skinny shoulders. "I'll deliver everything faster than, than, than ..." he faltered.

"Faster than I can say, 'cabbage,' right?" Mr. O'Connor prompted.

"Yeah! Faster than that!" Hamish agreed. Then he peered into the grocer's face. "But only if I can get some bread first. My legs need bread to run."

Mr. O'Connor chuckled and chucked the boy under his chin. "Of course, they do, laddie. Of course, they do."

***

By the time the sun hung beneath the drifting banks of ragged cloud, painting them orange and red with its sleepy rays, Penny and Hamish were back in their home. They lit a fire in the coal stove—thankfully there was still a bit of coal left—and chopped up the greens, adding them to the pot full of soup bones bubbling away on top. The delicious warmth radiated into the damp, musty room, and Penny felt herself coming slowly back to life.

"Help me get these soggy blankets over the chairs, so they can dry out some in front of the stove, Hamish."

He sprang into action, seemingly anxious to make himself useful. Penny's heart ached. What had he been doing with himself all that time she'd been staring at the ceiling, wishing it was all a bad dream?

She pushed the thought aside. It wouldn't help to dwell on that. Instead, she focused on getting the soup cooked and the house tidied as much as she could. Then she and Hamish sat down on the floor and filled their bellies with hot, nourishing food. Despite the constant gloom shrouding her thoughts, a full belly and heat made Penny feel a little better.

With the dishes washed and the leftover soup set aside to cool for the next day's meal, Penny sat on the floor in front of the stove and wondered what to do next.

"Tell me a story, Aunt Penny, please." Hamish plopped himself in her lap and leaned against her shoulder. Instantly, tears sprang into Penny's eyes.

She had no story to tell.

Somehow, in the days of black despair following her sisters' deaths, she had forgotten the way to the magical world of make believe she had escaped to so often before.

"I ... I'll try," she said, loath to disappoint Hamish, and closed her eyes. For a few long minutes, she sat like that, but her mind was like a dark forest full of unnamed dangers and unidentifiable shadows.

"It's all right, Aunt Penny," Hamish said, clambering out of her lap and crossing the room. "Maybe we can find one in here. There's stories in here too, sometimes, I think." He picked up one of the old newspapers Mr. O'Connor had given them as kindling for their coal fire.

You dear, sweet boy, Penny thought, blinking back tears. *Your mama would be so proud to see you now.*

She opened up the clunky periodical on the floor and turned the large pages one by one. There didn't seem to be anything other than bad news, so she kept going until she got to the small advertisements. She began reading them out loud, one by one, hoping she would find some inspiration for a story there.

"Esteemed lady of highly respectable house seeks parlor maid and governess for long term employment. Applicants should have at least two years of experience. Governess should have necessary training in childcare and possess at least three years of experience in private tutoring."

Penny stopped reading. The ad reminded her too strongly of her own shortcomings. She scanned further down the page.

"My name is Mrs. Sally Morgan. I have a cousin whose wife recently passed. He's needing a good woman to take care of his home and his baby daughter. It doesn't matter how plain she is, as long as she has a good heart, knows how to keep a house fairly clean, and loves babies."

Penny stopped again, but this time her eyes did not scan further down the page. Instead, she stared at the petition she had just read. It was such a simple, heartfelt plea. Penny could imagine Mrs. Morgan would be a good woman herself. One who loved her cousin like a brother. Perhaps he was so grief stricken over the death of his wife that he could not bring himself to pen the words, and so she had come to his aid and done it in his stead.

"You love babies, don't you, Aunty Penny?" Hamish's thoughtful voice startled her out of her reverie.

"Well, yes, I do," Penny said absentmindedly, the seed of an idea slowly germinating in the back of her mind. She looked at the ad again. There were two more lines. She read them silently to herself.

My cousin, Mr. Hunter Blakely, owns and runs a successful Quarter Horse stud ranch in Arizona, so she'll be well taken care of. For the sake of doing things proper, she'll have to be willing to marry him, even if it's just so folks don't gossip.

"Are you thinking about a new story, Aunt Penny?" Hamish asked into the silence, his voice sounding tired. Penny looked down at him. Her heart began to beat a little faster. The seed germinating in her mind was starting to look like a flowering possibility, a wildly fortuitous way out for herself and her precious nephew.

"Maybe I am, Hamish," she said, feeling a little terrified at her own words and yet keenly aware of the inexorable pull of the promise of a life so far removed from their pitiful existence. It felt just like one of her fairy tales. And yet …

What am I thinking? Marrying a man I've never met. It's unthinkable, is what it is. Then again, I suppose beggars can't be choosers. It would be nice to live on a horse farm, to be sure. Hamish has always loved horses.

At that moment Hamish yawned. Penny brushed his curly mop out of his droopy eyes. It was clear a full stomach and ample warmth was all he needed to lull him to sleep tonight. Penny slipped one arm under his knees and the other around his back. With a groan she hoisted herself to her feet and arranged Hamish's unresisting, skinny arms over her shoulders.

Grabbing the heaviest of the now dry blankets, she fashioned it one-handed into a crude bed in front of the stove before laying her nephew gently into the scratchy but warm folds.

"Aunt Penny?" Hamish slurred sleepily.

"Yes, sweetheart."

"When is Mama coming back?"

Penny only just managed to catch the sob in her throat. She couldn't remember what she had told him about that. Right now didn't seem the time to try to explain that he would never see his mother again. She didn't know if she could even bear thinking about it, let alone trying to explain it to a five-year-old.

"I don't know, we'll have to see," she said, her heart condemning her for the lie she told to spare his innocent heart.

"I hope it's soon," he mumbled and then his eyes fluttered closed.

Penny turned out the lantern and cried herself softly to sleep.

***

They managed to survive for another four weeks doing odd jobs for Mr. O'Connor and accepting his gifts of partially wilted vegetables, bread and oatmeal that had sat too long on the shelves of his store. Penny wasn't convinced that he only ever gave them his castoffs. There were times when the carrots were crispy and juicy enough to eat without cooking them, and the bread was still soft on the inside.

Penny sent in another story to *Our Little Men and Women*, only to receive another rejection. The day she received the letter, she sat rocking sadly in her favorite chair while Hamish played at cowboys with a horse he'd fashioned out of castoff clay from Mr. Newman's pottery shop and a doll Evie had made him from the sweatshop offcuts.

It seemed there was nothing for it but to find a job at a sweatshop. Penny's stomach tightened into a knot at the thought. As much as she'd pestered her sisters to let her take their place for a day or even get a job sewing coats together herself, she hadn't done it because she thought it would be a jaunt.

Memories filled her mind of a little girl being boxed about the ears for daydreaming when she should have been replacing empty thread spools on the machines, or snipping off loose threads, or scrubbing the sweat shop floor. Penny shuddered at the thought of Hamish being subjected to the same treatment. Even the endless, dreary hours of mind-numbing work was something she could not bring herself to even consider putting him through.

The very day Evie found out about how Penny was being manhandled, she had arranged for a neighbor, Mrs. Headley, to take care of Penny instead. Mrs. Headley, a retired schoolmistress, had taught Penny to read. But where would Penny send Hamish while she worked insanely long hours? Mrs. Headley wasn't alive anymore, and everybody else was too busy. Asking the O'Connors was out of the question. They were already helping so much, and their store kept them occupied all hours of the day.

A sharp knock at the door interrupted Penny's restless thoughts, and she started to her feet. Hamish looked at her questioningly. She shrugged and headed for the door. Opening it, she found herself looking into the shrew-like face of Mr. Ives from the ground floor.

"Evening, Miss Penny," he wheezed. "Looks like this is for you." He held out a pale blue envelope with her name and address written in a bold, round hand. "Postman got it mixed up with our lot," Mr. Ives muttered by way of explanation and turned away before she had a chance to say anything.

"Thank you, Mr. Ives," she called after his departing back and shut the door. Turning over the envelope, she read the return address. It was from Arizona.

Penny's heart began to pound. She hurried back to the rocker and sat down. For a few moments, she stared at the envelope, almost too scared to open it. Hamish, apparently oblivious to what was happening, went on making neighing sounds and saying cowboyish things in as deep a voice as he could muster.

Penny took a deep breath, steeled herself, and ripped open the envelope with shaking fingers. She removed the letter and opened it. Two fifty-dollar notes fell out onto her lap. Penny gasped and stuffed the money back into the envelope as if she were afraid it might disappear into thin air if she didn't keep it safe.

She bit her lower lip, smoothed out the letter and began to read:

Dear Miss White

It sure made me happy to read your reply to my advertisement. You sound like a dandy young lady, and I'm mighty sorry to hear about your sisters passing. Of course, Hamish is welcome to come along. I wouldn't dream of asking you to give him up.

You're to take the train to Prescott and then board the stage for Four Horse. My husband and I will meet you at the general store, where the stage stops. Just be sure and wire the stage company when you leave, so they can let us know when to expect y'all.

I'm including the money for your train fare and the stagecoach, since I reckon you won't have the spoons to pay for it yourself. There should be enough to buy y'all some food along the way, too.

I'm looking forward to meeting the both of you.

Mrs. Sally Morgan.

P.S. Mr. Blakely's struggling with a little problem at the moment. We're working on it, though, so I figure it won't be a problem for long. We'll talk about it when we meet you at the stage station.

Penny closed her eyes and lay back in the rocker. A little problem? She wouldn't mind only having little problems. Whatever it was, it was sure to be more bearable than the one she had now. She let her mind drift, contemplating the rosy future opening up before her like a Shasta daisy opening its snowy petals to the sun. Everything had happened so fast, it almost seemed too good to be true.

What if it is?

Penny's eyes snapped open. What if it was?

She stared down at the envelope in her lap that held more money than she could remember ever seeing in one place at one time. It would be easy to simply take that hundred dollars and live off it for a while until some other, more sensible solution, came her way. Only, she would never be able to live with her conscience if she did that. She'd have to do the right thing or suffer for it.

But what if this unfolding real life fairytale really was too good to be true? She sighed and lay back in the rocker once more. There really was only one way to find out.

Chapter Three

"Look, Aunty Penny! Have you ever seen so much ..." Hamish faltered, his eyes rolling upward and sideways as they did when he was looking for a word to describe something.

Penny left him to find it himself. Her body and her head ached too much to bother trying to express anyone's thoughts but her own. Eight solid days of rocking and jolting in a crowded, stuffy third-class car, seated on a wooden bench and trying not to listen in on everybody else's conversations had eroded much of her usual good humor. Thankfully, for the last leg of the journey, by stagecoach, she was spared the endless clackety-clack of the train's metal wheels on the rails that seemed to pound a hole in her head.

Hamish broke in on her thoughts as he finally came upon the word he was looking for. "I know. Have you ever seen so much *nothing*." His heavy emphasis on the final, evasive word and the uncanny aptness of it, elicited a wry smile from Penny.

She stared past Hamish's head out at the Arizona countryside jostling past the stagecoach window. *Nothing* was a good way to describe what she saw. And perhaps calling it the Arizona countryside was a little ambitious for what was clearly a desert.

Pale, sandy soil littered with rocks and dotted with clumps of sagebrush, prickly pear cactus and strange, twisted trees that looked like arrangements of bent and frazzled floor mops stretched out in all directions. The desolate blanket of earth was draped over a range of large hills, protectively enveloping thicker growths of the same vegetation as well as a few gnarled and stubby pinon pines within their folds.

Far above, a pale, silent sky brooded, a few wisps of cloud scudding across it like goose down feathers blowing in the wind. As Penny watched, a bird of some kind circled the arc of the heavens. Penny thought she heard a shrill, plaintive cry, partly snatched away by the wind. She let out a sigh and imagined she was wheeling up there alongside that bird, whatever it was. Its lonely cry echoed in her heart as she closed her eyes and wished to soon be asleep in a soft bed surrounded by utter silence.

"I think we're here, Aunt Penny," Hamish said, excitedly shaking her shoulder. Penny started up and immediately winced as a sharp pain shot through her neck and up into her temple. She'd fallen asleep while sitting upright and not even realized it.

"Here? You mean in Four Horse?"

"Uh-huh."

At that moment the driver called out, "Whoa! Steady on there," to his team, and the coach slowed to a swaying halt. Penny heard a thump as the man's feet hit the hard, dusty ground outside, and the next minute his weathered, sun browned face appeared at the window.

"This here is your stop, Miss White," he drawled, his face creasing into a distracted smile. "I'll just be taking the mail in, then I'll get your bag down."

"Thank you very much, sir," Penny said, sitting up straighter and tightly clutching the small cloth bag she had kept with her. It held the remainder of the money Mrs. Morgan had sent her and a few precious keepsakes that had belonged to Evie and Sarah. Someone up top threw a large canvas bag to the driver, which he deftly caught and carried into the store they had stopped in front of.

Penny peered at the sign above it. *Granville & Sons General Store*, she read. A pickle barrel and a few bales of hay were lined up against the front wall beside the entrance. It seemed a strange place to have a stage station. Perhaps that was a clue as to just how tiny the town of Four Horse was.

Penny didn't know how to feel about that, just as she didn't know how to feel about anything else that was happening to her. She felt numb, almost detached from any emotion other than a deep, constant, hopeless sadness that seemed to follow her around like a big black shadow.

Hamish slipped his hand into hers. "Are you scared, Aunt Penny?" he asked a little tremulously.

Penny regarded him thoughtfully. "I don't know, Hamish," she replied honestly. "Are you?"

"A little bit," he admitted.

The brisk thunk of boots on the boardwalk told them the driver was returning. A moment later, the door swung open, and he held out his hand to help Penny down, then bodily hoisted Hamish out of the coach by his shoulders and deposited him on the boardwalk.

"I sure hope you'll be happy in Four Horse, ma'am. It's the dandiest, sleepiest little town in all the Black Hills," he said as he caught the carpet bag tossed to him by the man on the roof and handed it to Penny.

"Thank you, sir," Penny replied automatically. She didn't have much hope that his good wishes for her would be fulfilled. She'd given up wanting happiness. All she wanted was for Hamish—and herself—to be safe and cared for. Happiness didn't really factor into anything.

The man, probably oblivious to her state of mind, doffed his hat and turned away. He leaped nimbly up onto the driving seat and slapped the reins over the horses' backs.

"Get up, there, Nifty! Starshine! Quit slacking!"

As the stagecoach rolled away, Penny squinted through the cloud of dust at what was slowly being revealed as an empty street. Mrs. Morgan had said she would be fetching them. Had she been held up? Was there something wrong?

It'll be just my luck if her cousin changed his mind or some disaster happened, she thought despondently. *I shouldn't have dragged Hamish out here. I shouldn't have answered that silly ad in the first place.*

"Is that Mrs. Morgan?" Hamish asked, pointing with a scrawny index finger at a woman striding purposefully along the boardwalk. Before Penny could reply that her guess was as good as his, the woman came to a stop in front of them. She was slim, primly decked out in a perfectly tailored dark green wool dress. Round spectacles, a lot like Penny's, perched on the middle of her sharp nose and made her pale gray eyes look a little too big for her long, narrow face.

"You must be Penny White and her nephew Hamish," the woman said, her middle-aged features expressionless. When she didn't say anything more, Penny decided it had probably been a question of sorts.

"Yes, ma'am, we are," she said. "Are you Mrs. Morgan?"

"No, I'm her neighbor, Mrs. Aylward. She can't drive a buggy in her condition and Mr. Morgan has been called away to an emergency on another ranch. Mrs. Morgan is far advanced in the family way, I'm sure you know. So, I've been asked to drive you out to the Blakely ranch."

"That would be so good of you, Mrs. Aylward," Penny replied as politely as she could.

In reply, Mrs. Aylward hurriedly shepherded them along the boardwalk to a livery stable, where she briskly hired a horse and buggy, and soon they were on their way.

As efficient as she was, Mrs. Aylward turned out not to be a very talkative travel companion. For the first few miles Hamish peppered her with questions about the town and the surroundings that were answered in monosyllables, if at all.

After that, he gave up and began pointing out things to Penny, who wasn't feeling too talkative herself. She did her best to respond in kind to Hamish's innocent enthusiasm, but it was a gargantuan effort.

At last, the buggy slowed, and Mrs. Aylward pointed to a large stone archway reaching up out of the vast nothingness. "Here it is," she said flatly.

The words, 'Blakely Quarter Horse Stud Ranch,' forged from steel and painted white, ran along the top of the archway in capital letters.

"This is as far as I go," Mrs. Aylward said pointing through the middle of the archway. "Just follow this track—it'll take you to the homestead." She sat bolt upright, staring out between the buggy horse's ears.

"Thank you kindly, Mrs. Aylward," Penny said. "May I pay toward the buggy rental?"

Mrs. Aylward's eyes flashed. "I won't take money from ..." she began and then clamped her lips tightly shut for a brief moment. "No. It's all right."

"Well, thank you again, and I hope we'll have the pleasure of meeting again." Penny forced herself to say as she picked up her carpetbag and stepped down off the buggy. As she turned to help Hamish down, she caught Mrs. Aylward looking at her with a strange expression. The lady immediately looked away, back at the buggy horse's ears.

A twinge of unease prickled the back of Penny's neck as she turned away and walked beneath the imposing archway. What did that look mean? Why had Mrs. Aylward not completed her sentence. *I won't take money from ...*

"Ooh! Look, Aunt Penny! Horses!" Hamish pulled his hand from hers and broke into a run. Up ahead a few curious equine heads had lifted from their browsing among the sagebrush and were watching their approach.

Penny had always had a healthy fear of horses. It was a survival instinct honed in the streets of New York City where she had occasionally had to jump out of the way of the four horse carriages of rich young men intent on showing off the power and speed of their draft animals.

"Hamish! Come back here!" Penny called out, fighting down panic. If anything happened to him, she would not be able to forgive herself. But Hamish was deaf to all pleas for caution. He reached the barbed wire fence and reached out a skinny arm to one of the nearest equines.

Penny hurried closer, preparing herself to snatch her nephew out of harm's way, but by the time she got there, one of the horses had stepped closer and was blowing gently on Hamish's outstretched hand.

"Ooh! His whiskers tickle!" Hamish giggled. Penny's pounding heart slowed to a steadier pace. The other horses were ambling closer, apparently curious about this small, squealing human. There was no malice about them. These were not the snorting, eye-rolling beasts she was accustomed to. Their intelligent, liquid brown eyes struck Penny as unexpectedly friendly, and she felt her muscles slowly relaxing.

Hamish was scratching the horses' muzzles, delighted by their attention. Only then did Penny take the time to look closely at the animals. They were a variety of colors: rich biscuit with dark chocolate points; flashy reddish brown; patchy black and white; there was even one with a curiously spotted coat that made him look a little like the Dalmatian dogs Penny had seen in some rich estates on the outskirts of the city.

They seemed fat and healthy, their coats glossy and their eyes bright and attentive. Penny couldn't help wondering how that was possible, considering the arid conditions they lived in. Despite herself and her fears, she felt a stirring of curiosity. Perhaps there was more to this place, and the man who lived here, than met the eye.

A sudden urgency to meet this Mr. Blakely filled her heart. "Come along, Hamish, dear," she said, trying not to sound too impatient. "I'm sure Mr. Blakely is waiting for us." She took his hand and pulled him gently but firmly away from the horses.

"Can we come back later, Aunt Penny?" Hamish pleaded, not taking his eyes from the horses still staring at him over the fence.

"I'm sure we can, love. Let's just do one thing at a time, shall we?"

"Okay, Aunt Penny," Hamish agreed and trotted along happily at her side. A flood of gratitude washed over her for his good, kind heart, and she felt a pang of guilt at her impatience.

They walked on for what felt like about half an hour, with Hamish chattering all the way about what he'd just seen and experienced. Penny was about to suggest they find a patch of pinon pine to rest in when they topped a rise and the homestead lay before them, spread out in the late morning sunshine.

Penny didn't waste time ogling at the extent of the place or the beauty of the stone ranch house, built from the same pale boulders that had formed the archway at the entrance to her new home. She wanted to get the formalities out of the way and then try to forget the tragedy and heartache that had brought her here.

Marching right up to the double front door she gave three sharp raps on the brass knocker. It was fashioned into the shape of a horseshoe suspended from a horse's head. The sound echoed on the whitewashed porch where she and Hamish stood as well as inside the entrance hall of the great house.

Penny looked down at Hamish, telling herself she wanted to encourage him, but knowing that it was really she who needed encouragement. Cleaning a tiny, one-roomed attic home was one thing, but this was a palace. And she had no servants to help her like Prince Hamish the Kind in her stories. A sense of dread began to fill her.

She looked up. There was no sound. No response. Penny fought down irritation and rapped on the knocker again. Harder this time. She waited again. Hamish fidgeted. The carpetbag in her hand felt suddenly heavy.

"Where's Mr. Blakely?" Hamish asked in a worried voice.

"I don't know, Hamish," Penny said, turning around and glancing around the empty yard. "Maybe he's busy somewhere." Standing on the porch, waiting, made her feel restless. "Why don't we go see if we can find them?"

Hamish brightened visibly. "Yeah, let's!" He spun around and headed for the yard.

Penny dropped the carpetbag on the floorboards and followed her nephew. He was making a beeline for the barn.

Probably hoping there's some horses in there, Penny thought to herself with a wry chuckle. Hamish entered the barn first and disappeared into the deep shadows that contrasted so starkly with the bright sunshine outside. Penny had taken only a few steps more when he reappeared, his eyes wide.

"There's somebody sleeping in there, Aunty Penny," he informed her in a hoarse stage whisper. "He looks real tired."

Penny frowned. Sleeping? In a barn? In the middle of the morning? That could only be a vagrant. But how was it possible that any place this far removed from anything would have vagrants wandering about? Still, alarm bells were ringing in her mind.

"Stay here, Hamish," she said in her most authoritative voice. She took a deep breath and stepped inside. As her eyes adjusted to the darkness, the form of a man appeared in front of her. He was sleeping, all right. Sprawled across a row of hay bales, his mouth hung open and his eyes twitched, as if he was dreaming.

He didn't look like a vagrant, though. His clothes, heavy blue denim trousers and a sky blue and black checkered shirt, were clean and probably hadn't seen more than two summers by the look of them. His hair was slightly long for a man's, but it was clearly also clean and fell across his sleeping face in auburn waves. His face, clean shaven—although there was a bit of a five-o'clock shadow forming—looked handsome in a boyish way, sprinkled with a light dusting of ginger freckles.

All this would have made for a charming picture, if not for the unmistakable reek of whiskey that hung around him like a noxious cloud. The memory of that postscript in Mrs. Morgan's letter drifted to the top of Penny's thoughts. *Mr. Blakely's struggling with a little problem.*

So, this must be the little problem, *I suppose,* Penny thought grimly. The fairytale really was turning out to be too good to be true.

Penny hovered over the sleeping man for a while, unsure what to do. The chance was very good that this was her intended, and yet she'd had no description of him from Mrs. Morgan. Since that good lady would have picked her up at the general store, there had been no need for descriptions.

"Is he all right, Aunt Penny?" Hamish's voice beside her made her jump. Only then did she realize that her temper was mounting. Had she come all this way to marry a drunkard? What kind of danger was she placing Hamish in? Was she to be a human shield to the tiny, helpless baby this man had fathered?

For a moment longer, Penny stood undecided, then she made up her mind. She'd lived long enough in the slums of New York to have experience with waking men from their drunken stupor. She needed answers, and she wasn't about to wait around until Hunter Blakely—if it was indeed him—surfaced from his nigh comatose state.

Glancing around the barn, her eyes rested on the item she was looking for. A steel bucket full of water stood beside the barn door. Penny briskly stepped over to it, gripped the handle and hoisted it up to waist height. Conscious that Hamish was watching her with big, worried eyes, she marched over to the sleeping man.

For a moment she paused. This wasn't the best way to be introduced to one's betrothed. Perhaps she should cut him a little slack, let him sleep it off while she and Hamish took some rest in the ranch house. Then she shook her head. That whiskey hadn't got down his throat by itself. If anything, he had it coming to him to receive a rude awakening.

With that, she set her lips in a determined line and dumped the entire contents of the bucket over the sleeping man's head.

Chapter Four

Cold water hit Hunter like the monsoon hit the desert, jerking him to dazed and delirious wakefulness. He lurched up from the bales of hay and fell forward onto his hands and knees, spluttering and gasping and spitting out water. Wiping his sleeve across his eyes, he barked out an expletive and coughed wildly, his lungs apparently still convinced that their owner was drowning.

"I swear by all the saints, Sally, that's the meanest trick you've pulled on me since we were ..." He didn't finish his sentence as he lifted his head and rested his eyes on a stranger. Two strangers.

A young woman stood watching him with a scowl on her face. Beside her stood a little boy looking dubious. About what, Hunter could only guess. In that moment his mind was too occupied with trying to figure out what a complete stranger was doing in his barn in the first place. What had inspired her to almost drown him was a mystery he didn't even want to plumb the depths of.

"Who in the blazes are you?" he coughed.

The young woman regarded him balefully and, for a moment, it seemed as if she wasn't going to answer him.

"My name is Penelope White, and this is my nephew, Hamish," she said at last, in clipped tones. She was clearly upset, and this added confusion to Hunter's own anger.

"And what in the blazes possessed you to come in here, into my barn, and toss water in my face?" he demanded, deciding he didn't like the belligerence of the woman at all.

"The blazes didn't possess me to do anything, Mr. Blakely," she said pointedly. "I had to wake you since your cousin,

Mrs. Morgan, wasn't able to come fetch us from the stagecoach as she promised she would, and nobody responded to my knock at the door of your house. That was the only humane way I knew how."

Hunter blinked rapidly and coughed again. Everything beyond her first sentence was lost on him. She knew his name? Was she new in town? What was she doing on his ranch?

The awful realization that this woman, who clearly felt intense disdain for his drunken state, had witnessed something nobody in Four Horse had the foggiest idea about. How soon would it be before she shared his little secret with the town gossips, like—heaven forbid—Mrs. Aylward?

Anger and confusion were now joined by red hot shame in the tumult of emotions that addled his brain.

"How do you know my name, anyhow, Miss, ah, Miss, ah, Miss White?" he growled, brushing back the tangled, sodden strands of hair that straggled across his eyes. It was a vain but instinctive attempt to make himself at least partly respectable past the throbbing headache and growing nausea that threatened to overwhelm him.

Penelope White's face registered shock. Her nephew shifted closer to her skirts, peering out at him fearfully.

"I sincerely hope that it is only the alcohol that has robbed you of your memory, Mr. Blakely," she said primly. "It seems rather unlikely that one would forget the name of the person one had agreed to marry."

If she had thrown another bucket of water at him, Hunter would have been less shocked than he was by those words.

"Marry?" He broke into another paroxysm of coughing. "I don't know what game you're playing at, little missy," he spluttered angrily, "but you'd better haul your sassy little carcass off my land before I ..."

"Hunter, who are you talking to?"

It was Sally's voice. Where had she been all this time? How had she let this woman wander onto his land?

The woman turned toward the door of the barn as Sally entered. The latter's face was creased with concern as she waddled closer, pushing Maisie in her baby carriage.

"This woman figures I agreed to marry her, but I swear I don't know her from Eve," he said, jabbing an agitated finger at the stranger.

"Penny? Penny White? And Hamish?" Sally said, focusing on the two strangers instead of on him.

Then the truth hit home like a sledgehammer. She knew their names. That could only mean one thing. She'd gone and done it. The thing he'd made her promise not to do.

"Sally," Hunter said darkly. "You and me, we've got to ..."

"Yes, we've got to talk, Hunter." His cousin's expression was an interesting mixture of serene and determined. She grasped his elbow and steered him away to the feed bins in the corner of the barn.

"You promised, Sally," Hunter whispered accusingly, his fists clenched.

"I promised I wouldn't answer any ads," Sally clarified. "And I didn't. Long before I made you any promises, I placed an ad of my own, and Miss White replied. You don't think I would have gotten a reply so quickly? It was only yesterday I made that promise. Or do you even know what day it is?"

Hunter ignored the jibe. He had bigger fish to fry.

"So, you knew she was coming, and you didn't tell me?"

"What would it have helped?"

"For one thing, I would have made sure I was respectable when she arrived, is what," Hunter snapped back.

"I was afraid you'd stop her coming here," Sally admitted softly. "Besides, shouldn't you be making yourself respectable for yourself and for your own family, more than for strangers?"

Hunter didn't have a reply for that. He turned away with a muttered curse and tried to slow his breathing. He had to get a handle on this temper of his. It didn't help matters any.

"Hunter?" Sally prodded. She was asking him to agree to her hare-brained plan, he could sense it. But how could he? He'd spelled it out to her already that marrying again was out of the question, and she hadn't listened.

"I don't know what to think, Sally," he said grimly. "You've done a number on me this time, sis."

"I'm sorry, Hunter, I knew you wouldn't agree, but I also knew that you wouldn't find anyone in town. Heck, even if Ellie Rhimes hadn't gone to Big Bug, she would've turned you down, anyhow, and you know it. You'd still be in the mess you're in."

Hunter wished she'd stop referring to his situation as a mess, but her words were condemningly accurate.

"I cain't think straight right now," Hunter turned to face his cousin. "You're asking me to make a life changing decision on a hangover. That rooster ain't going to crow. I need more time."

Sally nodded earnestly. “That’s fair enough,” she acknowledged. She glanced back at Miss White and the little boy. “What do you want me to tell them?”

Hunter huffed. “The truth, Sally. Tell them what you did and tell them I ain’t made up my mind yet if I agree to all these shenanigans.”

Sally pressed her lips together. “Could I tell them they can stay here until you’ve decided?”

Hunter squinted at her. She was trying to get a foot in the door on their behalf, that was plain as the nose on her face, but Hunter knew why. Sally had always been the one caring for the poor drifters that sometimes wandered through their area. She was a natural saint. He could learn a thing or two from her about mercy. Him and his temper.

He nodded grumpily. “Until I’ve made up my mind. Not a day longer.”

Sally patted his arm with a knowing smile that lightly grated his nerves. Then she walked back to where Miss White and little Hamish were standing. She began speaking to them in a hushed tone. Hunter watched them, still trying to make sense of what had just transpired. The throbbing in his head was ever present, but the nausea had dissipated a little.

He focused on Miss White, finding himself wondering about the self-contained young woman. Where had she come from? Why would she have answered a mail order bride advertisement? Why would she have her nephew with her? The most logical explanation was that she’d had a death in the family.

Miss White was nodding now, as Sally spoke, and a look of greater understanding began to dawn on her face. Sally said something, and Miss White smiled tiredly, pushing her round, wire-rimmed spectacles higher on her button nose.

Her eyes were almond shaped and a melancholy olive green in a milky white, oval face. Pitch black locks of hair framed that face like a glossy mane, even though they were tied back and pinned behind her head.

She ain't half pretty, Hunter found himself thinking. In that moment, almost as if she'd heard his thoughts, Miss White glanced in his direction. Hunter quickly looked down, scowling deeply and pretending to be checking the contents of the feed barrels where he still stood. His neck flushed hot, and guilt washed over him in waves. What was he doing, admiring a young woman's looks with Amy not yet a year in her grave?

Get ahold of yourself, Hunter Blakely, he told himself crossly.

"Hunter, I'll take Miss White and Hamish to the house and get them settled in one of the spare bedchambers," Sally broke in on his thoughts. "Then we'll start on dinner together," she added.

Oh, great, Hunter thought, *she's wasting no time getting the girl in training.* Already the nagging feeling was growing in him that Sally was going to have her way. He almost wanted to tell Miss White she needn't worry, she wouldn't be going anywhere anytime soon.

Instead, he grunted, "Yeah, sure," and strode past them, out of the barn. He needed to get cleaned up and sobered up so he could order his thoughts. If there was any way out of this, he had to find it and right soon. But he couldn't do that as long as the devil was pounding at his brain with a blacksmith's hammer.

***

By the time Hunter had washed up and shaved after reluctantly downing another of Sally's prairie oysters, Miss

White and her nephew had deposited their single carpetbag of belongings in the spare bedchamber furthest from his. Thankfully Sally had had the presence of mind to do that. Make sure they were far removed from each other.

When he came downstairs, the two women were in the kitchen chopping carrots, onions, potatoes and celery and talking. At least, Sally was doing most of the talking. The girl stood quietly, giving short answcrs. Maisie was in her baby carriage, with young Hamish cooing over her with a rattle. Hunter stood watching them for a moment, then turned and left without a word.

He needed to get outside to the sun and the open spaces and his horses. The distinctive aromas of horse, leather and sagebrush never failed to calm his nerves when he was overwrought. He walked out to where his prize stallion grazed with his mares. Big Red was a flaming chestnut, his coat shimmering in the noonday sun. Hunter's pride and joy.

"Hey, there, old buddy," Hunter crooned, alternately stroking and patting the sleek animal's neck. Big Red responded by rubbing his forehead against Hunter's shoulder. "I sure wish my life was as simple as yours."

Big Red nickered and nuzzled Hunter's pockets. Hunter chuckled guiltily, rubbing the pure white star under the horse's forelock.

"Sorry, buddy." He sighed. "There ain't nothing there." He'd always made sure he had a couple of apples and carrots ready for his horses whenever he went out to spend time with them. Lately, he had been forgetting even that. His stomach twisted into an uncomfortable, guilty knot. The signs were small, but they were there. He needed to get his life on track, and he would need help doing it.

His thoughts wandered back to the new arrival in the kitchen. She was a way out, no doubt about it, but was she the best way out? What would he do with her when he was back on his feet? And the boy? He closed his eyes as his head began to spin and rested his forehead against Big Red's neck.

"What do you figure I ought to do, Red?" he muttered tiredly.

The horse gave no response. Not that Hunter had expected one. He leaned against the powerful animal and drank in the life that seemed to radiate from Big Red's burnished coat. Little by little the agitation in his mind and the alcohol in his body dissipated until he began to make sense of his own thoughts.

Sally had spoken truly. As much as he hated to admit it, her idea was better than anything he had managed to come up with. If he'd been smart, he might have gone along with her and at least been able to pick his bride himself. The thing was, he'd been so wrapped up in his own sorrows, he'd come to the point of taking his cousin and her selfless kindness completely for granted. He sighed and buried his face in Big Red's mane.

"Reckon I better face it," he groaned. "There ain't no way out of this. Sally's got me in a corner, and it's the one I painted myself into." As hard as he tried to steel himself, as hard as he tried to find the choicest words to use to send that uppity Miss White away, he knew it was all hot air.

Big Red nickered again and gave Hunter a hefty nudge with his muzzle. Hunter gave another chuckle, a wry one this time. He knew it was probably pure coincidence that the horse had shoved him in the direction of the house, but it felt uncannily as if old Big Red was telling him something.

"You reckon I ought to give her a chance? That what you're telling me? Help out the poor widows and the orphans?" Somehow saying it that way made it feel more like he was the benefactor instead of what he felt like: a drowning man clutching at a straw.

Big Red nickered and nudged him again. Hunter hesitated a moment longer, staring out over the rolling Black Hills that had been his home for as long as he could remember. At least he had a home. He'd be a doggone dog in a manger if he begrudged sharing it with two poor orphans. That's all it would be, if he let Sally have her way.

For a while longer he stood, fighting down his pride. Then he patted Big Red's well-muscled neck one last time, turned on his heel, and strode back to the house. Sally had forced his hand this far, but, by all the saints in heaven, he was going to be the one in control from here on out.

He marched into the kitchen to find the place filled with the delicious aroma of roasting meat and vegetables. Sally, Miss White, and the boy sat on the wooden chairs that surrounded the table. Miss White had Maisie in her lap and was feeding her applesauce under Sally's watchful eye. They all looked up as he entered.

"Sally, a word with you," he barked, avoiding Miss White's eyes.

Sally nodded, gave Miss White a smile and patted her arm, and then promptly joined his side. Hunter led his cousin out to the porch.

"Tell me about this Miss White," he said. "What do we know about her?"

"She's from New York," Sally replied without skipping a beat. "Her sisters died a little over a month ago when the sweatshop they worked in collapsed on them. She's only eighteen, and she's left all alone, no family, nobody to take care of her, and a five-year-old depending on her for food and shelter."

"Eighteen? She's still a child, herself."

"I know, but she's seen a wagonload of hard times already. Her ma and pa were killed in a train accident when she was a wee babe. Her two sisters were all the family she ever had. She basically raised young Hamish herself, since his mama was forced to work all day to keep a roof over the family's head and food on the table."

Hunter nodded, staring off into the rolling Black Hills in the distance. That kind of life tended to toughen folks up. Make them more mature than their years. His twenty-five years of life hadn't been rosy either, although they didn't compare to the kind of life Miss White seemed to have had. If she was telling the truth.

Still, even his small struggles had made a man of him. Losing his parents at eighteen and having to shoulder the full responsibility of a successful Quarter Horse ranch. Eighteen. The same age as Miss White was now. It felt like a sign.

Sally seemed to mistake his silent staring for stubbornness. She began to speak a little more forcefully. "I told you plain, Hunter, I cain't keep cleaning up your messes. You need someone to take care of Maisie, so you can be free to run the ranch. Pa would turn like a spinning top in his grave if he could see how you're letting things slide around here."

"That's enough, Sally," Hunter said softly. He didn't need to hear any more. He knew as much as anyone that it would be purely selfish to expect Sally to keep housekeeping for him. And he really had no other options. At least Sally had thought ahead and got things done, which was more than he could say for himself.

"I've done made up my mind," he said flatly, turning back to face her, his arms crossed over his chest.

Sally drew in a breath and held it, her eyes locked on Hunter's. He knew she was praying silently in her thoughts.

"Miss White and her nephew can stay and I'll, ah, I'll marry her."

Sally's face relaxed into a grateful, relieved smile.

"But don't any of you go thinking this is a real marriage, mind," Hunter cautioned her. "I know how you womenfolk are, your heads up in the clouds and all. She's here to mind my daughter and keep my house clean. She'll keep on sleeping in her own bedchamber at the other end of the hall." He stopped, aware that his cheeks were growing hot. The thought of a woman in his house, other than Sally or Amy, God rest her soul, made him feel decidedly self-conscious and uneasy.

"You won't be sorry, Hunter, I promise you," Sally said, her eyes brimming with joyful tears. Then she flung her arms around his neck and hugged him.

"I hope you're right, sis. I sure as heck hope you're right."

Chapter Five

Penny spent the rest of the day determined to simply focus on Hamish and baby Maisie. The latter wasn't too big of an ask; the little girl was a delight to care for. She smiled and gurgled happily, only screwing up her little face into a silent cry when she had soiled her diaper. Feeding and bathing the tiny human carried Penny back to the days she had done the same for Hamish, before he became a curious, independent five-year-old.

On the one hand, the memories made her feel happy. On the other, they reminded her of what she'd lost, and she had to blink back tears, hoping that Mrs. Morgan, who now insisted that Penny call her Sally, wouldn't see her crying. She didn't want the dear lady to think she was ungrateful. Sally had been so kind to her, which was a far cry from the treatment she'd received from the thoroughly unlikeable Mr. Blakely.

Blakely almost sounds like bleakly, she thought to herself. *Ironic. I wonder if that is any indication of my future here.*

But her gloomy thoughts were soon crowded out by an impromptu tour of the house and the outbuildings, Sally's endless prattling about the history of the ranch—which Penny only heard with half an ear and promptly forgot—and the important matters of taking care of the needs of two young children.

That night, as she lay staring at the darkened ceiling in the soft bed she had wished for on the stagecoach ride, she found she couldn't sleep. Memories seemed to crowd around her like a gaggle of ghosts, haunting her dreams and poking at her heart till it ached.

She didn't know when she'd fallen asleep, but when she did wake again it was to more poking. Only this time it was her ribs being poked. By Hamish.

"Aunt Penny! Aunt Penny!" he was saying, "Aunt Sally says we're to hurry and dress. We're going into town."

Penny hoisted herself blearily onto one elbow, trying to shake off the cobwebs of sleep that still clung tenaciously to her brain.

"Town? Why? What time is it?" Penny mumbled, punctuating her list of questions with a yawn.

"I don't know, we just got to get a wiggle on," Hamish said and giggled.

"Get a wiggle on? What in heaven's name are you talking about, Hamish?" Penny felt completely disoriented.

"It's what Aunt Sally taught me. It means we have to hurry," Hamish said.

Penny fought back a sudden burst of irritation only partly successfully. "Aunt Sally? It's Mrs. Morgan to you, my dear. We've barely been here one day, and already your manners are ..."

"Aunt Sally said to call her that, since we're going to be a family now."

Penny shot erect on the deep, soft bed as if Hamish had struck her with a thunderbolt. The wedding. She was supposed to be getting married today. Her eyes snapped to the drapes. Bright rays of light were streaming through the chinks between the heavy folds.

"Hamish! Why didn't you wake me sooner?"

"I tried, Aunt Penny, but you didn't listen."

Shame clutched at Penny's heart. Here she was supposed to be in this house to help, and she was sleeping well past sunup. It was unthinkable. Unacceptable. She'd better toe the line or Mr. Bleakly, ah, Blakely, might change his mind about letting her stay. Not that staying was what she particularly wanted. He was a drunkard, after all, and she'd never seen a woman happily married to a man like that.

Pushing aside the jumble of thoughts tumbling through her mind, Penny scrambled out of bed. "Tell Aunt Sally I'll be down in ten minutes," she said, vaguely aware that Hamish was fully dressed and seemed to have had his face washed and his hair slicked back with something or other that made it look wet.

"No need to fret," Sally's voice preceded her as she stepped through the doorway into Penny's chamber. "I was just monkeying about with the young man here," she added with a chuckle. "He's a bright little button, is our Hamish."

Penny gaped at the woman. She seemed to have no boundaries at all. It was clear she'd already made up her mind that Penny and Hamish were her family, and she was treating them as such. Penny wasn't used to that. In the city, people were far more guarded, more like that Mrs. Aylward who'd fetched her and Hamish to the ranch the day before.

Still, she had to admit it felt pretty good to be so unconditionally accepted.

"We have plenty of time," Sally was saying as she stepped blithely over to the window and opened the drapes. "Isn't it a lovely day?" She stood by the window, looking out at the rolling hills beyond and gently stroking her distended belly.

"I suppose it is," Penny replied, frantically gathering her scattered thoughts.

“Now, Penny,” Sally said, turning back to face her, “there are some clothes in this closet for you. I’m sure they’ll fit—at least, most of them will. See what you like, and you can just give me the others later, and I’ll have Hunter put them back in the attic. As soon as you’re washed and dressed, I’ll have breakfast ready for you, and then we can make our way to town.”

“Why, thank you, Mrs. ... I mean, Sally,” Penny said, embarrassed that the heavily pregnant woman in front of her was the one making breakfast for her.

“You’re more than welcome, sweet,” Sally smiled, her face glowing. “I figured you’d had yourself a real hard time of it in the last couple of months, and then that awful train ride out here. It’s no wonder you slept the sleep of the dead.”

Penny nodded, feeling close to tears. The woman’s kindness and understanding should be making her feel happy, so why was she wanting to cry all the time?

“I’ll leave you to your washing up,” Sally said and the next moment she was gone, the door clicking softly closed behind her. It took Penny a moment to realize that Sally had taken Hamish with her. In that moment, Penny buried her face in the colorful flying geese quilt and cried like a baby.

***

Penny sat beside Hunter on the driver’s seat of his buggy when they drove into town. It was the natural thing to do, but Penny had wished she could rather sit in the back of Sally’s husband’s buggy. She’d introduced him as Matt, and he’d been quite comfortable to have her call him by his first name, too.

They were both such warm, personable people. Cheese to the chalk of her soon-to-be husband’s brooding silence. At least, that’s how he was around her. Hamish, sitting in the rear seat of the buggy and watching over Maisie in her Moses basket, seemed to be making more headway with getting Hunter Blakely out of his shell.

From the moment the little boy clambered up into the buggy, he let loose with a barrage of questions about Hunter's horses. Penny tried to shush him a few times, afraid that he'd talk Hunter's ear off and put him in a worse mood than he already seemed to be in, but Hunter said, "Don't fret yourself Miss White, I like talking about my horses," while he stared off into the distance, avoiding her eyes.

So, she let the menfolk natter away about coat colors and how fast horses could run, though Hunter said horses didn't run, they galloped. Penny let their conversation float over her head, vaguely surprised at how much detail Hamish seemed to understand about what Hunter was telling him. Instead of listening, she took the time to study her betrothed.

His boyish handsomeness was even more pronounced, now that he was fully sober, although he looked a bit down in the mouth. Probably because he'd had to stay away from the bottle that morning, as well as the night before. Still, the clean, square cut of his jaw and the faint freckles on his tanned skin drew her eye. His auburn locks, which covered his ears and swept the collar of his rugged but rather becoming tan deerskin jacket, shone like copper in the sunlight.

Penny realized she hadn't noticed the color of his eyes before. She'd been too busy noticing the anger in them. They were deep, rich brown, like the color of hazelnut shells. She also saw something else in them that she hadn't seen before. A deep melancholy that, in a flash of recognition, mirrored her own. As quickly as it came it was gone and the curtain of detachment descended once more.

He hadn't even really looked at her, yet somehow, she knew that he knew she was watching him. Feeling silly, Penny looked away, staring at the desert around her but not really seeing it.

"You don't have to go through with this, ah, marriage if you don't want to," Hunter said, out of the blue. "There ain't a red-blooded woman alive who'd want to be hitched to a feller roostered half the time. I don't blame ya."

Penny didn't look at him, just let his words wash over her.

"You could stay at Matt and Sally's until you find something that's more to your liking," he added.

Penny fought back tears of anger. What was he thinking? Until she found something more to her liking? As if she were an overindulged child who didn't like that taste of her dinner and kept whining for dessert. As if she were spoiled for choice with an endless array of options.

Oh, there was no doubt that the thought of living with a man who apparently got what he himself called "roostered" on the regular was a deeply troubling one, but what was she to do about that? He was her only option, and she was going to have to make the best of a horrible situation. And pray that it didn't end in some terrible tragedy.

Heaven knew, if Hunter Blakely ever did anything to harm Hamish ... She left the thought unfinished, giving him a furtive glance. His eyes were riveted to the track in front of them. He really didn't seem like a violent person. He'd certainly been angry when she woke him in the barn, but she had not once felt threatened or feared that he might strike them, despite his intoxicated state.

"We came all the way out here on Sally's dime. We may as well stay and give it a try," Penny said, relenting from her inward burst of anger. "Besides, Hamish seems to like you."

"Can I be your stable boy, Mr. Blakely?" Hamish chimed in eagerly.

"I reckon you can," Hunter agreed, much to Hamish's obvious delight.

Penny thought she caught the glimmer of a smile on Hunter's lips, too, before he relapsed into what seemed to be a habitual long face. She had wondered before why Sally hadn't told her about Hunter's drinking problem if it wasn't his usual bent. She had also wondered how often he drank himself senseless, but she hadn't felt comfortable to ask Sally those questions.

Now she wondered what it could be that was driving this man to drink. His departed first wife? But surely his grief would be soothed by the presence of a beautiful baby like Maisie? There was something despairing about his drunkenness, and it resonated with something in herself.

Still, he was a stranger, and he was clearly not in control of his drinking habits. She would have to tread lightly and stay watchful. For her own safety and Hamish's.

"Well, here we are," Hunter said with a sigh. Penny looked around to find that they had already entered the town and stopped in front of a quaint little chapel. She had been so wrapped up in the complexities of her situation and the man she was marrying that she hadn't even noticed where they were.

"I'll just go see if I can rustle up the reverend," Hunter said, leaping nimbly from the buggy and wrapping the horse's reins around the hitching post. "Sally and Matt'll be a while. They had to drive a mite slower than us because of Sally being so far along and all."

"All right," Penny said. She could have sworn a shadow of guilt crossed his face when he said that last bit.

It didn't take long before Hunter emerged again with the reverend in tow. The man looked a little flustered, as if he hadn't been expecting to have his services required, least of all by Hunter, but he quickly recovered and greeted Penny and Hamish warmly when Hunter introduced him as the Reverend Harvey Wickham. Then he hurried them all inside the chapel.

By the time the reverend had his papers and books sorted out, Sally and Matt had arrived and deposited themselves in the first pew beside Hamish, who was still watching over Maisie, very serious about his new responsibility. Penny glanced back at them while the reverend began the nuptials. Sally gave her a warm, encouraging smile. Penny turned back to face the reverend.

He was talking rapidly, as if he wanted to get the business over and done with as quickly as possible. Penny's stomach twisted. She felt like she couldn't breathe. The reverend's words drifted meaninglessly around her like fall leaves in a windstorm. Penny glanced around, instinctively looking for a place of escape.

Instead of a way out, she noticed a man, standing outside one of the floor-to-ceiling windows. He was tall and lean, dressed in a deep royal blue wool suit with a pitch-black necktie and a dazzlingly white shirt. On his head he wore a black Stetson trimmed with silver. His face was as lean and long as his body, and the look on it sent a chill through Penny. She was about to lift her hand to point him out and ask who he was, when he disappeared.

Penny stood beside Hunter, hearing him repeat his vows after the reverend's rapid prompts, wondering if her eyes had just deceived her. Had she really seen someone? Or was her mind playing tricks on her? Who would stand glaring through the window of a chapel at a hastily proceeding wedding ceremony?

Shaking off the strange appearance of the man, Penny dragged her attention back to the reverend just in time to hear him prompt her with her vows. She repeated what he said, giving no thought to meaning of the words she was saying.

What did it matter anyway? It wasn't Hunter she was doing this for. It was for Hamish to have a hope for a future. Her own future didn't matter. She owed everything she was to Evie. Evie had given Penny a home, treated her like she was her own daughter, gone through the most heinous abuse, and staunchly protected Penny from it. Penny vowed she would do the same by her sister's son. Even if it killed her.

Chapter Six

"Y'all take care, now," Sally said breathlessly as Hunter helped Miss White up into the buggy. He reached out to steady young Hamish as the lad scrambled up to his seat at the back where Hunter had already deposited Maisie in her Moses basket. Turning back to face his cousin, he took a deep breath. He needed a drink and the knowledge that he couldn't have one only poured salt on his thirst.

"We sure will," he said, trying not to grit his teeth. Having Miss White there had been okay while Sally was around. Now the awful reality was leeching into his consciousness. If not for Hamish, he might have upped and changed his mind right there.

The boy proved his worth on the ride home, just as he had driving into town, keeping up a nonstop stream of questions. Sometimes he launched into his own observations and musings, and Hunter found himself beginning to thoroughly enjoy the little tyke.

"What are those funny trees that look like witches' brooms?" Hamish said when they were halfway home. He was pointing to a clump of the rather aptly described plants growing a distance from the wagon track.

"Those? Why, they're cholla cactus," Hunter informed him. "They look all soft and fluffy from far, but if you go close enough, you'll see that cottony-looking mop head is a mess of pretty dang sharp, pure white thorns. Some folks call 'em jumping cholla, 'cause you only need to come close in a strong wind to get a couple of them mean little barbs under your skin."

"You mean they can jump off the tree and burrow into my skin?" Hamish's eyes widened and he shivered, apparently imagining the sharp prickles leaping off their branch and burrowing under his skin like little white moles.

"They don't really jump," Hunter assured him. "But they sure do burrow. They got lots of little barbs facing the wrong way, too. Makes them powerful difficult to pull out once they're inside ya."

Hamish shuddered. "I'm going to stay far away from those witches' brooms," he vowed.

Hunter had to hand it to the boy. He'd chosen a name that suited the spiny cactus better than its official label, in Hunter's opinion.

"What does that word mean, *cholla*?" Miss White asked.

Hunter jumped slightly at the sound of her voice. He'd managed to shut her out, focusing on Hamish and things he could easily talk about. Things that didn't awaken memories. Now he was forced to remember.

"It's Spanish for skull," he explained, trying not to look at her too closely. "I guess 'cause they're all white and they make those round bunches. Maybe they looked like skeletons to the Mexicanos."

"Oooh! That's so spooky!" Hamish exclaimed, shuddering again.

Hunter laughed. "You could say so," he agreed.

"I was wondering how the town's name came about, too," Miss White said. She seemed to be warming to the conversation. On the way out, she'd sat in almost total silence, apart from when she'd tried to hush her nephew in the beginning.

"Four Horse?" Hunter said, searching his memory.

“I think that’s a funny name for a town that has lots and lots of horses, not just four.” Hamish knotted his brows in an apparent effort to understand the conundrum he had just presented.

“There’s folks that joke that it should have been called One Horse, since it’s such a small town.” He glanced over at Miss White to gauge her reaction. A smile tugged at the corners of her mouth, and she pushed up her spectacles again. She was such a pretty picture sitting there on the buggy seat, loose tendrils of jet-black hair being whipped about by the wind, caressing her alabaster skin.

As soon as the thought shot through his mind, his neck felt hot under his collar. He looked away and closed his eyes tightly for a second, trying to erase the image.

“But who called it Four Horse?” Hamish brought Hunter’s churning thoughts back to the subject at hand.

“Nobody really knows for sure. The story is, it kind of just happened. See, back when this land was first settled, my pa and three other fellers decided they liked these hills and claimed the land for their ranches. They all set to raising beef and planting melons and such, but soon they all turned to what they all loved most.”

“What was that?” Hamish asked, clearly fascinated by the tale.

“Horses,” Hunter said simply.

“I love horses the most, too,” Hamish declared proudly.

“I don’t doubt it for a minute.” Hunter smiled at the boy, wondering if he had ever been so grateful for the presence of a child.

Almost instantaneously, the gut numbing thought occurred to him that, in fact, he had. When Maisie was born, he was sure Heaven had become one angel poorer. And then, only a month later, Amy died, and Maisie was there to remind him, day by day, moment by moment, of the crushing loss he had suffered, the burden of guilt he had brought upon himself.

"So, there were four horse ranches here before?" Miss White herded his thoughts back to his story.

"Yeah. Four horse ranches. When a settlement sprung up between the ranches, folks used to call the place, 'the four-horse ranch town.' Well, that soon got shortened to Four Horse, and I guess it just stuck."

"Like a thorn from the witch's broomstick," Hamish interjected.

"Just like that," Hunter agreed with a chuckle.

"Sometimes the truth is more like a story than any story I could dream up," Miss White said pensively.

"What happened to the other horse ranches?" Hamish asked, looking as if the thought had just occurred to him.

"They went back to barley, melons, sheep, beef, that sort of thing," Hunter said, watching old Billy turn and trot under the stone archway without Hunter so much as twitching the reins. "Only my pa stayed with the horses. Became the best Quarter Horse breeder from San Francisco clear across to the Great Plains." In his mind's eye he could see the homemade trophies and ribbons lined up on the shelves of the small office in the barn. Prizes he and his father had won at many a county fair and harvest festival.

Decades of selective breeding were behind those prizes, matching just the right stallion with just the right mare to produce the fastest, smartest, steadiest, most driven Quarter Horses that ever ran a race or took part in a roping contest. And it had paid off, and then some. Folks from many neighboring Territories had come to buy his father's horses.

Hunter glanced around the yard as Billy trotted briskly toward the front porch. All at once, he found himself keenly aware of all the little signs that proper care and attention was not being lavished on the stud farm with such a proud legacy. Weeds growing between the cobblestones of the yard, a broken window here, a loose corral railing there, fading whitewash on the stable walls.

He sucked in a deep lungful of air. Sally was right. If Pa could see the place now, he would be turning in his grave, for sure.

The ever-present hopelessness that permeated most of his waking thoughts grew thicker, as if it was a live thing trying to suffocate him. How was he ever going to get back to where he'd been? Right at that moment, he was already imagining where he had stashed his latest supply of Old Farm Pure Rye. Until the memory of a pail of water being dumped over his head flashed through his mind. He didn't want that happening again.

More than that. It was time he stopped painting his throat, if only for the sake of his own dignity. But that was much easier said than done. If only he knew he could make himself stop, he'd just take one drink. Just to settle his nerves. But he'd been through that pantomime enough to know that whiskey was a wagon that had no brakes. It was better not to get on at all than to try to jump off halfway to having a brick in his hat.

"Hunter, could you help me down, please?" Miss White's voice broke in on his musings. He realized he was sitting on a stationary buggy, staring into nothingness.

"Oh, sure. Sorry, Miss White," he said, jumping to his feet and taking her hand. She froze. So did he. Her hand felt so small and yet so warm and strong between his clumsy fingers. For a moment their eyes locked, and then she looked down, her cheeks flushing irresistibly pink.

"I can understand you might not want to call me Mrs. Blakely," she said, "but perhaps it would be better to just call me Penny instead of Miss White. Most people do."

"Ah, sure. Yeah, I, ah, reckon that's fair enough," Hunter stammered, feeling foolish. "Begging your pardon, Penny."

Her name sounded happy on his tongue, without him trying to make it sound that way. Penny. It suited her. He wondered if she had a middle name.

"You can let go of my hand, now, Hunter," she said, and he realized she was already down on the ground.

Beginning to feel more foolish than he could ever remember, he handed Penny the Moses basket with his sleeping child and helped Hamish down.

"I'll turn old Billy out and park the buggy," he said unnecessarily. Penny nodded and walked into the house, the Moses basket slung between both arms as it rested on her hip and Hamish running ahead to get the door for her.

Hunter slapped the reins over Billy's back and sent the horse trotting to the barn. All through unhitching Billy from the buggy, rubbing the old boy down, and walking him out to the big corral at the back of the stables, he pushed away thoughts of Penny.

What was wrong with him? He never let his eye wander like that. What was it about this girl that was messing with his head? Again, he saw her before him, her guileless green eyes echoing the sadness that permeated every fiber of his body.

She seemed at once so sure of herself and so aware of her vulnerability, so purposeful and resourceful and yet so resigned to her fate.

Hunter wandered along the fence of the corral, absentmindedly tracing the rough, whitewashed rails with his index finger. He didn't want to go back to the house, and yet he felt drawn there by an invisible force. He wanted to know more about her, and yet he couldn't bear to be close to her. Just like Maisie.

The numbing truth began to dawn on him that if he was going to get back to where he was before, he would have to let go of Amy. He would have to release her to fate, or God, or whatever it was that had taken her, no, snatched her, from his life. But that was so hard to do.

He hadn't thought it possible to love a woman—to love any human being—the way he had loved her. Loving anyone else would be an insult to that person and a betrayal of his love for Amy. Or, at best, a poor replacement.

Black Bess, his oldest brood mare, came ambling closer, whickering throatily. Hunter's father had intentionally named her after Dick Turpin's horse in William Harrison Ainsworth's, *Rookwood.* She certainly had the heart and determination of the mythical horse and had birthed many foals who carried that same stamina and strength of character.

"Howdy, old girl," Hunter crooned softly, sliding his hand along her neck and under the thick, wavy mane that covered her entire neck. He drew his fingers through the locks, combing out tangles and the odd twig and burr. Soon Bess's mane was flowing free again, and Hunter stroked the black, glossy waves.

Before he could stop it, an image of Penny and the ebony, wavy crown that adorned her head, rose up in his mind. He wondered how it would feel to run his fingers through that mane.

As quickly as the thought appeared, guilt and self-condemnation followed closely on its heels like a pack of wolves after a jack rabbit. He jerked his hand away and stuck both hands under his armpits. Tramping angrily away from the horses, he headed for the top of the nearest hill.

Amy would have wanted you to be happy, Sally's words of only two days before echoed in his mind as he slogged up the hillside. Hunter's jaw clenched convulsively. He didn't want to be happy without her. He couldn't be happy without her. He wasn't supposed to be happy without her. He reached the top of the hill and let his hands drop down to his sides, balling them into frustrated fists.

"Don't you get it?" he roared at the brassy heavens. "She shouldn't have died! She should have been here, with me and Maisie! She wasn't supposed to die! Oh, God, it's all my fault. This is all my fault!"

The lonely cry of a prairie falcon echoed across the sky. Hunter fell to his knees on the rocks and wept, his only witnesses the saguaro cacti reaching their supplicating arms to Heaven.

Chapter Seven

A few hours passed before Hunter felt composed enough to make his way back to the ranch house. He tried not to think too much about the fact that he was a married man. Come to think of it, he'd never once thought of himself as not married after Amy's death. Seeing himself as single, or worse, a widower, would have forced him to accept that she wouldn't ever be coming back. He wasn't ready to do that just yet.

Without any idea how long he'd been out on the hillside wrestling with God like Jacob in the Bible, he stepped into the house, his ears and eyes alert. It was quiet. For a split second he wondered if Penny had decided to up and leave. A humorless smirk drifted across his lips. Theirs would be the shortest marriage in history if she had.

A growl from Hunter's stomach interrupted his musings and he looked at the clock on the half-moon table in the entrance hall. Three o'clock. He'd missed dinner, and his body felt it. Walking softly, trying not to creak a floorboard—he wasn't quite sure why he felt the need to do that—he entered the kitchen. The lingering aroma of cooking still hung about, making his mouth water.

A short search revealed a plateful of beef stew kept hot in the warm oven of the large coal stove. For a moment, Hunter hesitated. Then he scowled at his own silliness. How come he felt like an intruder in his own home? Just because some girl and her nephew had taken up residence with him? Of course, this meal was meant for him.

He took the plate, fetched silver from the sideboard and sat down at the kitchen table. Inhaling the fragrant, herby aroma, he tucked in. It was good. Real good. Either that, or he was powerful hungry.

He didn't notice Penny's entrance until she pulled out the chair opposite his and sat down. Hunter jumped, almost stabbing his cheek with the fork and just barely managing to escape choking on the mouthful of beef, rice and vegetables he'd just begun to savor.

"Oh, I'm so sorry," Penny said, sounding like she meant it. "I didn't mean to startle you."

Hunter shoved the food into his cheek so he could reply. "No harm done," he said, feeling foolish and looking around for a napkin to wipe his chin that was now covered in gravy.

Penny jumped up and fetched one for him. She handed it to him and sat down again.

"I'm glad you knew where to look for that," she said, her eyes on his plate of food. "We couldn't find you anywhere."

He had to hand it to her. She was taking her role seriously. That made him wonder exactly how seriously she was taking it and how clearly Sally had explained it to her. He swallowed and set down his fork.

"Yeah, I reckon I sort of disappeared for a while. Guess I should've told you I wouldn't be home for dinner." How he would have done that, he didn't know. He himself hadn't known he would be out there so long. It just felt like the decent thing to say.

Penny was tracing the woodgrain of the tabletop with her index finger. "No, no, not at all," she said. "This is your home. You should be free to come and go as you please."

Something about her manner struck Hunter as disingenuous. As if she was trying to be something she wasn't. The image of her standing over him with the bucket she'd just used to dump a gallon of water over his head didn't quite reconcile with the servile, mouse-like woman sitting across from him.

"While we're on the subject," he said, leaning back in his chair, "I reckon it would be good to hammer out what we can expect from each other. I don't know what you'd rightly call 'em. Rules make me think of boarding school. Terms of agreement, maybe?"

Penny looked slightly uncomfortable, but she nodded, and Hunter plunged right in.

"I ain't sure what Sally's told you, but one thing you need to know for sure. This, ah, thing ain't going further than you being a nurse for Maisie and helping me to keep house."

The words sounded more abrupt after they'd left his mouth than they had been in his head, but it was too late to do anything about that.

Penny pressed her lips together and nodded her agreement. She didn't take her eyes from his face, their warm olive green showing only the slightest bit of spark and sass behind her round spectacles. Beyond that was still the aching melancholy he remembered from the chapel.

"See, I ain't fixing to marry again. Ever." He paused. He could almost imagine her reminding him that he had just that morning got married. "I mean, not real, honest to goodness marry. The only woman I'll ever love, well, she ain't here anymore, and I'm forced to make changes I never had a notion to make. If you're, ah, ever looking to get out of this, ah, thing—say you find yourself a beau that sets your heart a'galloping like a quarter mile winner at the state fair—well, I'll be happy to let you go your way, and I'll go mine. Long as you first help me get another nurse and housemaid in."

Penny's eyebrows rose ever so slightly, and she blinked a couple of times. "You mean you'd divorce me and take another mail order bride? Whatever would the town have to say about that?" she asked and then immediately looked like she regretted it.

Hunter eyed her, trying to think of something to say that would put her in her place, but her words struck him suddenly as being so comical, so hysterically true, that he couldn't come up with anything.

A thin wail drifted through the doorway of the kitchen, instantaneously arresting Penny's attention. It saved a relieved Hunter from having to reply at all, especially when, a second later, Hamish ran into the room, his face stricken.

"Maisie's crying! Make her stop, Aunt Penny! I don't know how!"

Penny jumped to her feet and Hamish gripped her hand. He all but dragged his aunt out of the kitchen, and Hunter let out a small sigh of relief behind their departing backs. Then he looked down at his food. It was almost cold. He wolfed down the rest, distractedly wondering if he should take a nap after he'd finished it.

Before he could make up his mind, Penny was back with Maisie in her arms and Hamish in tow, the latter still looking concerned. The baby was still fussing a little even though Penny was cooing over her. His new wife looked up at him and gave him a smile.

"I think Maisie's missing her papa," she said and moved closer as if to hand the baby over to him.

Hunter stared at his child. She was the spitting image of Amy. Strawberry blonde curls hung about her soft-skinned face. Her wide, cobalt blue eyes looked up at him with unabashed curiosity. She smiled, and a single dimple dented her left cheek.

Penny may as well have thrust the fork on the table right through his heart. He stood up, taking a step backward. “Likely all she needs is her diaper changed, and that ain’t a job for a man,” he snapped. At the sound of his own words, shame engulfed him, even before the look of wounded confusion sprang into Penny’s eyes.

His gaze went back to Maisie. She was screwing up her eyes as if she was going to start crying again. He longed to hold her, to feel her soft warmth, her baby frailty, the trusting way she used to lean into him when he held her. Only, the sight of her awakened the ravenous guilt and sorrow that had eaten away at his soul for too long.

He turned and fled the room, not knowing or caring where he was going, as long as it was away from Penny and Hamish and Maisie. Soon, he found himself in the ranch office. He paced up and down, trying to remember if he had any Old Farm Pure Rye in the desk drawers.

At first, he resisted searching, but Amy’s face danced before his eyes, taunting him, reminding him that he would never again hear her infectious, musical laughter; never again race her across the valley on horseback; never again dance with her on the porch and kiss her by the tender light of a blood red, setting sun.

The next thing he knew, he’d found a half full bottle under a pile of old saddle blankets and was already almost finishing it. His pain blunted, he stared at the amber liquid and managed to think clearly for a moment or two before the drink rendered him oblivious.

Something’s got to give. Lord, help me. I cain’t keep going round this mountain. Something’s got to give and powerful soon.

***

At least Hunter managed to be sobered up before supper, although he was uncomfortably aware that the odor of old whiskey still hung about him a little. He poured himself a large cup of coffee from the pot before he sat down to the light meal of boiled egg salad, cornbread and preserves that Penny had prepared.

She peered at him from beneath her lashes, apparently waiting for him to do something. In a flash it dawned on his still slightly alcohol pickled mind that she was waiting to say grace. He couldn't remember when last he'd done that and had to fight off another flood of crippling guilt.

Hamish stared at him with wide, all too comprehending eyes. The boy seemed to know exactly what ailed his new landlord. In the physical sense, at least. Hunter cleared his throat and rapidly mumbled the grace he'd heard his father say so many times it was imprinted on his brain.

"For what we are about to receive, may the Lord make us truly thankful. Amen."

"Amen," Hamish and Penny echoed in unison.

Hunter looked down at his plate which Penny took and began dishing up for him. Unbidden the question flitted through his mind, *Am I truly thankful?* He knew he should be thankful. For Sally, for Maisie, for the ranch, for his beautiful horses, even for his newly expanded household. But he didn't know how to be.

Teetering between self-recrimination and self-pity, he had lost his grip on gratitude. After wallowing in negativity for so long, how did a body find his way back to thinking happy thoughts?

"I suppose I should have asked if you like boiled egg salad," Penny's voice brought him back from his internal journey.

Hunter raised his eyes to hers, taking a while to register what she'd said. He realized that she and Hamish had already begun their meal, and he was still staring at his plate, now full of food.

"Oh, ah, no. No, I like it well enough. I was just thinking of ..." he trailed off. It really wasn't her business what he was thinking of. A little twinge of irritation at himself stirred in his mind. Why had he felt comfortable enough to share anything with her? It had to be the lingering effects of the whiskey.

"Thinking of what, Mr. Blakely?" Hamish was looking at him with round, innocent eyes. Eyes that looked surprisingly similar to Maisie's, except they were a slightly deeper blue.

"Nothing, really," Hunter lied.

"I hope you won't mind my asking, but I was wondering about Maisie's mama," Penny said. "I was looking at your family pictures on the wall today in the drawing room. Maisie looks an awful lot like her."

Hunter clenched his teeth for a moment. He could almost hear Sally in his head, telling him to be nice to the poor orphaned girl.

"Her name was Amy," he said flatly, his eyes fixed on the fork he was loading with lettuce and tomatoes. "She was the schoolmarm at the one-room ranch school up at the Urquhart's place."

That was all she needed to know. It was more than he wanted to share. Hunter shoved the forkful of salad into his mouth and hoped she wouldn't ask any more questions.

"Oh, wonderful!" Penny said with what felt like forced cheerfulness to Hunter. "I love teaching, too. Do you mind my asking what happened to her?"

To her credit, her eyes held a look of sincerity when Hunter snapped his gaze from his plate to her face, but of all the questions she could have asked, she had to ask that one. Once more the boiling magma of anger at his lot rose to the surface and spewed its scalding fury all over an innocent.

“Yeah,” he snapped. “I sure do mind. You think I like thinking about it? The way she died? The way she upped and disappeared out of my life forever? Of course, I *mind*!”

The skin of his face burned with shame as much as with anger. Even as he spoke the words and saw that horribly familiar wounded look filling Penny’s eyes, he hated himself, but was still powerless to stop the torrent.

Hunter dared not look at Hamish. He could already imagine how he must be frightening the little chap, and he really didn’t want to. The boy deserved it even less than his aunt. The latter had now reverted back to her little mouse persona and sat frigidly pushing the remainder of her salad around on her plate.

The atmosphere was so thick, Hunter felt sure he could have cut it with his butter knife. He pushed back his chair. “Thanks for the grub,” he muttered. “Reckon I’ve had enough.”

Penny didn’t look up. Simply nodded her acknowledgement of his words.

Hunter stood up and left, his legs as leaden as his heart. He headed directly for his study and collapsed with a huff into the old leather chair that had belonged to his father. Leaving the room unlighted, he sat staring out of the window at the gathering gloom.

It had been a calamitous day. His wedding day. He harrumphed to himself at the irony. And then the guilt set in again. Those words he'd said at the altar, he had tried so hard not to think about what they meant.

The last time he'd said them, Amy had been standing in front of him, her sparkling blue eyes dancing with joy, her salmon pink lips parted in an ecstatic smile, her strawberry blonde hair piled up on her head in a mess of perfect curls dotted with baby's breath flowers.

Saying them again, to a perfect stranger this time, had taken every last ounce of willpower he had, but the knowledge that only hours later he had imagined combing his fingers through that stranger's silken, raven black hair made a nauseating sense of betrayal pulse through him.

"The girl and her nephew are desperate," he muttered to himself, trying vainly to mollify his conscience. "And Sally, I reckon I'd about wore out all her generosity, me being such a burden on her and all. It ain't like I even had a choice."

Tears stung Hunter's eyes as the betrayal morphed to waves of powerlessness and he reached reflexively for the bottom drawer of the great old mahogany desk that he sat behind. His fingers folded comfortingly round the tapered neck of a brown glass bottle, and he drew it out. For a while he sat looking at the label, telling himself that it wasn't a good idea to pull that cork. But his heart refused to believe him.

Four glasses later he had convinced himself that marrying Penny was an act of unadulterated charity and in no way a betrayal of his only true wife's memory. Somehow, though, the image of Penny's soulful, guileless eyes behind their darling wire-rimmed specs, refused to budge from his memory.

Those eyes echoed a sadness in his own soul that made him feel like she would understand him, like he could pour out all his pain to her, and she'd soothe it with the salve of her sympathy.

Hunter shook his head. It was feeling fuzzy. He had to stop those unwanted thoughts, but the whiskey seemed to have blunted his willpower as well as his pain. He rose from the chair and went to the open window. It was almost dark, that time of day when everything looked a little surreal, and it was hard to see where things ended, and their shadows began. A cool breeze drifted past and around him.

From the study, Hunter could look over the yard. A movement near the stables caught his eye. Peering into the dusky shadows, he thought he could just make out the form of a man. A tall man dressed in dark clothing, his pale face staring malevolently out from under a black hat that could have been a bowler.

Hunter shook his head and blinked a few times, then he peered into the gathering darkness again. The man was gone. Combing the yard and outbuildings with his eyes, Hunter tried to see where the man had gone to, but there was no trace of a living being in sight.

With a curse, Hunter looked down at the bottle still clutched in his hand. "Demon drink!" he muttered to himself and threw the offending amber liquor out the window with all his might. The bottle smashed onto the cobblestones below, splintering into a thousand pieces.

Chapter Eight

Penny lay staring at the wall of her bedchamber. It was rough, whitewashed adobe, from what she could tell, and somehow always felt cool to the touch, no matter how hot it might be outside. The featherbed beneath her felt like a cloud, reminding her of the story she'd told Hamish only hours before her sisters had been plucked from her life.

"No! No! I mustn't think about that!" she whispered crossly to herself, turning over and sitting up. Only then did she realize how light the room was. Her heart began to race. She'd done it again. Overslept. What were the Blakelys going to think of her?

She was trying so hard to be a good housekeeper and nurse. Just as hard as she was trying to keep a rein on the witticisms that had always made her sisters laugh so much. Sleeping late every morning was going to do nothing to inspire them to keep her on, no matter how hard she worked or how respectfully she spoke.

"Hamish?" Penny's eyes darted around the room. His cot in the corner was empty. Baby Maisie still seemed to be sleeping, although she would probably be waking up soon, and likely she'd be ravenous.

Penny leapt from her cozy down cocoon and frantically washed and dressed. She was just done when Maisie began to stir. Thank goodness the babe was already sleeping through the night, just like Hamish at the same age. Only, it felt like somewhat of a mixed blessing to Penny in that moment.

As she washed and changed Maisie, she hoped Hamish wasn't up to any mischief. She wondered why he hadn't woken her when he got up. Try as she might, she couldn't even remember hearing him wake and move about, let alone leave the room.

At last Penny clattered down to the kitchen with Maisie on her hip, the latter happily playing with a loose strand of her hair. Bursting in at the doorway, out of breath and feeling flushed, Penny's eye fell on Hunter already there. He was just lifting a full pail of frothy cow's milk onto the table.

"Oh, I'm so sorry, Hunter. I completely overslept," she huffed.

Hunter looked up, his face registering slight confusion.

"I said I'd come with you to the milking this morning, so you could show me how to do it," Penny explained with a bit of a question mark in her voice, wondering if he remembered.

Hunter's expression deadpanned, and he nodded his understanding. "Don't fret yourself about it," he said in a phlegmatic tone. "I found young Hamish trampoosing about outside. He turned out to be a fine assistant, the finest I've ever had."

"Really, Uncle Hunter?" Hamish said, having just come in at the kitchen door, a swathe of chicken feathers clutched in his hand.

So, it's Uncle Hunter, now, Penny thought to herself. *Hamish is settling in better than I am. I suppose that's something to be grateful for.*

Hunter smiled down at Hamish as the little boy came to stand beside the big man, squaring his skinny shoulders and imitating Hunter's stance. They made a beautiful picture. That and Hunter's unexpected smile sent Penny's heart into a little leap in her chest. He really was handsome when he smiled.

She shook the thought loose from her mind as soon as it entered it. No. Those weren't the kind of thoughts she should be thinking. He had made it abundantly clear that he would be quite happy to see the back of her if she happened to find a beau elsewhere.

Quickly she composed herself. "I'm happy to hear that," she said, forcing herself to smile, too. "I promise I'll be ready on time tomorrow morning."

"Oh, you can come help us tonight, Aunt Penny," Hamish informed her happily. "Uncle Hunter said I can try milking Mabel myself! Won't that be just dandy?"

"Dandy?" Penny echoed. "Why, Hamish, I do believe you're already turning into a country boy." This time she didn't need to force her smile.

Then she caught Hunter's eye. He didn't look amused.

"Of course, there isn't anything wrong with being a country boy," Penny added hastily. "I'm rather looking forward to becoming a country girl, myself."

Hamish ran around the table and hugged Penny around her knees. The look on Hunter's face hadn't changed, and Penny felt even more compelled to make up for her tardiness.

"Here," she said, holding Maisie out across the corner of the table to the little one's father. "Why don't you hold Maisie while you tell me what the next step is with the milk. It's meant to be strained through muslin now, isn't it?"

Hunter stepped back as if she had thrown boiling oil at him, inexplicable fear wrestling with the desperate longing swirling about in his eyes. Maisie gurgled and cooed.

"My hands ain't clean," Hunter protested.

"I'll hold her, Aunt Penny!" Hamish offered, reaching out eagerly.

Penny let him take the baby and went to fetch one of the muslin cloths she'd seen in the scullery. This was the second time Hunter had made an excuse not to hold his own child. She tried to remember if he'd ever picked her up on his own volition and couldn't recall a single instance of that happening. Strange.

Shrugging off the thought, she returned to the kitchen with the muslin and a large colander. Hunter had fetched a clean, empty pail and placed it on the table beside the one full of milk.

"It's real easy," he said, his voice a little gruff. "Just pop that muslin in the colander, put it on top of the bucket and pour."

Penny followed his instructions, readying the colander and muslin, while he lifted the heavy pail and did the pouring. The warm, sweet scent of freshly drawn milk filled Penny's nostrils. It was a strangely comforting scent.

She looked at Hunter. He was focused on his task, his hazel eyes peaceful in his freckled face, the auburn curls in his neck willing her to slide in a finger and pull them out from under his shirt collar.

Penny sucked in her breath. The last of the milk sloshed into the colander. Hunter looked up at her, his gaze searching. "Something wrong?" he asked. For a moment the guardedness, the simmering anger, the cool aloofness were gone.

"Ah, no, no, nothing at all," Penny said turning her focus to the colander as she lifted it up and shook it a little. It was more an effort to get ahold of her thoughts and her racing heart than to shake out the last drops of milk from the muslin. She hoped Hunter wouldn't notice.

Penny moved over quickly to the washbasin standing beside the stove and dumped the colander inside. "I think I'll feed Maisie first before I wash this out," she said. "Some fresh warm milk will do her good. I think she must be famished by now, what with my tardiness and all."

"Sure," Hunter said, although he didn't sound very sure.

"Hamish, won't you get me her bottle from the scullery?" Penny said. "Let Uncle Hunter hold her for a while. I'm sure he'd like to give his little girl a proper good morning."

"I'll get the bottle." Before Hamish could respond to Penny's instruction, Hunter set off in the direction of the room in question. Penny frowned to herself. That was the third time. Why was he so averse to holding his own baby? Or was she just being oversensitive to read that into his behavior?

Hunter soon returned with the bottle. Penny filled it from the pail on the table, conscious of his eyes on her.

"I, ah, I'm, ah, awful sorry for the way I snapped at you yesterday," Hunter said, almost making Penny slosh a ladleful of milk over her hand instead of into the bottle. "I reckon I'm all out of sorts. Ain't used to sharing my space with, ah, strangers."

Penny set down the half full glass bottle. She forced herself to look him in the eye, even though his apology was as unexpected as his smile, and it made her heart flutter. "We are still strangers, aren't we? And I do ask an awful lot of questions. Evie always told me I need to learn to allow people their privacy and not be such a busybody."

Hunter nodded. "Still, I had no cause treating you so mean."

Penny felt herself soften. She gave him what felt like a slightly sheepish smile. “No hard feelings,” she said.

In that moment it struck her that there was no reek of whiskey hanging about him. She’d heard the bottle smash on the cobblestones of the yard the night before, heard him storm from his study to his bedchamber and slam the door. Perhaps he was fighting the urge. Could he be doing it for Hamish? For Maisie? For her?

Her heart fluttered again, and she cleared her throat self-consciously, realizing that her gaze was still locked onto his. That aching but resigned melancholy she’d had a glimpse of during the buggy ride to their wedding was back. She almost began to believe he wanted to bare his heart to her, but the next instant he turned away and began washing the colander and the muslin cloth in the basin.

“Oh, no, please, I’ll do that,” Penny said, suddenly filled with a desperate need to be kind to him, to make his life as simple and easy as she could. Hunter paused in mid scrub and lifted his head, but he didn’t turn around. Penny picked up the baby bottle and hurriedly forced the feeding tube over the open end of the bottle.

She pinched it under her arm and strode over to where Hamish sat playing with Maisie on the floor. Picking up the little girl, she hurried to Hunter’s side.

“Here, why don’t you feed her? I’ll show you how if you haven’t done it before. It’s really quite simple.”

Hunter’s eyes, when he turned to look at her, were full of shadows. He took a step backward again. “No, I, ah ...” he faltered, then his face lost all expression. “No, thank you, ma’am,” he said stiffly, clearly working hard not to snap at her. Penny’s heart sank as her confusion returned.

"Why not, Hunter? I don't understand. I feel certain you love her, so why would you not want to hold her?"

Hunter's eyes glistened as they rested on Maisie who was squirming in Penny's arms. His hands clenched into fists at his side. He took another step back.

"Sure, I do," he croaked. "But how's a feller like me supposed to know the first thing about babies? Next thing you know I'll have her passing on my conscience, too."

His eyes looked haunted and angry at the same time, but Penny didn't get the sense that the anger in them was directed at her. His words echoed in her mind as she tried to make sense of them.

"I said I'd show you how, and I promise I will," Penny said pleadingly. If only he could get past his irrational fear, he could know the unequalled joy of nursing an infant. Not just any infant. His own flesh and blood.

Hunter simply shook his head and brushed past her, making a beeline for the outer door. "I'll be back for dinner," he said as he passed by her. In a matter of seconds, he was gone, marching across the yard with strides that ate up the ground.

"Hunter! Wait!" Penny cried out. Maisie began to fuss and whimper in her arms. Hunter had already reached the barn. "You haven't even had breakfast yet," Penny said softly, knowing there was a good chance that he wouldn't hear her even if she screamed at the top of her lungs.

"Can I still have breakfast, Aunt Penny?" Hamish's innocent voice drifted up to her from where he stood tugging at her sleeve. "I sure am hungry. So hungry I could eat a whole cow."

Penny looked down at her nephew, trying to banish the image of a departing Hunter from her mind. "I don't have a whole cow, but I'll scramble you some eggs, Hamish, how about that?"

"Ooh! Yes, please! I love eggs!"

Penny did, too. Only, that morning, she had absolutely no appetite. Maisie began to bawl lustily in her arms, and Penny wished she could sit down on the flagstone floor and join her.

Chapter Nine

The days that followed were fraught with a strange atmosphere. To Penny, it felt not unlike an armistice. Penny didn't try to get Hunter to hold Maisie or play with her, and Hunter treated her with stiff deference. He didn't meddle in her housekeeping. In fact, he was hardly ever at the house, spending most of his time with his horses.

An almost desperate industriousness possessed him. Penny would watch him from the top story of the house sometimes, working like a Trojan as he, repaired loose shingles, mended splintered corral rails, and cleared the weeds from amongst the cobblestones and around the outbuildings.

Penny got tired just watching him some days, but she dared not offer her help, convinced that he would simply refuse it. She had the impression he was inflicting some sort of punishment on himself, although he did let Hamish buzz around him like an excited honeybee, jabbering away non-stop but executing with deadly earnest each task that Hunter gave him.

Sometimes Penny would take out a pitcher of lemonade and some oatmeal cookies that she'd baked. She'd discovered the previous Mrs. Blakely's recipe books, shoved in the bottom of a pantry shelf and covered in dust, and they were an absolute gold mine.

Whether Hunter recognized the recipes of his daughter's deceased mama, Penny had no way of knowing. He didn't say anything, so she went on using them, grateful for the clearly written instructions and measurements. Her resources had been limited in New York, unlike the well-stocked Blakely pantry, and she desperately needed the help.

Often, Penny would simply sit watching Hunter and Hamish working and wonder what the former had meant by that strange remark in the kitchen the last time she'd offered to have him hold his baby.

Next thing you know I'll have her passing on my conscience, too.

Did he really think Maisie was so frail and fragile that his simply holding her would crush her to death? Surely, he had held her as a tiny newborn. All fathers did. Even if they didn't change diapers or nurse them or bathe them. What in the world could he have meant by that?

On the fourth day after the unannounced truce had begun, which happened to be a Saturday, Hunter announced during dinner time that he was going to visit Sally and Matt, and that Penny was welcome to tag along if she had a notion to.

"I'd love that," Penny replied with a gracious smile. She looked at her nephew who was obviously all ears. "Wouldn't you, Hamish?"

Hamish nodded vigorously, his mouth full of pumpkin pie and his eyes shining.

"Well, then. We'll hit the trail in an hour," Hunter said. Then he cleared his plate and excused himself from the table in short order.

The ride out was just what Penny needed. She'd been longing for even a small change in the routine, but, more than that, she'd been longing for some female company. Now that life was progressing and taking her further and further from the last time she'd sat around the coal stove in the attic room with Evie and Sarah, telling stories and laughing together, she became keenly aware of her need for a woman to unburden herself to.

Hunter and Hamish chattered away incessantly all the way into town and Penny simply listened, silently turning over in her mind all the questions she had to ask Sally and wondering if it was even a good neighborly thing to do. The dear lady was far advanced in the family way, after all. More than likely, she wouldn't be up to having a veritable stranger pepper her with endless questions.

"Well, here we are," Hunter said, interrupting Penny's thoughts.

He parked the buggy and helped Penny and Hamish down. Then he unhitched old Billy, as Hamish had told her the buggy horse was named, and walked beside Penny toward the Morgan residence, with Hamish skipping along ahead of them.

It was a happy reunion, with Matt and Sally thankfully doing most of the talking. Hunter seemed to relax more in their presence. Penny was grateful for that, but her mind kept wandering to the roiling questions in her mind and she had a hard time keeping her focus on the lighthearted conversation going on.

When the tea and flapjacks were finished, Sally sent the men, including Hamish, to do the washing up and motioned to Penny to come closer.

"Penny," she whispered conspiratorially, "Matt and I were talking, and we figured we'd like to buy some new clothes for Hamish. You wouldn't mind, would you? It'll sure be an honor for us, after all you've done for Hunter and me."

Penny blinked. "Oh. I don't know what to say," she replied honestly. "Of course, I won't mind, I just, well, I can't ..."

Sally held up a finger to her lips. "It's a gift," she said and patted Penny's hand.

On hearing that he was to be measured for some new clothes, Hamish's eyes stretched big as saucers in his face and his grin threatened to split his head in two.

"Uncle Hunter and Uncle Matt can both go with you, Hamish," Sally said, clearly enjoying the little boy's delight. "That'll give us girls some time alone. I'm sure Penny's had about all she can take of you fellers, right, Penny?" She gave Penny a wink.

Penny laughed but didn't reply.

The *fellers* left, with Hamish's mouth still going nineteen to the dozen. They were barely out the door when Sally turned to Penny, her hands gently stroking her rounded belly. It seemed to be a habit and Penny couldn't help thinking that the baby who would soon be born was going to be one of the most well-loved children in all the world.

"Penny," Sally said, her voice velvet with heartfelt kindness. "I know Hunter ain't a picnic to live with—I grew up with him, after all, so I've seen him at his worst."

"And he's at his worst right about now, isn't he?" Penny said softly.

"Pretty much." Sally gave Penny an understanding smile. "If I weren't in this condition, well, I'd be over there every other day, no doubt about it. I do hope you'll come on over anytime you're needing some time away from him."

Penny shook her head. "Hunter is trying his best, I can see that," she said softly. "I've just been missing my sisters." She paused. "I can imagine it would be even worse for Hunter, having lost his wife. I can tell he truly loved her very deeply. He must miss her horribly."

Sally's eyes misted up with tears. "We all do," she said with a catch in her voice.

Then she shook her head as if trying to dispel the sadness that threatened to overwhelm her. Penny knew that feeling all too well. Before she could order her thoughts to share them with Sally, the older woman patted her arm.

"I'm sure you must have questions about Hunter and Amy. I hardly think he'd have shared much with you."

Penny blinked. "Why, yes, I do," she said, immediately wishing she hadn't responded so eagerly. "Well, I do wonder about some things, but I can understand if he doesn't want me to know."

Sally smiled. "More likely he just doesn't want to talk about it. There ain't a reason in creation you shouldn't know all there is to know, seeing as you're his wife."

"Not his *real* wife," Penny reminded her quickly, feeling her cheeks tingle.

"Still, you're living in the same house as him. You'll need to know how not to step on his toes and if he ain't giving you pointers, well, I reckon it's my duty as his adopted sister to pick up the slack."

Penny stared at Sally waiting for her to say something more, until the questioning look in her new friend's face made it clear that Sally was waiting for her to begin with the peppering she'd thought a woman heavy with child would not want to hear. Sally had even stopped stroking her stomach, her full attention riveted on her guest.

"Well," Penny began hesitantly. "I surely can understand why he wouldn't want to talk about ... what happened to Amy."

"Ah, yeah," Sally said, a tender sadness coming into her eyes. "He wouldn't. I'll just call a spade a spade. It was childbed fever. Took her real fast. The doctor came soon as he could, but she was too far gone ..." her voice trailed off.

"Childbed fever," Penny repeated thoughtfully.

"Yeah. The dangdest thing is, Hunter figures it's his fault she died, and he won't budge on that nohow, no matter how much any of us try to talk reason to him."

A light was slowly dawning in Penny's mind. *Next thing you know, I'll have her passing on my conscience, too.*

"But surely, he couldn't have done anything to save her?"

"He says he should've seen the signs sooner, should've sent for the doctor sooner, should've had her birth in Prescott." Sally shook her head. "I've told him a heap of times there ain't a thing he could have done, but he won't listen. He's still taking it real hard."

"That's why he drinks, isn't it?" Penny said.

"Yeah. I hope he hasn't been looking too deep in the bottle since I left." Sally gave her an apologetic look.

"I don't know for sure when last he drank anything, honestly, but I do believe he's going all out to resist temptation," Penny felt happy to report.

Sally looked relieved. "Things'll get better, you'll see," she said leaning back in her chair as she resumed stroking her belly. "He's truly a good man, is our Hunter. Just wading through a bad patch now, is all."

"I believe you," Penny said, once again feeling the bitter guilt of having survived while her sisters perished. "I've often wondered why Evie had to go instead of me. If I'd only disobeyed her and gone to the factory in her place that day. Then at least Hamish would still have his mama with him."

"He's blessed to have you, though. And it really wasn't your fault the building collapsed," Sally reminded her, placing a gentle hand on her shoulder. "Not that it makes missing your sisters any easier, knowing that." She paused, staring past Penny. "Amy was like a sister to me, you know? I still can't get used to the idea that she's gone, and it's already been nearly nine months."

"Do you think it ever gets any easier?" Penny asked, feeling as if she'd known Sally forever and wondering if it was God's way of giving her a sister in place of Evie and Sarah, someone who could understand her pain.

"I don't know," Sally said, tilting her head to one side. "I reckon the only way for us to find out is just to go through it."

Penny smiled at her. There was a sort of resignation in Sally's eyes, too, just like in Hunter's. It was a different kind, though, more hopeful, as if she were looking for the rainbow after the storm.

"I hope it gets easier for Hunter," Penny said. "I sometimes feel like a bit of an albatross about his neck even though I'm trying hard to give him all the support I can."

Sally's eyes twinkled. "Don't you mind him, Penny. Having you and Hamish here is a blessing he'll thank me for later. You mind my words."

Just then, Maisie stirred in her Moses basket on the floor beside Penny. She blinked and yawned. When her sleepy gaze focused on Penny's face, she reached out her chubby hands and gurgled happily.

"Looks like that little miss wants to join the confabulation," Sally said, her eyes brightening. Then she jumped, her hand on Penny's shoulder returning quickly to her stomach. "Oh, and so does this one!"

Penny laughed from her belly for the first time in longer than she could remember. “Maisie likely wants to go crawling around, too. I’ve had all my days trying to keep her from crawling clear out of the house. Was she that mobile when you were still at the ranch?”

“Oh, all the time! All the time,” Sally laughed. “I reckon she’s about ready to start walking.”

“So do I,” Penny agreed. “She’s been pulling herself up on everything in sight. It’s a wonder she hasn’t injured herself dragging the crockery from the dining table yet. I feel like I need to grow eyes in the back of my head sometimes.”

As she spoke, Penny lifted Maisie out of the basket and deposited her on the floor. Almost at once, the baby girl crawled away, clearly eager to explore her new surroundings. Penny let her go, keeping a watchful eye for anything that could pose a danger to the adventurous infant.

The sound of men’s voices, interspersed with Hamish’s excited chattering drifted in from the porch, and moments later, Penny watched as Hunter entered his cousin’s parlor. At the sight of Maisie propelling herself determinedly across the floor, he stopped in the doorway and stared at her. Maisie, who’s neck had been craning upward, also paused.

For a moment, Penny’s heart stood still. From what she could tell, father and daughter had locked their gaze, and she felt a shiver of anticipation run through her. Maisie reached out a hand and gripped the leg of the Queen Anne chair beside her. With a little grunt of effort, she pulled herself up.

Penny held her breath.

Maisie reached out her free hand to Hunter, talking excitedly in her baby gibberish. Hunter didn’t budge, his eyes still riveted on his only daughter.

Penny's heart ached. If only he would move toward her. If only he ...

In one lightning quick movement, Maisie pushed herself away from the chair and took a shaky but purposeful step forward.

Her very first step.

For a breathless moment she teetered there, and as if time had slowed to a crawl, Penny saw the child begin to topple forward.

Penny froze, knowing instinctively that she was too far to catch Maisie. Her heart leapt into her throat, strangling the cry of alarm that tried to escape her.

In that moment, Hunter took a giant step forward, reached out his strong arms and hoisted his baby to safety. Penny half expected him to keep her at arm's length and carry her back to her basket, but instead, his face crumpled, and he pressed the child against his chest.

Penny watched, transfixed, as silent tears began to stream down her new husband's face. Maisie was patting his damp cheeks, jabbering away in her birdlike manner.

Tears sprang into Penny's own eyes as she watched. For an ethereal moment she, Hunter, and Maisie were the only people in the room. Everything else ceased to exist for her. There was no doubt in her mind that the awe that filled her was the same kind she would have felt if she were witnessing a miracle of healing performed by Jesus Himself on the streets of the Holy City.

***

Penny lay on the soft luxury of her bed and stared into the darkness above her while tears trickled down the sides of her face. The events of the afternoon played through her mind like a pantomime on a stage, Sally's words echoing in every image.

Don't you mind him, Penny. Having you and Hamish here is a blessing he'll thank me for later, you mind my words.

Penny couldn't deny that she wanted Sally's prediction to be true.

If only things could have been different. If only she could have written a beautiful romance for herself and the alluringly mysterious and deeply troubled soul she now found herself irresistibly drawn to. But real life and fairytales were two very different things.

It all felt so unfair. Now that Sally had answered her questions, Penny felt an uncanny solidarity with Hunter. They shared the same pain, the same guilt, the same hopelessness. Surely two people who understood each other so well would be able to live in a more harmonious state than anyone else?

And yet a deep foreboding hung over her heart and mind. She and Hunter were clearly two broken souls, bereft of the most precious people in their lives. Any romance between them would be doomed to more heartache. Broken vases could cut deep wounds, no matter how many flowers they held.

No. In reaching for her own happiness, she might very well become a curse in his life.

I have a role to play, she reasoned. *I'm here to ease his burden for the time being. And I'll do that, faithfully and diligently, until his heart has healed enough to love again, and then he'll find someone blithe and carefree. Some innocent girl who'll shine joy and laughter into his life. That's something I'll never be. Not anymore. No more fairytales for me.*

Chapter Ten

Hunter could hardly believe the blessing he'd had bestowed on him. The gift of seeing his precious daughter take her first step was like sign from heaven. It got him thinking that maybe there was a God after all. A God who was giving him a second chance to be the father he yearned to be and yet despaired of becoming.

The bittersweet joy that had filled him when he held Maisie for the first time since her mama passed was a sensation he began to crave, and he found himself making all sorts of excuses to stop in at the house during the day, just so he could see her. For so long, he'd been racked with guilt at the knowledge that his daughter needed him, and he was failing her. Now he saw how much he needed her.

Maisie seemed only too happy to help him bridge the chasm of his own making, and her first step became the forerunner of many, many more. Most of them took place where he was present, holding out his hands and ready to catch her if she showed even the slightest sign of falling.

"If only your mama could see you now, sweetheart," he whispered to her one day as he lifted her up into the air. She laughed and kicked her happy little feet.

Hunter swallowed down the unbidden lump in his throat, remembering how excited he and Amy had been when they'd found out they were soon to be a family of three. They'd talked about moments like this.

Hunter could hear her voice again as if she were in the room with him once more.

"I want you to be there for all her firsts," Amy said, her eyes shining like polished sapphires. "Her first step, her first words, her first everything!"

"Well, you'd better be sure to call me when you see things heading in that direction, love," Hunter teased.

Amy laughed. "Never. You'll have to hire someone else to take care of the horses and the ranch. Our Maisie needs you more than they do."

Hunter smiled at the memory as he swung Maisie down to the floor again and held her hands while she beat her stockinged feet energetically on the rug. At the time, he'd argued that it would take too long to teach somebody else exactly how he liked his horses cared for and trained. Now he felt ready to follow Amy's suggestion in a heartbeat.

"Thing is, I reckon we have Penny to thank for even making it possible for me to spend time with you, princess," he said to the top of Maisie's head. Maisie responded with a squeal of delight, almost as if she understood her father's words.

A twinge of conviction made him draw in his breath sharply. He'd underestimated Penny's role in his life. Grossly.

On impulse, he carried Maisie through to the nursery where Penny was teaching Hamish to read.

"'F', fff, 'I', ie, 'G', guh, f-i-g, fig!" Hamish said with a triumphant flourish at the end.

"Excellent, Hamish!" Penny praised her student.

Hunter cleared his throat, and she spun around, looking inexplicably guilty.

"Oh, is Maisie hungry? Does she need her diaper—"

Hunter held up a hand, cutting her short. "Maisie ain't the reason I'm here," he said, trying not to notice the endearing way she looked searchingly into his face. "Well, if I'm honest, she really is, but it ain't her diaper I'm here about."

"Oh," Penny said, looking nonplussed. Hamish left his reading book and reached out his arms for Maisie. The latter was only too happy to be relinquished to Hamish's care.

"I reckon I owe you a debt of gratitude," Hunter said, hoping Penny would see how sincere he was.

"Me? Whatever for?"

Her round, innocent eyes drew him in like a cottonwood leaf in an eddy on the creek. "For reminding me that I need to be part of my daughter's life. 'Specially now, while she's still a tiny tyke hitting milestones like her first step and all. It's you who made me realize how important that is."

Penny smiled bashfully. Then a little spark of impishness twinkled in her eye. "She hasn't got her milk teeth yet. You might not want to thank me for anything once she reaches that stage."

Hunter stared at her, unsure what to make of her words.

Penny laughed a bubbling laugh that could have belonged to a water nymph. It made Hunter feel instantly happier than he'd felt in months. He couldn't help but laugh, too, and in that moment, Penny ceased being a stranger.

Hunter stepped to the window, unsure what to do with the feelings darting around in his chest like swallows before the rain. Only days before, he hadn't expected to feel happiness for years to come and yet, here he was, laughing into the lively green eyes behind Penny White, no, Penny Blakely's perfectly round spectacles.

She came to stand beside him, and they gazed out at the shimmering blue haze of midday heat that hung over the hills around the homestead.

"I'm afraid I can't take credit for making you realize anything, Hunter," Penny said, her voice slightly husky. "You did it all yourself."

Hunter shook his head, but he didn't contradict her. For some reason he felt an extreme aversion to arguing with the petite, vivacious woman beside him. Instead, he let his mind drift to happier times and his lips involuntarily shared those memories with his new wife.

"I was scared out of my wits when Amy told me she was expecting," he said, once more feeling the terror of that heavy burden of responsibility. "I didn't know dang all about being somebody's pa. Figured I could never be as good a pa as mine was, especially since he weren't around to show me the ropes no more."

"That's how Evie felt when she knew she was expecting Hamish," Penny said with a wry chuckle. "And Sarah and I, too. I was just thirteen when he was born, and I knew Evie and Sarah wouldn't be able to stop working at the factory. Especially not with another mouth to feed. I can't tell you how terrified I was at the thought that I'd have to take care of a tiny, helpless babe, and me still a child myself."

"I can only imagine," Hunter said, looking at her with new eyes. Then he corrected himself as the full desperation of the picture Penny had painted became gradually clearer in his mind. "No, I cain't even do that."

It was true. His circumstances had never been that dire. After his parents died, he'd always had Sally and then Matt, too; not to mention the ranch and his horses. And now he had Penny and Hamish. How had he not seen before how blessed he was?

Most likely my brains were too pickled to even think straight, he thought wryly.

For a long moment, he and Penny stood silently side by side, and he wondered at how comfortable he felt with her around. It was almost as if she were meant to be there. He looked at her hand resting on the wooden, whitewashed windowsill. At once the urge filled him to take that hard-working but gentle hand in his own.

His pulse throbbed erratically in his neck as he fought the feelings that now threatened to break loose from him, and he forced himself to keep his breathing calm and steady. What was happening? Thinking about combing his fingers through her hair was one thing, a silly, boyish fantasy. Wanting to take her hand felt more like an act of deep adoration than mere physical attraction.

She couldn't possibly feel the same. She was just being kind. He'd seen her do that since the day she walked in. The way she'd guarded her speech, resisted becoming overly familiar. It had been so obvious. Why were these feelings being awakened?

Whatever the reason, they couldn't be tolerated.

Hunter was about to turn away from the window when Penny's voice cut through the storm in his heart like a bolt of lightning that illuminates the world in a flash of clarity.

"I was thinking of taking Hamish and Maisie for a walk this evening when it's cooler. You could join us if you're so inclined." Her eyes were soft, her voice trilling slightly, pulsing with some underlying energy that buzzed around him and made him feel lighter than a cloud.

In that flash of clarity, he knew he wanted nothing more in all the world than to go on an evening walk with Penelope Grace Blakely. He didn't care who tagged along.

No! his rational, pragmatic self protested vehemently. *It's too of a sudden! I ain't done grieving yet. It's just a hankering after what I lost, is all. It ain't about Penny, nohow. I got to watch myself. For her sake and mine.*

He shook his head, looking down at his boots. "No, I, ah, I've got a heap of work waiting."

"Oh. All right."

The disappointment in her voice cut through him. For the teeniest heart stopping moment he imagined himself relenting and telling her that he'd give his eye teeth to go on a walk with her. Instead, he cleared his throat and turned his back on her, striding swiftly to the door but feeling like he was walking upstream in a rushing river.

What if she really was disappointed? On the other hand, what if she was just being kind? Anybody would be disappointed at a purely platonic friend turning down their invitation to spend time with them. There was no reason for him to think she might be feeling the same giddy pleasure in his presence that he had begun to feel in hers.

It was a pleasure he craved and yet feared. How could he indulge in that pleasure when his heart still belonged to Amy, when he still caught himself speaking to her as if she was in the room with him? How could he entrust his heart to the hands of a woman, so soon after it had been shattered by Amy's death?

The old thirst for whiskey gnawed at his throat, and he had to force himself not to search the house mentally for a forgotten stash of Old Farm Pure Rye hidden in some obscure corner. He marched blindly from the house alternately wishing for a drink and wishing humankind had never discovered how to distill alcohol.

No self-respecting woman would look twice at a man so weak that he tried to drown his sorrows in a whiskey bottle every time a bad memory arose in his mind. With a sense of crushing failure, he realized that he didn't even deserve Amy anymore. Even if she was raised from the dead by some stupendous miracle, he'd be too ashamed to offer her his hand.

He would never have imagined it possible that he could sink so low. His father hadn't raised him that way. Even after his pa had died, he'd walked in the ways of decent Christian morals. There had never been any doubt in his mind that he was an upstanding member of society. Not perfect, certainly, but not a floundering, closet drunkard.

How did I get here? Hunter silently asked nobody in particular. A flash of lightning zig-zagged across the sky, bringing him back to the present moment, and he realized he'd walked out to the horses without thinking. Big Red was nuzzling at his pockets, once again devoid of apples. Hunter absentmindedly patted the horse's soft, warm neck. The wind was chilly against his skin, and the southwestern sky had turned an ominous dark gray.

Monsoon time, he thought, conscious that he should probably be looking for shelter. For some reason he couldn't fathom, he chose to stay in the open, watching the bulbous, rain burdened clouds rolling closer across the wilderness. Thunder rumbled. Another flash of lightning cracked open the sky.

The mares and yearlings were getting skittish. The foals, some newborn, some between one and two months old, stuck close to their dams' sides like big furry burrs as the horses moved about restlessly, already beginning to clump together instinctively for protection.

Big Red lifted his head and sniffed the wind. He gave a grunting whinny and began to round up his herd. Squealing and snorting, he drove them to the shelter of a thick stand of juniper and canyon live oak growing in a coulee nearby.

Hunter watched them go, but still, he didn't budge. Towering thunderheads now completely obscured the sun, plunging the landscape into an almost nocturnal darkness. Large drops of rain began to fall just as Big Red ushered his herd into the shelter of the trees. The flashes of lightning came closer, the vibrations of the thunder rumbling tangibly across the ground under Hunter's feet.

A skittish yearling colt broke away from the herd, bucking like a bronc and kicking up his heels. He could clearly feel the same electricity in the air that Hunter felt. Big Red charged at the youngster, his head snaking low to the ground, his teeth bared, and his ears laid back. Nipping at the rebel's heels, Big Red drove him back to the herd.

Satisfied that his charges were safe, the stallion trotted back to where Hunter stood and lowered his head, placing it firmly against Hunter's chest. Then he whinnied and headed back to where his mares stood, looking over his shoulder at his owner as he went. Hunter shook his head. He still didn't know why, but he felt no compunction to flee the storm.

Perhaps the storm inside him was drawn to the storm around him. Perhaps he deserved the lashing he'd surely get. The large drops became more frequent. Tiny hailstones stung Hunter's skin through his shirt, which was becoming more soaked by the second.

Then he heard the roar as the wind rudely plucked his hat from his head and hit him like a wall, alternately plastering his clothing against his skin and then whipping it away as he stepped backward to keep from being blown over.

Seconds later all he could see was a curtain of pelting sheet rain like an endless waterfall all around him. He screwed his eyes shut and lifted his face to the sky, ignoring the sting of the hailstones as he let the deluge wash over him.

All at once he heard his father's voice in his memory. At first, he wasn't sure what he was saying, but soon the words crystalized in his mind.

When thou passest through the waters, I will be with thee; and through the rivers, they shall not overflow thee: when thou walkest through the fire, thou shalt not be burned; neither shall the flame kindle upon thee.

The words echoed over and over in his mind while the rain soaked him to the bone, running down his neck and back and into his boots. As the cold water coursed over him, he could almost feel old stains being washed out of his skin and his clothing. Whiskey. Shame. Grief. Guilt. Confusion. Anger. Hopelessness.

With a start he realized that only moments earlier he'd stood there internally willing the storm to drown him, the lightning to strike him and end his misery. Instead, it was cleansing him.

Hot tears joined the ice-cold rain running down his cheeks as he lifted his hands in surrender. His deepest innermost being unclenched its fists, and he released Amy to the heavens. In an instant he felt lighter than a feather. A sense of deep peace settled over him as the rain softened, and a single shaft of sunlight lit up the faraway hills.

Chapter Eleven

"Uncle Hunter, I want to learn how to ride. Will you teach me?"

Hunter looked up from his fried eggs and potato cakes into Hamish's eager face. He heard Penny draw in a sharp breath and turned his focus to her. Her eyes held a look of barely subdued fear.

"I don't know, Hamish," he said carefully, keeping a watchful gaze on Penny's face. "Did you ask Aunt Penny how that sits with her?"

Penny gave him a grateful half-smile and Hamish turned his attention on his aunt.

"Please can Uncle Hunter teach me to ride? Please, Aunt Penny?"

"I'm a little worried for your safety, Hamish," Penny said, clearly trying very hard not to outright put her foot down and forbid him from ever going near a horse. Her eyelids fluttered slightly as she looked into Hunter's face again. "Of course, I do trust Uncle Hunter to take good care of you, but, well, horses are so ... unpredictable. So dangerous."

Hunter's heart skipped a beat at her words. She trusted him and was willing to say so in his hearing. That had to mean something.

A flicker of hope caught flame in his heart, but he quickly doused it. He might have released Amy, but he still felt fragile, not entirely healed. If he was reading things into her words and actions that weren't there, he'd have more than just egg on his face.

Besides, even if she did feel what he felt, there was still the possibility of Penny suffering the same fate as Amy. What if she had a difficult birth, and he couldn't get the doctor in time? He felt his neck grow hot as he realized he was thinking of Penny birthing his child.

"You'll make sure I don't get hurt, won't you, Uncle Hunter?" Hamish brought him back from his foray into the impossible future. "And I'm real strong, too!" the boy added, flexing his puny arm muscles for both adults to see. "And quick!" He jumped off his chair and darted across the kitchen, then skidded to a halt and looked at them both expectantly.

Penny laughed, the sound making Hunter's toes curl involuntarily. "I'll do my dangdest to keep you safe, buddy," he promised, smiling and feeling sheepish. He glanced over at Penny. Her eyes were full of hope. The sight caught him flat footed for a moment. It was the first time he'd seen that expression there.

"I suppose if he could ride your gentlest horse, it would be okay," Penny said hesitantly.

Hunter nodded, anxious to allay her fears. "Black Bess is my best brood mare, but she's also the wisest old dame you ever did see. And gentle as a lamb," he assured her. "I'll lead Hamish around the corral on her."

"Thank you," Penny said, and Hunter could see that she meant it. His insides tingled as he momentarily lost himself in her eyes. Then he gave a cough, reminding himself he had to break the spell. For both their sakes.

Penny readjusted her spectacles and cleared her throat. "Well, then, let's finish up breakfast, and I'll see to Maisie while you boys have yourselves a grand old time out there." Her eyes were downcast as she speared a piece of potato cake, and her mouth showed no expression. The flushed cheeks and smiling lips he'd hoped to see never materialized. Perhaps she was just happy for Hamish's sake. That was perfectly reasonable.

"You'll come watch, won't you?" Hunter said before he could stop the words coming out of his mouth.

"Oh, yes, please come watch me, Aunt Penny! You'll be so proud of me!" Hamish added eagerly.

Penny smiled, her eyes settled firmly on her nephew. "Of course, I'm always proud of you, Hamish. And I'd love to watch you take your first horse ride."

Hamish set to finishing his breakfast so quickly that Hunter worried he might choke, but the task was completed without any major mishaps and soon Hunter and Hamish left the house. As they strode toward the stables, Hunter noticed that Hamish had his right thumb hooked into his belt and was almost unbalancing himself with the huge strides he was trying to take. He breath came in huffing gasps from the effort.

Hunter looked down and noticed that he had his right thumb in his belt, too. He couldn't even remember hooking it there. Shortening his strides to make life easier for his young companion, he smiled to himself as the hazy memories of his own boyhood drifted through his mind. More than likely, he had also imitated his father's actions.

A thought struck him. What if Hamish needed him? What if being at the ranch was not only good for giving the boy a roof over his head and food in his belly? *Every boy needs his father.* The words rang with truth in his head, even though he wasn't sure when he'd heard them or who had said them.

An idea was growing in his mind, one that added to his burgeoning sense of purpose. Even if he couldn't be a husband to Penny, there was nothing stopping him from being a father to Hamish for as long as the boy lived under his roof. Maybe even longer than that.

"Here we go," Hunter said as they reached the stables. "First I need you to help me let all the horses out into the big corral over there and then we'll saddle Bess for you."

Hamish giggled joyfully and skipped ahead a few steps, before falling back in line and hooking his thumb back in his belt.

He was a worthy assistant, just as he had been at the milking, his face cast in a grave, deeply serious expression as he proceeded to promptly execute every instruction from Hunter. Soon they had Bess saddled, and Hunter hoisted a beaming five-year-old up onto her patient back.

Bess turned her head to blow on Hamish's leg and Hunter knew it was going to take some coaxing to get her going faster than snail's pace. She was almost impossible to get going when she knew there was an inexperienced rider on her back. Hunter had always marveled at how she seemed to know. The old mare would literally tiptoe along, as if she was carrying a load of fragile crystal ware that could smash to bits at the slightest jolt.

"Here, you can hold the reins," Hunter said, handing Hamish the braided leather thongs. "I'll still keep ahold of the lead rein, though, so no need to fret."

"Oh, I ain't fretting," Hamish assured him in a very grown-up tone. Hunter had to bite his lip to keep from laughing at the boy's use of cowboy slang.

Hunter clicked to Bess, and just as Hunter had expected, she stepped out as if she were walking on eggshells. All along the corral rails they went with Hamish sitting ramrod straight in the saddle, his hands gripping the reins, his eyes staring straight ahead of him.

"You all right up there, kiddo?" Hunter asked, noticing that Hamish's habitual babbling was conspicuously absent.

"Yeah, right as rain," Hamish responded. Hunter smiled to himself again and then began to give the boy tips on holding his hands up, keeping his heels down, and using the reins to put pressure on Bess's neck so she'd turn the way he wanted her to.

By the third turn around the corral, Hamish had relaxed and turned his tongue loose again.

"I sure hope Aunt Penny comes out in time to see me ride," he said, swaying in time to Bess's gently thudding hooves. "It'll make her happy."

"I hope so, too," Hunter agreed, thinking that Hamish would never know just how much he hoped so.

"She's been real sad, you know, Uncle Hunter. Since Mama and Aunt Sarah went away. But she's getting better now. Before she didn't even want to get up in the morning. She just lay in the sleeping corner on the blankets and slept an awful lot or just looked at the roof. I don't know what she was looking at. She didn't want to read or play with me or even go for a walk. She didn't even want to tell me a story, and she loves telling stories the best."

Hunter looked sharply at the boy. He wondered if he should let Hamish go on or tell him to stop. Would Penny want him to hear all these things? And yet, he found himself desperately wanting to know more.

"Honest to goodness, Uncle Hunter," Hamish went on, apparently mistaking Hunter's reaction for disbelief. "She didn't even want to eat. I ate all the food Mrs. Madison brought us. She's the lady who lived on the ground floor of the tenement house. For days and days and days Aunt Penny just lay there. I got so scared."

Hunter's heart broke. He knew that suffocating paralysis of loss only too well. Thinking back, he could almost feel it again. He gave himself a little shake at the unwelcome memory.

"You're safe now, Hamish," he said, keen to change the subject. "Both of you."

"Yeah, we are," Hamish confirmed happily. Then a shadow crossed his face. "I hope Mama and Aunt Sarah come back soon, though. I really miss them. A whole heap. I think Mama will like it here."

A deep, aching sorrow gripped Hunter's heart. Hadn't Penny explained to Hamish what had happened to her sisters? Then again, he couldn't blame her. How would a body do such a thing? Tell a child that his mother was dead? He couldn't imagine how he might have explained Amy's passing to Maisie if she had been five years old. He hardly understood death himself, for all his grown-up cognitive capacity.

"Aunt Penny! Aunt Penny!" Hamish cried out suddenly, dropping the reins and waving both his arms. Bess's ears flickered backwards, and her step faltered a little, but she stayed steady as the rock she was.

Hunter looked in the direction of Hamish's gaze to see Penny hook her arms over the rails of the corral. Maisie's baby carriage stood beside her. Maisie was sitting up, looking about her with wide eyes full of wonder.

"Look at me ride, Aunt Penny! Look at me ride! Bess is so pretty, isn't she? Oh, riding is so much fun!" Hamish babbled while Hunter retrieved the reins and handed them back to the exuberant child.

"Why don't you show Aunt Penny what I taught you about riding?" Hunter suggested.

"Uh-huh," Hamish nodded vigorously, taking the reins from Hunter's hands and settling himself down again. The ecstatic grin was once more replaced by stern concentration.

"Heels down, hands up. Right, Uncle Hunter?"

"Right." Hunter kept his features as somber as his pupil's and led Bess around to where Penny stood. All the while Hamish was telling Penny everything Hunter had just taught him while Penny listened with rapt attention.

Hunter tried to keep a tight rein on his heart, but it was galloping in his chest like a runaway mustang.

"Oh, my, Hamish, you look like you were born on a horse," Penny lavished her nephew with praise that the boy fairly blossomed under.

"He's got a real natural seat, if ever I saw one," Hunter told her as he drew Bess to a standstill opposite her. "And real good balance, too."

"There, you see? I was right," Penny said, smiling proudly at Hamish. "One day you'll be teaching Maisie here how to ride." Maisie squealed happily and reached out to Bess.

Hunter watched Penny while Hamish told her about their first few rounds and how steady and gentle Bess was. Hunter hardly heard him. All he saw was Penny's eyes full of tender love and genuine admiration. She had lost so much, all through her difficult life, and yet she still clearly had so much love to give. So much adoration.

She'd make a feller doggone happy, that's for sure, he caught himself thinking. All at once the desire rose up in his heart to be that doggone happy fellow. His neck felt hot. His heart ached, it was beating so fast.

No. Such a blessing was not his to be had.

She's only on my ranch because she's got nowhere else to go, and I'll do well to remember that, he reminded himself sadly. *Anyhow, a woman like her ain't looking for a man who turns to drink as easy as I did. Ain't no telling when liquor'll slam it's claws into me again, and I'll be no use to her. No use to anybody.*

Still, he couldn't help wishing she would turn those loving, admiring eyes on him; bathe him in that gentle, tender acceptance that radiated out from her like the rays of the rising sun.

If wishes were horses, beggars would ride, his mother had always said.

Hunter sighed inwardly and tore his gaze away from Penny's beautiful face. He'd have to make work of focusing on Hamish. If he couldn't love Penny, he'd love her nephew like his own son and give him everything he planned to give Maisie. It was the least he could do.

But would that be enough? For him? No. For Penny? He hoped so. And yet, his rebellious heart clung stubbornly to the pale hope that she would want more. That she would want as much as he wanted.

And he wanted all of her.

Chapter Twelve

When Penny and Hamish walked away from the corral, once Hamish had eventually—and reluctantly—agreed to focus on his letters and arithmetic for the day in exchange for another ride in the afternoon, Penny felt her heart soaring. Seeing Hamish looking so happy up on the back of that huge but gentle horse was a balm to her soul. If Evie was looking down on them from Heaven, she would surely be pleased with her baby sister.

"Can I push Maisie, Aunt Penny?" Hamish asked, still skipping along beside her excitedly.

"Of course, you can, dear," Penny said. She stopped and stood aside so Hamish could take hold of the handle of the baby carriage. He gripped it manfully and strode forward.

"I can't wait for my next ride," Hamish said. "Maybe Uncle Hunter will let me ride that big red horse. Did you see him, Aunt Penny? He was in the big corral."

"I did," Penny replied. She had seen that horse all right, cantering up and down the length of the corral, his mane and tail flying like shiny satin banners in the wind, his hooves lifted high and proud, striking powerfully at the earth with each restless stride. He was beautiful. Breathtaking. But oh, so dangerous. "I'd rather you didn't ride that horse just yet. He looks rather more spirited than old Bess."

"I bet he can run real fast," Hamish said, increasing his pace. Penny laid a gently restraining hand on his arm.

"Now, Hamish, keep a handle on yourself. It's not a good idea to take off running before you can walk. Like as not you'll fall flat on your face."

Hamish giggled but slowed his pace.

"When you can handle Bess and some of the other horses by yourself, I'm sure you'll be able to ride the big red horse," Penny told him, not wanting to completely squash his enthusiasm.

"All right, Aunt Penny," Hamish happily accepted the conditions she stipulated. But for the rest of the day, all through reciting his alphabet, scribing his letters and ciphering his arithmetic, he kept harping back to his first time on a horse and daydreaming out loud about what he would do one day when he was a first-class horseman like Uncle Hunter.

We've been here but a couple of weeks, Penny thought to herself while she watched him jabbering away, *and already he's quite positively idolizing Hunter.*

The thought made her smile. She'd seen that thumb in his belt, just as Hunter's habit was, the way he copied every move Hunter made. It was touching, and she really couldn't think of a better role model.

Nor a more handsome one.

She jolted a little at her own thought and her cheeks flushed.

Well, it's not a lie, she mollified herself, remembering the way he'd absentmindedly stroked the old mare's neck. She never knew such large, strong hands could be so gentle, so caring. What would it feel like to have such a strong, gentle hand close around her own?

Penny shook her head, feeling her heart ache. No. There was no sense in these kinds of daydreams. How long would she have to keep reminding herself that Hunter had made it abundantly clear that he had no intention of getting involved in a romance with her? Or anyone else, for that matter.

Even if she did manage to carve a niche for herself in his heart, there would always be the ghost of his late wife casting a shadow across their love. Was that what she wanted? Could she be happy with such a relationship?

No, I couldn't, she admitted silently to herself. *If I were to love Hunter Blakely, I'd want him to be free to love me with all of himself, and no ghosts between us. He's let Maisie back into his heart, but she's his own flesh and blood. That's different.*

Perhaps it would be better to follow Hunter's suggestion to actively seek another beau she could lavish all her affection on without reservation, without living in the shadow of a memory. Another mail order bride ad? No. She might very well end up in the same situation, and she didn't have the gumption to face it twice.

Besides, they'd made a vow in a chapel, before a minister of the gospel. That mattered to God, even if it didn't matter to Hunter, and Evie had deeply instilled in Penny that a vow was made to be honored. She could lie about it for the rest of her life, but even if nobody else knew, she would.

And then there was Hamish. How could she possibly wrench him away from Hunter, the man he already looked up to like a boy might look up to his father? Leaving might relieve her of the cloying emotions she had to fight day and night, but it would bring so much more harm to so many others.

Penny sighed. She hadn't planned for things to get quite so complicated. But there it was. People weren't puppets she could move around at will. Besides, the last thing she wanted was to have a puppet for a husband.

Her thoughts wandered back to Hunter. The wildness around him seemed to be in his very bones. He looked so at home with the horses, so confident and free out on the rolling hills. Trying to tame a spirit like that would feel like a sin against the Creator Himself, not only His creation.

The sonorous gonging of the grandfather clock downstairs in the entrance hall clanged through Penny's thoughts and jerked her to her feet.

"Oh, my hat! Is it twelve o'clock already?" she asked without expecting an answer. "I'd better start dinner, or I'll be late!"

Hamish looked up at her like one coming out of a dream. Penny realized he'd abandoned his schoolwork and begun playing cowboys with his toys again.

"Oh, goodness, Hamish, whatever am I going to do with you?" She stopped, seeing his confused look. "Myself, I mean, whatever am I going to do with myself?"

That correction didn't seem to clear anything up for Hamish. He still sat watching her with a slightly discombobulated look on his face.

"Oh, never mind," Penny said, giving him a flustered smile. "Won't you keep an eye on Maisie, dear? I'll have to go down and get dinner going lickety split."

Hamish nodded and obediently scooted closer to where Maisie sat in a playpen, mesmerized by a rattle. "I'll read to her," he said.

"That's a good idea," Penny said distractedly and left the nursery.

Down in the kitchen, while she peeled and chopped vegetables and put water on to boil the potatoes for shepherd's pie, she berated herself for getting lax again. She'd managed to drag herself out of bed earlier in the mornings, but still, she didn't seem to have the energy for anything.

Everything she did took twice as long as it used to, and she was forgetting too many things.

Just the day before, she'd forgotten to close the chickens' feed bin and the next thing she knew the greedy fowls had knocked the thing over, spilling its contents across the yard behind the kitchen. Hunter hadn't said much, but she'd felt horrible for causing such unnecessary waste.

Her mind wandered back to the days of her black melancholy, when she'd lain on a damp pile of blankets, listening to the mournful drip of rain leaking onto the floor around her and wishing she could have been the one to die, instead of Evie and Sarah.

A pang of longing shot through her heart with such force that a sob caught in her throat before she knew what was happening to her.

"Oh, Evie! Sarah!" she whispered hoarsely. The tears welling up in her eyes spilled over her lashes and onto her cheeks. "I miss you so much! And I don't know how to tell Hamish he'll never see you again."

She paused, blinking down at the potato she was peeling. Tears blurred her eyes, so she could hardly make out the shape anymore, let alone see where the peeled bit ended, and the skin began.

"I'm not sure I've managed to explain that to myself, honestly," she added, still in a whisper. "How am I ever going to pull myself together again?"

She sat down on a nearby chair, tears dripping onto her hands, the potato still a distorted brown and white blur. If she had any intention of making Hunter's life easier, she'd better get her act together. But how? The same downward spiral of hopelessness and grief that had dragged her down to the depths of despair after her sisters' deaths, whirled around her once more, sucking her spirits lower and lower.

Dark thoughts flitted through her mind, like ominous clouds blotting out the sun that had begun to shine ever so tremulously in her heart. She loved a man who would never love her back, but she couldn't leave because Hamish was already clearly attached to him. She would never see her sisters again, and she could never hope to find happiness.

Only days earlier, she hadn't cared about that. She'd cared only for Hamish's safety and Hunter's happiness. Now a kind of panic seemed to be taking hold of her at the thought of becoming an old maid. She shook her head.

"I won't be a selfish ingrate," she told herself crossly. "Just because my prospects are gone, doesn't mean I can't be happy for Hamish and Hunter and do everything in my power to add to their happiness. Regardless of my own."

It made her feel strangely better to hear the sternness and strength and determination in her own voice. Setting down the vegetable knife, she took off her eyeglasses and wiped away her tears with the corner of her apron.

"No sense in bawling like a big baby when I have so much to be thankful for," she chided herself for good measure and then briskly resumed peeling the potatoes.

She couldn't deny, even though it wasn't for lack of trying, that a fearful heaviness still brooded in her chest. For how long could she keep secret her feelings for Hunter? Would it become a problem if she inadvertently started to show them? Would it cost Hamish a father figure and a chance at a future doing what he clearly already loved? Working with horses.

"I won't let myself do that to him," she vowed under her breath. "If that's the cross I have to bear, then so be it."

***

That evening, at the supper table, Hamish still had much to say about his ride and what he was going to do the next morning on his second ride. Hunter merely nodded and made agreeable noises, apparently having run out of things to say on the subject.

"Well, Hamish," Penny said, as she pierced a canned peach with her fork, "you're a step ahead of me in country living now. I've never ridden a horse in my life."

She wasn't sure why she'd said that. Perhaps it had something to do with her wanting to offer every smidgen of encouragement she could possibly come up with.

Hunter snapped to immediate attention but didn't say anything.

Hamish didn't skip a beat. "Uncle Hunter could teach you, too, Aunt Penny," he said. "I'm sure he could. It ain't hard."

"It isn't hard," Penny corrected him.

"Yeah, that's what I said," Hamish replied, immediately turning his attention back to Hunter. "You could teach her, right, Uncle Hunter?"

Penny couldn't help but notice that Hamish's face and tone sent a clear message that he believed Hunter capable of re-hanging the moon, should the need ever arise.

"Sure, I could teach you, Penny. Easy as tie your shoes," Hunter said, not looking overly eager.

"Why, thank you. I'll remember that," Penny said politely. He clearly didn't mean it, and she didn't intend to take him up on it. It was obvious to her that he was keeping her at arm's length, and she didn't mind too awfully much. It was better that way. Hopefully Hamish would forget about it by the time morning came.

When the meal was finished and the washing up done, Penny didn't hold out much hope for that, either. Hamish prattled the entire time about how they could have their riding lesson together in the morning and that she didn't have to worry, Hamish himself would show her exactly what to do if she felt scared or confused.

Penny smiled at him, loving him for his kind and sincere heart.

"You're a darling, Hamish," she said. "Let's see what happens tomorrow, shall we?"

"Okay, Aunt Penny," he replied, giving her a hug around the knees. Then he looked up at her and spoke the words she had dreaded for a long time. "Tell us a story before we go to bed, Aunt Penny. Pleease!"

"That sounds like a dandy idea," Hunter said. "I'll fetch a book from the library.

Hamish spun around to face him. "Oh, no, not a book story. Aunt Penny has a whole library of stories in her head, don't you Aunt Penny?"

In mid-sentence he'd spun back to face her. Now he fixed his pleading blue eyes on her. She didn't dare say no, even though her mind had gone blank in an instant. A story? The last story she'd told was the last one her sisters had heard her tell. How could she ever tell another story again?

And yet, how could she disappoint Hamish?

Chapter Thirteen

Caught between two evils, Penny chose the lesser and nodded her head, her heart pounding uncomfortably in her chest. A spark of intrigue glimmered momentarily in Hunter's eye before he turned away toward the kitchen door. "All right, then," he said over his shoulder, sounding a trifle bored. "I ain't bothered either way. A story is a story, I reckon."

"Oh, Aunt Penny tells the most bestest stories you've ever heard," Hamish boasted, skipping along at Hunter's heels.

Penny stifled the apprehension and embarrassment rising up in her chest and followed her menfolk to the parlor. All the time her head was spinning. What was she going to tell? She could hardly remember the old stories she'd told Hamish. Even if she could, she was sure he would recognize them, and he clearly wanted a new story.

Dear God in Heaven, what am I going to do? the desperate but silent plea cried out from her spirit.

As she settled down in the settee with baby Maisie sound asleep in her Moses basket and Hamish already curling up beside her, his head in her lap, a memory flashed in her mind. Evie had often read Bible stories to Penny when she was a child. It was during those times that Penny had first fallen in love with the drama and the beauty and the mystery of storytelling. Frantically she searched her memory for a Bible story she could draw inspiration from.

Just when she had begun to despair, it came to her in an almost audible voice.

Queen Esther.

Of course! That was perfect! A good story always had a king or a queen in it. Or both.

Taking a deep breath, Penny settled back on the settee. She closed her eyes, trying not to think about Hunter's attentive gaze, those observant brown eyes she knew were now resting on her, watching her every move.

"Once upon a time there was a young woman who was an orphan and lived with her uncle. She was very, very beautiful, but desperately poor. Her country had been invaded and her people taken captive by a tribe of minotaur who were well known and deeply feared by all who knew them."

Penny opened her eyes and glanced down at Hamish. His eyes were riveted on hers as he drank in every word, never satiated but always hungry for more.

"The woman's name was Myrtle, and she loved her uncle dearly. He was a kind and wise man, and he raised her as if she was his own daughter. His name was Quinn. One day the minotaur king, Tudor, sent out a decree that all the most beautiful young women of the land must come to his palace, so he could see them. He was seeking a new bride."

Hamish gasped. "If Myrtle marries the king, what will happen to her uncle?"

"Why, we'll have to wait and see, won't we?" Penny replied, giving him a wink. Hamish hugged himself in anticipation, his eyes not leaving his aunt's face for a second.

Out of the corner of her eye, Penny could see Hunter leaning forward slightly in his chair. She could feel his eyes on her, and she wondered if he were sniffing out her ill-concealed deception. Holding her pose, she went on.

"Myrtle cried and cried, begging her uncle to let her run away, to escape the terrible fate of being married to the terrifying minotaur king, but he refused. He knew she would be found and that the punishment for defying a royal decree would be harsh and cruel. 'It's better that you go to the palace. We will pray that there is a more beautiful young woman than you who will steal the king's heart.' Her uncle meant every word. He truly loved Myrtle like she was his own daughter, and it broke his heart to think that he might never see her again."

Hamish gave another gasp and frowned worriedly but didn't interrupt this time.

"As it happened, the king chose Myrtle to be his bride, and she wasn't even allowed to go home say goodbye to her uncle. She cried for a whole week, but then she put on a brave face and made up her mind that, whatever happened to her, she would walk tall and make her uncle proud. Especially when she heard that her uncle had managed to convince the king's court to employ him as a scribe, one who writes down the stories of the king's conquests in war and all his great accomplishments."

Hamish let out a small, 'ah,' of admiration. Penny glanced over at Hunter. His eyes were riveted to her face, his expression one of studious attention. Penny quickly looked back down at Hamish and absentmindedly stroked his curls back from his forehead as she resumed her narration.

"Then one day, when Quinn was walking through the marketplace, he overheard a general in the king's army talking about a plot to kill all the humans in the land by leading them to a place where they would fall into a secret chasm filled with boiling lava. Only minotaur would be left alive, and the few people who were kept as slaves and servants at the king's palace. Including, of course, the new queen, Queen Myrtle."

"Oh, that's awful!" Hamish exclaimed, struggling up from Penny's lap.

"Yes, it is, isn't it?" Penny said. "Quinn instantly sent a message to Queen Myrtle and urged her to speak to the king and warn him about the plot. Queen Myrtle was horrified and terrified all at the same time. She knew the general, and he was one of the king's most trusted friends and counselors. Her new husband, King Tudor, would never believe her that the general was plotting such a terrible thing."

"But what if the king loved her?" Hunter asked, his voice making Penny jump.

"Yes, what if the king loved her?" Hamish echoed, hope leaping into his eyes. "Would he believe her then?"

"That was the only hope that Myrtle had to cling to," Penny said, her heart fluttering about in her chest like a bird in a cage. "She knew the king loved her, just as she had learned to love him. Living as the king's wife had taught her that, beneath the hard, brutal exterior was a man who needed love as much as she did. A man who had a heart of gold. Still, she didn't know for sure if their love would be strong enough to survive such a test."

Penny paused. Her story, even though it was a hasty and crude adaptation of someone else's, was inching closer and closer to home. Her chest felt tight, and tears threatened to spill over onto her cheeks. Her audience waited silently with bated breath for the next scene to unfold from her lips.

"That evening, Queen Myrtle asked to spend the night with the king. He was tired and irritable from weeks of planning many new military campaigns, but he graciously allowed her to enter his chamber. Myrtle brought many gifts, all sorts of things that she knew were the king's favorites. Fruit and sweetmeats and singing birds and a band of musicians. The king and queen danced the night away. Then, when both grew tired and the king was reclining on his couch with his queen in his arms, she decided to reveal the terrible news and weather whatever storm broke loose from that revelation."

Hamish squeezed his eyes shut, muttering something in a rapid whisper. Penny could only imagine that he was praying for the poor queen in her story. Blinking away the fresh onslaught of pesky tears, she continued.

"As soon as King Tudor heard about the plot, he jumped up from the couch, his eyes blazing with anger. Queen Myrtle bowed down before him, ready for the saber strike that would take her life. Instead, King Tudor tenderly stroked her cheek and helped her to her feet. His eyes were still blazing, but they were filled with love. 'My Queen,' he said, 'nobody who threatens your people will survive my anger. Nobody who threatens the lives of your loved ones will see another sunrise.'"

Hamish let out a sigh of relief and Hunter sank back in his chair.

"So, the general was thrown into the very chasm he had planned to use to kill Queen Myrtle's people, and her Uncle Quinn became the king's chief advisor. The king and queen had many beautiful children, and they ruled the kingdom with justice and wisdom and love, for the rest of their days."

A soft silence hung about the room after Penny's final words faded away. Then Hamish spoke in a voice filled with awe.

"That was your bestest story yet, Aunt Penny," he said, his eyes sparkling with wonder.

"It wasn't all my own," she admitted, not wanting to take credit where it wasn't due.

"A whole heap of it was, though, wasn't it?" Hunter said. His voice was subdued and thoughtful.

Penny dared not look at him. She longed to share her heart with him, to tell him how deeply her own story had moved her, but she couldn't get past the lump in her throat to say anything at all. Instead, she gave him a barely perceptible nod.

"Well, I think it was one of the most topping stories I've ever heard," Hunter said with extravagant conviction.

Penny smiled. If only he wouldn't be so nice and make it so hard for her to stick to her vow. She was still searching for something to say in response, when Hunter addressed her nephew.

"Hamish, seeing as you're such a big lad now, learning to ride and all, you reckon you'd be up to getting yourself ready for bed?"

Penny stared at him, wondering what his intention was.

"Your Aunt Penny looks like she could do with a wee break, anyhow. She works real hard cooking and cleaning and all, don't you think?"

Hamish sat up and swung his legs off the settee. "Yes, sir!" he said, his childish features contorted into an almost comical look of proud self-sufficiency.

"Good man," Hunter said, rising from his chair to give Hamish's shoulder an affectionate squeeze.

Hamish started to stand, but then hesitated. "I'd really like for you to tuck me in, though, Uncle Hunter."

Penny had to blink back a fresh flood of tears when she heard that. She looked up at Hunter, silently begging him to say yes.

"You bet ya I will, buddy," Hunter replied, giving Penny a look that made her feel giddy. "Wait here, Penny, I'll be right back, soon as I've tucked this big feller in."

Penny smiled, hoping she didn't look as fragile as she felt.

Left alone for a few moments she wondered what it was that Hunter had on his heart. He clearly wanted to speak with her. The way he had made certain they could spend some time together without little ears about to hear the grown-ups' conversation was a dead giveaway. Penny looked down at the angelic features of the still sleeping Maisie in her basket and tried not to think too much.

Moments later, Hunter's footsteps on the rug made her look up. He deposited himself beside her on the settee, but with a healthy gap between them. Penny felt only slightly surprised at how much she wished he would close that gap.

"That was your version of the story of Queen Esther, wasn't it?" Hunter asked, a glimmer of gentle humor in his voice.

"You found me out," Penny admitted bashfully.

"Do you wish you could be her?"

His question startled her. All the humor was gone from his voice and his eyes held an intensity that was utterly unexpected.

"Yes, yes I do," she said. The tears were spilling over now, and she did nothing to check them. "I wish I could be her. A queen with the power to stop the killing of those she loves. I can barely let Hamish out of my sight, I'm so afraid something might happen to him. I cringe every time he walks out the door for fear that he won't come back through it again, just like Evie and Sarah. Maybe I can save him, maybe I can't, but there's for sure nothing I can do to save my sisters even though I would exchange my life for theirs in a heartbeat!"

Hunter pulled out his hanky and handed it to her. She took it and pressed it over her nose and mouth while she held his gaze, all at once filled with a reckless boldness. Hunter's eyes were brimming with tears, too. He shifted closer, closing the gap between them, and put his arm around her, drawing her head to his shoulder.

"I loved them so much, Hunter, and now they're just gone," Penny sobbed, feeling Hunter's warmth melt her last reserves of resistance.

"I know," was all he said, but it was more than enough. It was all she needed in that moment. Just for someone to know what she couldn't put into words. Somehow, she knew that he truly did understand.

"We ain't all that different, you and me," Hunter said hoarsely. "I sure wish I could be that King Tudor who put a stop to the killing."

Penny didn't need to wonder if she believed him.

"If I could have only stopped Mr. Murphy from putting my sisters in danger," she said sadly. "Then they wouldn't be ... gone. And I wouldn't feel so horribly guilty. But I'm not sure why I feel guilty, when he's the reason they're not with me anymore."

"You ever had the thought someone bigger than Mr. Murphy was to blame?"

Penny hesitated. It felt sacrilegious even to think it. "You mean God?"

"Uh-huh." Hunter looked conflicted himself.

"I wouldn't ever dream of blaming God." Penny felt a little shocked.

Hunter looked away. "Yeah, well. I tried it for a few minutes. Didn't sit right. Felt like I was just looking for a scapegoat. After that I just figured He weren't there, until I had to admit how He'd given me a second chance at being a good father for Maisie. If Sally hadn't got you and Hamish out here and gone off to town to have her own baby, why, I'd likely still be painting my nose every night, trying to forget yesterday, when tomorrow was waiting for me with open arms."

Penny pulled back so she could look into Hunter's eyes. "A second chance," she echoed, not daring to share what the second chance was that she craved and would most likely not be granted. "I'll be happy for Hamish to have a second chance at being part of a family," she said instead.

"Yeah." Hunter shifted, his arm dropping from her shoulders. "Penny, I, ah ..." he trailed off.

"Yes?" Penny dried her eyes and looked expectantly into Hunter's face. He seemed suddenly unsure of himself. Then he stood abruptly to his feet.

"I think you're a grand storyteller. You should write books someday."

The atmosphere in the room had changed again, and Penny didn't know why.

"Thank you, Hunter," she replied, wishing he would sit down beside her and hold her again.

"I'll carry Maisie upstairs for you," he said. "I reckon it's time we all got some shut eye."

"Yes, yes, of course," Penny said, standing to her feet too.

Hunter picked up the basket and Penny followed him from the room and up the staircase. Had she let her guard down too much? Did he think her forward? What had caused the sudden change in his demeanor?

She racked her brains trying to think of something she might have said that could have made him feel pressured or made him think she had designs on him. That comment about her wanting Hamish to have a family, perhaps. Did he think she had meant for Hunter to be the father of that family?

The truth was, if he had, he wouldn't have been wrong. Now that she was thinking about her words clearly, she had to admit that she might as well have said what she originally wanted to say. That she wanted a first chance at romance.

What she did know for sure was that Hunter's reaction had just told her all she needed to know. She'd been right all along. He would never love her the way she wanted him to. The way she loved him.

The thought drove a dagger of despair through her heart.

How had she let things get this far? Her silly romantic notions had brought her dangerously close to ruining all Hamish's chances of growing up in a loving family.

She had better not let a slip like that happen again. Whatever she felt for Hunter had to be put to death as quickly as possible. If only she could get her heart to cooperate.

Chapter Fourteen

Hunter knew he should leave Penny's bedchamber immediately, but, against his better judgement, he paused at the doorway, watching Penny gently bundling Maisie out of her Moses basket and into her crib. The infant stirred and mumbled in her sleep. Penny shushed her softly and began to hum a haunting, lilting tune.

It tugged at Hunter's heart, just as her story had. And, oh, what a story, so skillfully adapted, with such imaginative twists. He wondered why she had looked almost desperate before she started her narration. Perhaps she had been searching for inspiration and found it missing. Hunter knew that feeling all too well.

His mind drifted to the drawings he'd done not too long ago. His horses had been his favorite subject, until first Amy and then Maisie had come into his life. After that, the two women in his life had dominated his sketchpad. Since the fever had taken Amy, he hadn't the heart to put pencil to paper other than to scribble a reminder for himself in his diary.

"Goodnight, Hunter," Penny's voice brought him back from his inner meanderings. She was standing in the middle of the room, looking a little ill at ease.

"Ah, yes. Goodnight," Hunter said, and swung abruptly away from the doorway. No doubt she wanted to get ready for bed, and there he was gawking into empty space.

Without thinking, he headed for his study. The leather creaked comfortingly as he settled into his father's old chair. His fingers seemed to find the key for the safe drawer in the desk all of their own accord and the next thing he knew, it was open, the contents making his chest throb with longing and sorrow.

Gently sliding them out, one by one, he studied the drawings, criticizing his technique here and there, appreciating a particularly well depicted form or shadow. Black Bess, Big Red, Scarborough, Dandelion, Sandy, Lewis and Clark. Yes, Amy had called a set of twin foals Lewis and Clark. Hunter shook his head with a fond, but tearful smile as he removed the next sheet of sketch paper.

And there she was. Amy. His eyes traced the contours of her face. A ghostly pain seared into his chest—the kind that people felt after a deep wound had formed a pink ridged scar, and they traced their finger over it. He reached quickly for the next drawing.

Maisie, as a tiny newborn, eyes screwed shut, lips puckered, fists clenched. It was the only drawing he had done of her. Before he'd had time to capture her features in graphite and wood pulp again, the fever had consumed her mother's slender body and snatched Hunter's reason for living away from him.

Hunter fought off the need for a tumbler of whiskey and gathered the papers together. It was just possible there was a bottle secreted away in that drawer. He would have to close it and lock it quickly before the call became too strong.

He was about to shove all the drawings back into the drawer, when something caught his eye. A bundle of letters. Tied together with a black velvet ribbon. Hunter reached out instinctively. Then he paused but briefly. Seconds later the ribbon was untied, and he held the first letter in his hands, reading his own words, feeling as if they belonged to a stranger.

My love

I long to hold you in my arms again.

Hunter paused, looking away to the window. He steeled himself and went back to reading.

I wish this was all over already. I wish you would break off your engagement to Wyatt. Surely by now he's seen your heart doesn't belong to him. Tell him you can't marry him and let's have done with this sneaking about. I want the whole territory to know you're my girl, Amy, so no other feller will ever darken your pa's doorway. Heck, I want the whole world to know.

There was more, but Hunter didn't read it. He already knew her reply, but he couldn't help opening the next letter, the fragrance of jasmine and sunlight washing over him, torturously sweet.

My beloved Hunter

You know I would love nothing more than to be in your arms right now. You also know why I can't yet break off the engagement to Wyatt. My pa will suffer for it and then some. I can't let that happen.

"Darn right you couldn't. You always were more levelheaded than me," Hunter whispered softly. "My anchor is what you were. And now I've got to go on and find me a new one."

If I can just find another place for pa, someplace where he isn't beholden to old Mr. Blackwell, somewhere he'll be safe, then I'll break it off and marry you in a heartbeat.

Hunter set down the letter and lay back in his chair. He stared up at the ceiling, watching a spider scuttle across the paneled wood, but hardly seeing it. He was remembering the night after he'd received her letter.

The night he'd held her to her promise. The night he'd gone over to the Smith homestead and sat down with Amy and her father. The night he'd promised Captain Smith he could live at the Bleakly ranch, doing whatever odd jobs Hunter couldn't get to. The night he and Amy had eloped.

The call of the whiskey was stronger now. Hunter leaned down, reaching into the drawer.

Something moved in the doorway, and Hunter jumped, banging his hand on the wooden frame that held the drawer in place. He cursed under his breath and snapped his head up.

Penny stood in the doorway, her slender figure wrapped in an embroidered robe. She pushed up her spectacles and gave a little cough. Hunter grabbed at the letters as she stepped over the threshold.

"How long've you been standing there gawking at me?" he growled, still raking papers together.

Penny froze. "Gawking at you? I wasn't gawking at you at all," she said, looking suspiciously at him and the papers on his desk.

"You just got here?" Hunter tried again, though his tone was still harsher than he intended.

"Yes. I remembered something I wanted to tell you and forgot, what with Hamish wanting a bedtime story at such short notice." She looked a little aloof, and yet something in her face made him think she was insatiably curious about the papers on his desk.

Not that he could blame her. He had reacted rather like a guilty man. Although she didn't have to know he had been reaching for a drink when she appeared in the doorway with such impeccable timing that she might as well have been the personification of his conscience.

"Tell me something," Hunter repeated, marginally less gruffly. "Like what?"

"I saw a man walking around here today." Penny took two steps closer and stopped again, looking uncertain. "It might not be important, but I felt uneasy, so I chose to err on the side of caution."

Hunter stiffened. "A man? Just walking around?"

"Yes. Hamish and I were gathering prickly pears up beyond the top corral, and Hamish saw someone down by the stables. We went over, but the man began walking away very quickly. Then he mounted a large gray horse and rode away without looking back."

Alarm raced through Hunter's body, relegating every other concern to the realm of unimportance.

"You recall what he looked like?" he pressed.

Penny tilted her head to the side. "I didn't see his face, but he was quite tall. Had a bowler hat on. I thought that was rather strange for out here. I think it's the first bowler I've seen since I arrived in Four Horse. And he was smartly dressed. Carried a cane, too, though he didn't walk like he needed it."

Hunter went cold. There could be no doubt about it. Wyatt.

Penny was still speaking. and he dragged his attention back to her words.

"I felt like I'd seen him before, and then I remembered the day we were ... were married, I thought I saw someone like that looking in at the window of the chapel. Only that time it felt more like a dream ..."

"You weren't dreaming. I know who that man is," Hunter said flatly, cutting her off. His stomach tightened into a knot. Penny's eyes grew wide.

"Is he dangerous?"

Hunter regarded her for a while, wondering how to answer that. Wyatt Blackwell dangerous? Perhaps threatening was a better word. Then again, what was he doing snooping around the Blakely ranch? What did he want? Why now?

Penny coughed and shifted her weight onto the other foot, her eyes clouded with concern.

"I don't rightly know if he's dangerous, truth be told," Hunter said. "Wyatt Blackwell learned from his pa how to make life real hard for folks if they didn't pony up on their rent, but I don't know that it's fair to call him dangerous."

Even as he spoke, he remembered the night he'd sighted a tall, lean figure in the shadows of the barn and thought it was a whiskey induced hallucination. A shiver of foreboding ran down his spine.

Penny seemed to relax a little, though, reassured by the words he wasn't even sure he believed himself. "What do you think he was doing here?"

"I'll be danged if I know," Hunter admitted.

"Do you know him well?" She had moved even closer now and stood with one hand resting lightly on the desk.

"Too well," Hunter shook his head and began folding up the letters at a less frantic pace.

"You have a history with him then?" Penny prodded.

A flash of indignation shot through Hunter's chest. "You sure are mighty nosey tonight, ain't ya?"

Penny shrank back. "Yes, I suppose I am. Begging your pardon, Hunter. It's just, I suppose being a storyteller I'm just too curious about everything and I really shouldn't ..." she trailed off, fading toward the doorway.

Hunter relented, suddenly feeling tired. "It figures," he said, gesturing to her to come closer again. "Ain't no harm in it. Why don't you sit down? You may as well know about my feud with Wyatt Blackwell. Now that you're family."

He said it before he thought about what it meant, but it was true. Penny and Hamish were his family now. If Wyatt was up to something it would be better for her to know who he was. It was Hunter's responsibility to prepare her before she came face to face with Wyatt at some juncture or another.

"If you don't mind sharing with me," Penny was saying as she moved hesitantly toward the other leather chair by the fireplace.

Hunter simply shook his head and motioned to her to be seated. She did, folding her hands in her lap as she did so and not taking her round, innocent-yet-wise eyes off his face for a moment.

"Wyatt Blackwell and I go back a long way," Hunter began with a sigh. "Since we both were no higher than a prairie dog, we never could get along."

Penny settled into the chair, seeming to detect the gravity in his voice or his countenance, he wasn't sure. Whatever it was, she responded with a look of solemn attentiveness, as if she instinctively knew that what he had to say about his relationship with Wyatt would impact her, too.

"When Amy's family came to Four Horse, it didn't take Wyatt long to start sparking her. Relentless he was. Amy's pa was a veteran of the War, just wanting a place to wait out his last days in peace. Wyatt's pa was their landlord and he made life real hard for the Smiths until Captain Smith gave in. So, Wyatt and Amy were betrothed."

Penny's eyebrows lifted and then lowered again, a strange indignant sadness filling her eyes.

"The truth was," Hunter went on, averting his gaze so her rapt, expressive face wouldn't distract him from his narration, "from the first day she set foot in Four Horse, Amy loved me, and I loved her. We'd meet in secret, until one day we decided enough was enough. Amy broke off her engagement, Captain Smith came to live here with us, and we got married. Wyatt kicked up a stink the likes of which the town of Four Horse hadn't seen since the first folks settled here, I'll wager."

Penny shook her head disbelievingly. "But why would Mr. Blackwell bother you now? Now that Amy's ... gone? If she was what he wanted, he wouldn't have any reason to come snooping around the ranch, would he?"

Hunter sighed again, pushing from his mind the image of the amber bottle in the drawer only inches away.

"That's what my common sense is telling me. Trouble is, Wyatt don't cotton much to common sense. He figures things his own way. No telling what's going on in the top story there."

For a while they just looked at each other. Ominous thoughts and fears were beginning to crowd Hunter's mind. What if Wyatt had heard about Penny? What if the old rivalry was stirring in his bones? What if he begrudged Hunter his new wife?

More importantly, what might he do to act upon that grudge?

The cold fist of fear closed around Hunter's heart. What if Wyatt hurt Penny or Hamish? Or both?

Wyatt had never set foot on his land before. Even when Amy and her father had moved there. Hunter had heard what Wyatt and his father had done to their tenants when they didn't toe the line. They'd never been caught, they were that clever, but all of Four Horse understood the cause of the seemingly freak accidents that happened on their rented lands.

What if Wyatt was getting bolder? Would he try such tricks outside his own territory?

Hunter was at once filled with the smothering thought that he might have to send Penny and Hamish away. For their own good. Only, this time, he didn't want to.

But if he didn't, there could be more blood on his hands. If something happened to Penny or Hamish because of his old feud, he would never forgive himself.

Chapter Fifteen

Hunter seemed to have disappeared into the world of his own thoughts as he seemed wont to do at the drop of a hat. Penny sat still, watching him for a while, guiltily appreciating his boyish ruggedness.

He made her think of a grown-up Tom Sawyer, except that any spark of fun and mischief he might have lurking in his eyes was hidden beneath a thick layer of sadness and self-recrimination, like heavy clouds that dim the light of the sun.

"Well, thank you for bringing this to my attention. I'll be sure to let you know sooner if I see any strangers on the ranch again," Penny said, rising from her seat.

Hunter blinked, as if he only just noticed her in front of him. His eyes were troubled.

"He said it was me who killed her, you know," he said, not seeming to have heard her at all.

Penny didn't need to ask who he was talking about. She wavered, unsure how to respond. How could she comfort him when she hadn't been able to forgive herself yet for the fact that her sisters no longer lived and breathed?

"Surely that's not so." Her words felt hopelessly inadequate, and yet she longed so to make him understand that Mr. Blackwell's accusations were false, could never be true.

Hunter looked suddenly old. "No. He ain't far off the target." He looked down at the letters and drawings in front of him on the desk. Penny could just make out a picture of a newborn who she guessed must be Maisie. From behind Maisie's portrait, the drawing of a horse's muzzle peeked out.

"We mustn't think such things, Hunter. It'll only drive us to distraction," Penny said firmly, remembering her promise to herself to make his life as easy as she could. To be the support and encouragement to him that she herself needed.

Hunter seemed to snap out of his trance. He pushed back his chair, stood to his feet and deposited the letters and drawings into a drawer. Closing the drawer with a bang, he locked it firmly, put the key in his pocket and stepped out from behind his desk. His face was resolute, his eyes hard.

"No. Wyatt was right, but I'll be danged if I'll let it happen again."

Penny stared at him as he marched past her toward the door, lantern swinging from one hand.

Was he saying he would make sure no harm would come to her? It was a thrilling and yet at the same time disconcerting thought. Did he think Mr. Blackwell would harm her? If he did why had he said he didn't think Mr. Blackwell was dangerous?

"We'd better call it a night and get some shut eye," Hunter was saying as he stood with his hand on the doorknob. That fierce determination was still there. It added to his masculine allure, and Penny's heart fluttered.

"Of course," she said, tearing her gaze from his face and setting her own features into a mask of resoluteness. She hadn't expected the look of strength and danger in him to set her emotions alight again.

She tried not to brush against him as she passed by him into the hallway, feeling like a June bug drawn to a bonfire that she knew would consume her if she touched it. Hurrying toward her chamber she set her lips in a firm line. She had to fight this raging attraction with everything she had.

"Goodnight, Penny."

She stopped and turned back to face him. His features were chiseled by the rays of the lantern in his hand, his tanned, freckled skin coated in golden yellow light. The auburn curls framing his face glowed like burnished bronze. He looked at once fragile and invincible. Her heart ached.

"Goodnight, Hunter."

Then she fled to her bedchamber, almost drowning in a flood of longing. She lay awake for what felt like hours, trying to rid her memory of his image in the pale lamplight.

***

Penny woke to her whole body feeling thick and sluggish. In her foggy mind, the pale memory of a dream still lingered. All she could remember of the dream was that she'd been at Murphy's when the freak windstorm hit, trying to hold up the creaking, swaying building. She had begun to grow smaller and smaller while the building grew larger and larger, until she was the size of an ant beside a colossal, threatening edifice swaying and groaning beneath a leaden sky.

Her head ached dully. Her eyes felt furry in their sockets. She rolled over with a moan and glanced around the room. It was light already. And Hamish was nowhere to be seen. She'd overslept again. Penny moaned again and pulled the coverlet over her head.

Perhaps I should take to sleeping on a blanket on the floor again, she thought groggily. *In the tenement I never overslept. Nothing like a cold, wooden floor to keep one's sleep light.*

Even as the thought staggered through her mind, she knew it wasn't true. She'd overslept on that hard attic floor, too. Almost every day since the day after Evie and Sarah had ...

Dear God, don't let my sisters see me in this state, she prayed silently. *It'll break their hearts.*

Dragging herself from the bed, she first took care of Maisie's toilet before stumbling through her own. When she reached the kitchen, she caught Hunter on his way out with an apple in his hand. A slight whiff of whisky hung on the air, but he didn't seem to be inebriated.

"Morning," he said gruffly when her footsteps alerted him to her presence. "I ain't hungry this morning, and I'm late anyhow. I'll see you at dinner."

"I'm so sorry, Hunter," Penny began, intending to launch into a long apology for being late and a promise to fetch some breakfast out to the stables for him, but he was already gone, striding over the cobblestone yard.

Hamish came clattering into the kitchen, carrying some fresh eggs in a basket.

"Look, Aunt Penny! I fetched the eggs all by myself after Uncle Hunter helped me milk Mabel."

He proudly held out the basket for her to admire the clutch of eggs with their rich brown shells.

"What would I do without you, Hamish?" Penny said, ruffling his curls as she smiled fondly and fought back the ever-present guilt. "You're such a comfort to me."

Hamish grew an inch taller as he set the basket down on the table. Only then Penny noticed the bucket of milk standing there, with the colander and muslin cloth still resting in it.

"How about I make us some omelets, Hamish?"

Hamish looked up at her, his eyes telling her yes before his lips did. "Can I fetch some fresh green things from the garden to make it look pretty?" he asked.

"That would be wonderful," Penny agreed.

Hamish scurried off, and Penny set to work gathering the needed utensils and ingredients for their breakfast. Doggedly, she went through the motions, although it was like wading through thick mud. All she wanted to do was escape upstairs to her soft, down bed and sleep away all the darkness and worry that clung to her like spider's webs.

She had begun to think Hunter wouldn't even begrudge her that, especially considering the whiskey fumes that had been following in his wake that morning. If he did, it would be rather like the pot calling the kettle black. Come to think of it, he hadn't once admonished her for being tardy at breakfast, or slow with her chores. Perhaps he understood. And yet she was routinely overcome with guilt for the way she was slacking on her duties.

Even though she had never voiced her vow to him, she couldn't bear to break it. Just as she couldn't bear to break her vow to take care of Hamish. It felt like those two vows were her last lifeline, a slim, but tenacious double braided cord of hope in a sea of ever-changing tides of emotions. For her own sake, as well as for the sake of Hamish and Hunter, she had to keep hanging onto that singular saving grace with all her might.

As she trudged her way through the day, her thoughts drifted from her sisters to Hamish, to Hunter and the smoky threat of the mysterious Mr. Wyatt Blackwell.

"Aunt Penny," Hamish's voice broke in on her thoughts, "I bet we've been here a whole year, haven't we?" He was holding Maisie by the hand while she practiced her walking on the patchy grass outside the kitchen.

Penny tried not to laugh as she hung out another diaper on the wooden clothes horse where it could be dried by the sun and wind. "No, not quite a year, Hamish. Barely a month, if I'm not mistaken."

She paused. To be honest, she wasn't even sure how long they'd been at Blakely Quarter Horse Stud Ranch. It could be one week or even one year. Time seemed to have melted together in one seamless lump of emotional turmoil and hopelessness.

"Well, that's also a long time," Hamish went on, his focus on Maisie as she squealed with laughter and lifted her foot up, apparently enjoying the tickling sensation of the grass against her soft, pink soles. "I think it's time Mama and Aunt Sarah came to visit us."

Penny's heart froze in her chest. Tears sprang to her eyes without warning.

I have to tell him, she thought, looking into her nephew's earnest, all too grown-up eyes. He was beginning to suspect something. She could tell by the way he studied her expression, his eyes questioning, pleading.

Penny looked away and finished rinsing the diaper in her hands. Then she wrung it out, aware that Hamish never once let his gaze drop from her face. She shook it out, hung it over a rung on the clothes horse and wiped her hands on her apron.

Walking over to where Hamish stood, she took Maisie's hand and sat down on the grass beside the two children. Her heart was beating wildly. There was no telling how he'd take it, but she couldn't lie to him anymore. He had to hear the truth. She would be there to help him pick up the pieces if he did fall apart as she feared he would.

"Hamish, your Aunt Penny hasn't been entirely truthful," she began. Hamish grew even more somber as he plopped down on the grass beside her. Maisie gurgled and dug her hands into the dirt, fascinated by the tiny clods of earth and the rough pebbles.

"That's okay, Aunt Penny," Hamish was saying. "You and Mama always taught me to forgive, so I'll forgive you, too."

Penny choked back her tears. "That's very kind and very brave of you, my boy," she said, squeezing his shoulder. "But I need to tell you the truth now. I won't be a good aunt if I don't."

"Okay, Aunt Penny," Hamish nodded, his innocent blue eyes fixed earnestly on Penny's face.

"There's no nice way to say this, so I'll just say it the way it is. Your mama and Aunt Sarah aren't coming back again. They've gone to a land so far away that we can't go there. Not for a long, long time."

Hamish sat bolt upright, his eyes round. "Are they in Prince Hamish the Kind's land?" he asked, his voice hushed with awe.

Penny stifled a sob. "Yes, I suppose you could say they are," she said. "Or somewhere like it. It's the place Mama used to call Heaven."

"And we'll see them one day?"

"I certainly hope so. But it could be a very long time before we do. You might be an old man before you see them again."

Hamish blinked rapidly. "I'll miss them," he said sadly. "I miss them so much already."

"Yes. So do I. But you have to be brave and wait for that day to come at the right time. And be sure to be the good, kind boy your mama raised you to be. Then, when you see her again, you can tell her all about your life and she'll be so proud of the man you've become."

He suddenly perked up. "I could write them letters, couldn't I? You said my writing is real good already."

"Letters cain't reach Heaven, Hamish," a male voice crashed in on Penny's hearing.

She looked up to see Hunter standing there, his hands on his hips. She scowled at him. Hunter didn't seem to notice. It didn't matter that what he had said was the truth. It wasn't his place to come barging in on her sensitive conversation with her nephew, an orphan, who needed to hear this news as gently as possible.

"Is that true, Aunt Penny?" Hamish turned his face back to hers, once again wide eyed.

"It is true, Hamish." Penny wasn't about to go back to lying to him. "But I'm sure you can ask the angels to read them and fly up to Heaven and tell your mama and Aunt Sarah everything you wrote."

His cherub face broke into a delighted smile. "Then I'll do that," he said. "Right away." Without another word he leapt to his feet and raced inside.

"Wipe your feet before you go indoors, Hamish!" Penny called after him, but he was already probably halfway across the kitchen.

Penny turned her attention to Hunter who had squatted down beside Maisie and was taking grass stalks from her mouth, much to her displeasure.

“I’d appreciate it if you’d not interfere when I’m speaking with Hamish on delicate matters,” she said stiffly.

“No point in lying to the boy,” Hunter said with a shrug.

“There’s no point in leaving him hopeless, either,” Penny retorted sharply.

Hunter hoisted a fussing Maisie onto his hip. “Ain’t like there’s all that much hope floating around here, anyhow, is there?” he said, his eyes dark.

“All the more reason for us to make sure Hamish, at least, has something to hope for, even if neither of us do.”

Penny spun on her heel and headed for the kitchen, her ire rising like a hot tide in her chest. It was only when she reached the washing up area and stood bracing herself with her hands on the table that she realized she had left the dirty diaper water in the washbasin outside and a diaper languishing in the pail of rinse water.

Reluctantly, she moved over to the window to see what Hunter was doing. It was more than she could bear to go out again with him watching her. As she peered through the windowpane, she caught her breath and paused, gazing at the scene beyond.

Even though the image was rendered slightly wobbly and hazy by the glass, none of its beauty was lost. Hunter was dancing with his daughter on his hip, with her giggling in utter delight. Round and round he went in a waltz step, whistling a melody Penny vaguely recognized. Perhaps one of the tunes she’d heard coming from the dance halls when she’d taken walks with Hamish on Sunday afternoons.

They always went to Central Park, where Hamish loved to watch the rich children playing on their velocipedes and tricycles, or sailing their toy boats on the waters of the great pond. She could still remember it like it was yesterday, Hamish skipping alongside her as they walked home.

"That boy who let me ride his vol, volcanopede, no, vel, velopsidee, he said they call them boneshakers! And they really do, Aunt Penny! I'm sure all my bones have been shaken loose now!"

Penny had to chuckle to herself, remembering, while she watched the father-daughter dance come to a close outside.

"Here, Aunt Penny, can you check it for me?" Hamish startled her out of her dream world. He stood beside her, holding out a sheet of writing paper full of large letters written in his childish hand and accompanied by some crude but painstakingly drawn pictures.

"Of course, I will, dear," she said, taking it from his hand.

At that moment, Hunter stepped inside with Maisie still on his hip. Penny tried not to look guilty for spying on his private moment with his daughter. She lifted her chin and held his gaze when he addressed her.

"Penny, I'll be going into town tomorrow afternoon after dinner," he announced. "If you're needing anything, or you'd like to tag along for the outing, you're more than welcome."

Penny hadn't expected that olive branch, but she wasn't deaf to how impersonal it sounded.

"Well, that's very kind of you to invite me, Hunter, but I ..." she didn't get any further.

"Ooh, please, Aunty Penny, can we go along?" Hamish was hopping up and down, tugging at her apron. Maisie began squealing and bouncing up and down in Hunter's arms.

"Looks like Maisie wants to go along, too," Hunter said with a lopsided grin that made Penny's heart melt like wax in the sun, but she steeled herself.

"Well, then, I suppose it won't do for me to stay alone at home by myself," she said with an intentionally nonchalant tilt of her head.

She didn't want to tell Hunter that notwithstanding the heartwarming display of tender care and affection she had seen him lavish on Maisie, she still couldn't bear to let Hamish out of her sight, even if it was to trust him into the hands of another adult.

Besides, Hunter wasn't just another adult. He was an adult still struggling to free himself from the talons of drink. As much as she admired his efforts, she knew what a relentless prison warden alcohol could be.

In her hand she held a letter written by a boy to his dead mother. If anything should happen to that boy, Penny knew she would never forgive herself. She would spend the rest of her life dreading the day she would have to face her sister in Heaven when her time came.

What she might actually do to save Hamish from any misfortune on the trip into town was a complete mystery to her. But staying behind, imagining tragedies all afternoon, would drive her positively insane.

But even more terrifying than that, what if that Wyatt fellow should show up again while she was all alone? She shivered and avoided Hunter's questioning eyes.

Chapter Sixteen

Hunter helped Penny down from the buggy in front of the general store and handed Maisie over to her. The street was quiet, with only a few folks going about their business at a leisurely pace. A couple of women across the road at Matt's carpenter shop seemed engrossed in conversation. Penny recognized one of them as the daunting Mrs. Aylward.

"See what you need for the house, and you're welcome to get anything you need for yourself or the children," Hunter said, looking distracted. "You can put it on my tab."

"Thank you," Penny said, studiously ignoring the way he'd said, "the children," as if they were a normal family.

"I'll be back in a few shakes once I've attended to business over at the miller." Hunter handed down the baby carriage as he spoke. Hamish clambered down from the buggy to join his aunt.

"Can I push Maisie, Aunt Penny?"

"Sure, you can, love," Penny replied, then stopped and giggled silently to herself. *I'm starting to sound like someone from around here,* she thought. Placing Maisie in the baby carriage, she watched the buggy clattering away, pushing aside the faint hope that Hunter would turn around and give her a parting look.

He didn't.

"Oh, my!" a female voice enveloped Penny as she turned to face forward, intent on entering the store. "Is that the Blakely baby?"

Bending over the baby carriage was a woman at least ten years older than Hunter, wearing a boldly striped pink and navy dress, her head covered with a bonnet festooned with red silk flowers in the shape of large lilies. Fiery red curls peeped out from underneath, clashing with the red of the flowers. The woman looked up at Penny and smiled, apparently awaiting her reply.

"Yes, ma'am," Penny replied, feeling immediately self-conscious. "Maisie Blakely."

"Oh, well, she is the spitting image of her mama, ain't she?"

Penny hesitated for only a second. She was going to have to get used to this. "I didn't know the first Mrs. Blakely, but from the pictures I've seen of her, Maisie does take very much after her mama."

The woman's attention was now firmly on Penny. "The first Mrs. Blakely?" she echoed. "Do you mean to tell me there's a second Mrs. Blakely?"

Penny's cheeks felt hot. "Yes, ma'am. That would be me."

"Hunter married again? So soon?" the woman blustered. "Well, I never! Who would have dreamed it?"

"Hunter married again?" another voice chimed in. Penny glanced over to see a gentleman stepping closer. "Did I hear you right, Abigail?"

"Yes, dear, you did," the woman replied. "I'd never have thought it possible, myself, not in all my born days. He was downright devastated when Amy passed on. Do you remember?"

"Yeah, I do," the woman's gentleman companion agreed. "I've never seen a feller so devoted to his wife. I sure am happy he's found love again, though. If anyone deserves happiness, it's Hunter Blakely."

Penny felt as if she was shrinking smaller and smaller, just a tiny speck in a world dominated by ghosts from the past.

"If you please, ma'am, sir," she said, wanting to get away. "It's lovely to have met you, but I've some errands to run, if you don't mind."

"Oh, where is my head?" the woman said, pressing one hand against her chest. "I didn't even ask your name!"

"It's Penny, Penelope Blakely, Mrs. Hunter Blakely." Saying those words filled her eyes with bittersweet tears that she blinked back quickly. In the same instant, she felt a hand tugging at her little finger.

"Aunt Penny! Aunt Penny, you should try these pickles! They're so good!" Hamish looked up at her, still crunching on the last pickle he had popped into his mouth. His other hand held out a fistful of the crisp green preserves for her to take.

"And this is my nephew, Hamish," she added, the heat rising in her face as she took the offered pickles from Hamish's hand.

"Lovely to meet you, Penny, Hamish," the gentleman responded. "The name's Jeremiah Winters and this is my wife, Abigail Winters. Welcome to Four Horse!"

"Yes, welcome to Four Horse, Penny. I do hope you'll be joining us for the Four Horse Fall Barn Dance that my husband and I are organizing?" Mrs. Winters leaned closer to Penny and whispered. "I'd sure love for you to twist Hunter's arm into coming, too. We ain't seen much of him around since Amy passed. I reckon it's time we got him out of his shell again, don't you?"

Penny felt overwhelmed. They were all assuming things that she couldn't bring herself to correct them on. The worst of those being that she had any sway or influence over the man she was married to.

"I'll do my best," she said weakly, giving her two gushing new acquaintances an embarrassed smile. Hamish had grabbed the handle of the baby carriage again.

"Did you try those pickles, Aunt Penny?" he said. "Do you like them? There's a whole barrelful over there. The man said they're free for the eating."

Mr. and Mrs. Winters laughed. Penny laughed too.

"Say goodbye to Mr. and Mrs. Winters, Hamish," she said, scrambling to take some control of the situation again.

Hamish paused and turned to wave. "Goodbye, Mr. and Mrs. Winters," he said, seemingly blithely unaware of his aunt's angst.

"Y'all take care now," Mr. Winters said as he took his wife's arm and the two hurried off down the boardwalk.

"And don't forget about the barn dance," Mrs. Winters flung cheerfully over her shoulder.

"I won't." Penny sighed. Then she followed Hamish into the general store.

The clerk took one look at Maisie in the baby carriage and the same conversation played itself out again. Everybody she happened across, all said the same thing. Penny tried not to get irritable, but it was taxing, to say the least. Time after time she would untangle herself, move Hamish along and head for another section of the store, only to be waylaid once more by inquisitive, though welcoming, townsfolk.

At last, her purchases made, Penny asked the clerk to watch her packages while she went across to the carpenter's shop owned and run by Sally's husband, Matt. She was anxious to hear news of Sally and the expected new baby. It felt strange to think that she was about to be an aunt for the second time, only this time by marriage.

"You betcha, ma'am!" the young man said as Penny steered Hamish from the store. The little boy was still adamant that he would push Maisie everywhere they went.

They managed to make it across the muddy street to the carpenter's shop without being accosted by any more curious townsfolk. Mrs. Aylward and her friend had, thankfully, already left, so Penny didn't need to face them as well.

"Well, howdy, Penny! Howdy, Hamish!" a friendly, familiar voice called out as they entered, the bell above the door jangling merrily. Penny relaxed instantly, letting out a long sigh.

"Hello, Matt, how d'you do?" she replied.

"Topping," Matt replied giving her a grin from behind his sales counter.

"And Sally? How's she doing?" Penny went on, watching Hamish staring at a display rack full of rows of brightly painted wooden toys.

"She's fine and dandy, Penny. Thank you for asking. The little one has us on tenterhooks, and no mistake. Taking his or her sweet time to bust on out into our world."

Penny laughed.

"How d'you like my shop, Hamish?" Matt said, diverting his attention to the rapt five-year-old.

Hamish turned awe filled eyes on Matt. "Oh, Mr. Morgan. It's the dandiest place I ever slapped eyes on!"

Matt laughed. “Well, dogies, Hamish! I’ll be danged if you don’t already sound like a born and bred Arizona cowboy!” he exclaimed, slapping his leg. “You ever done a spot of carving before?”

He stepped over to the rack that had caught Hamish’s attention. The toys cast angular shadows in the light of the kerosene lamps suspended from the rafters. Carefully selecting a large horse in the act of galloping, he picked it up and held it out to Hamish.

“What do you think of this here wild mustang?” Matt asked, giving Hamish a wink. “Made him with my own two hands, I did.”

Hamish’s eyes widened. “He looks just like Big Red!” he said, his voice full of awe. “Look at his mane flying in the wind, Aunt Penny!”.

Penny couldn’t help but smile as she watched him turn the horse over and over in his hands, stroking the flowing mane and tail with his fingers, making it gallop through the air while he made a wild whinnying sound in his throat.

“Why don’t you keep him, then?” Matt said, a generous smile splitting his face and creasing his eyes.

“Keep him?” Hamish whispered turning disbelieving eyes on Matt and then pleading ones on Penny.

“What do you say, Penny? We can call it a welcome gift,” Matt said, his eyes twinkling. It struck Penny that the simple act of giving the boy a gift was a source of pure joy to him.

Penny turned her gaze on Hamish. “Of course, that’s a lovely gift and a lovely gesture. Be sure to say thank you.” She gave him a wink.

"Oh, Mr. Matt, uh, Mr. Morgan," he said. "Thank you! Thank you kindly! I'll never forget this, as long as I live. I swear it. I ain't never owned such a beautiful carved horse in all my life!"

Penny inwardly cringed at his grammar, but she let it go for the sake of the moment. Mostly because she was distracted by having to blink back tears for the second time that afternoon. How Evie would have enjoyed the sight of her precious boy receiving such a beautiful gift. If only she could have.

Penny pushed aside the numbing pain clawing at her heart and tended to the business of asking Matt if he could make a larger playpen for Maisie.

"I don't like to leave her to herself too often, but, when I do, I'd like her to have more space to crawl around in," she confided in Matt.

"Well, that'll be easy as pie," Matt replied. "You just give me the measurements, and I'll have it knocked up for you in a couple of days.".

Penny and Matt pored over a notepad he produced from behind his shop counter while she gave approximate dimensions, and he drew a quick, deft sketch. Behind them, Penny could hear the sounds of a little boy playing with his new toy horse and, by the sound of it, a few other toys as well.

"Yes, yes, I think that'll do the trick," Penny said at length, surveying the completed sketch. "We'd best get back to the general store, so we don't keep Hunter waiting."

"Of course," Matt replied.

"Do give my love to Sally, Matt."

"I will, thank you, Penny. And say howdy to Hunter for me. I'll see y'all again soon, when I deliver Maisie's new playpen!"

Penny and Hamish left, traipsing across the street once more, Hamish still making his horse gallop through the air while he added the sounds of clopping hooves.

Matt's easy manner had helped Penny relax after the stress of having to introduce herself as Hunter's new wife to what felt like half the town. She didn't notice the man standing on the boardwalk outside the general store until she walked up the steps and almost bumped into him.

"Oh, dear! I'm so sorry, sir," she stammered, gripping Hamish's shoulder to stabilize herself.

"Amy Smith," the man said, his voice faraway and husky. He was staring at Maisie in the baby carriage.

Penny felt a tremor run through her. She looked closer at the stranger. He was tall, wearing a dark blue pinstriped suit and a black bowler hat and holding a cane loosely in one hand. His face was lean and sharp, like a hawk's. His eyes were watchful and piercing. It was the exact same face she'd seen in the chapel window on her wedding day. She had to stop herself from audibly sucking in her breath in shock.

Was it him? Was it Wyatt Blackwell?

"Actually, sir, the baby's name is Maisie. Maisie Blakely," Penny said, deciding not to let her fears run away with her.

"I know that," the man snapped. Then, as if coming out of a trance, he lifted his eyes to hers and his face relaxed into a benign smile. "I'm sorry. That was rather rude of me. I meant, yes, I know the baby's name. It's just that ..." he trailed off, looking stricken.

"Oh, that's all right. I've been hearing it all afternoon, how she looks so much like her mama, and how nobody expected her pa to marry again," Penny said, softening a little.

Perhaps Hunter was right. Perhaps Mr. Blackwell wasn't dangerous. Perhaps he was merely disturbed, shaken by the child's likeness to her mother. After all, he had been engaged to Amy, according to Hunter's telling, and that lady seemed to have had a way of making men lay down their lives for her.

It was an alien concept to Penny. She had no idea how one went about winning the undying loyalty of men. All she'd ever managed to procure in her short life was lewd comments and shrewd appraisals as if she were nothing but a work horse or a pleasure pony. And she'd never even thought of trying to attract any masculine attention. Her books had always been better companions that any young buck she'd ever met.

"You must be the new Mrs. Blakely," the man was saying as Penny surfaced from her private thoughts.

"Yes. Yes, I am. Penelope Blakely. But most people call me Penny." She placed her arm around Hamish's shoulders. "And this is my nephew, Hamish."

"Well, well, well, old Hunter must count himself a very lucky man, landing himself a ready-made family, no less."

Penny wondered at the implication of his words, but before she could ask what he meant by them, he continued speaking.

"I dare say I'm very pleased to meet you, Penny, and young Hamish." He stretched out his hand to Hamish who took it and shook it with a very grown-up look on his face. "I'm Wyatt Blackwell. Hunter and I go back a long way. I feel sure he must have mentioned me by now." Mr. Blackwell inclined his head in a show deference.

Penny felt as if someone had thrown a pail of icy water over her. Wyatt Blackwell was being uncommonly kind and courteous, but something in his manner chilled her to her core.

“I think he did,” she said, feeling only slightly surprised at the glimmer of satisfaction in Mr. Blackwell’s eyes.

“It figures,” Mr. Blackwell said, leaning on his cane and hooking a thumb into his vest pocket. “I’ll wager he told you I was betrothed to Amy before he stole her away from me.”

Penny didn’t know what to say. She looked down at Hamish, wondering if it was a good idea for him to hear all these things.

“Oh, don’t worry, I’m not losing any sleep over the matter,” Mr. Blackwell went on with a dry chuckle. “All’s fair in love and war, as they say in the classics.”

“Yes, I suppose it is,” Penny felt compelled to agree. She couldn’t help but feel that Mr. Blackwell attached a peculiar meaning of his own to that saying, and the thought filled her with unease.

“Well, then, don’t let me hold you up any longer,” Mr. Blackwell said, straightening up and tapping his cane on the boardwalk. “I’m sure you still have some errands to run, and we wouldn’t want to keep Hunter waiting.”

“Oh, yes, it was lovely to meet you, Mr. Blackwell,” Penny forced herself to say.

“I’m sure we’ll meet up again sometime, Penny. Perhaps at the Fall Barn Dance.”

“Perhaps. Goodbye, Mr. Blackwell.”

“Please, call me Wyatt.”

Penny opened her mouth to reply, but he had disappeared into the general store, the lingering scent of his cologne the only evidence that a man had stood before her seconds before.

The rattle and jingle of a buggy and harness drew her to face the street. Hunter was driving up, his face looking like a storm cloud.

"Who was that man, Aunt Penny?" Hamish asked, looking up at her curiously.

"I don't think I truly know the answer to that question, Hamish," Penny replied, an unnamed, leaden fear pressing coldly on her heart.

Chapter Seventeen

"What in the blazes do you think you're doing, talking to that varmint?" Hunter fumed as he drew the buggy to a standstill in front of the general store. He couldn't believe Penny hadn't known who she was in conversation with. No doubt Wyatt himself would have made sure she knew who he was. So why had she even given him the time of day?

Penny managed to look flustered and indignant all at the same time. "I'm sure we can discuss it at home, since it probably wouldn't be wise to make a scene in the middle of the main street of the town," she said crisply. "To say nothing of upsetting Hamish and Maisie."

She held his gaze while he stared back at her, trying to think of something to say in return, but coming up empty. She had a point, even if he didn't want to concede that point. He would have to swallow his pride along with his temper and discuss the matter at home, as Penny had suggested, out of earshot of the children and the townsfolk.

Without answering, he wrapped the reins around the foot guard railing of the buggy and jumped down to help load the parcels in moody silence. The sight of her talking with Wyatt, looking as if it were a perfectly ordinary conversation with a perfectly ordinary citizen had catapulted him into an immediate fury.

He would not have admitted it if anyone had asked, but the sharpest edge of his anger had been whittled by sheer jealousy, seeing Penny in Wyatt's company. He tried to tell himself it was perfectly natural. Sure, they weren't lovers, but she was still his wife, and it was a man's instinct to be wary of those who might break up his household.

The journey home was silent and fraught with tension, the adults both locked up in their brooding thoughts. Hamish contented himself with chattering away to Maisie, who responded with chuckles and gurgles. She even seemed to be trying to imitate some of Hamish's words. Rather than being an irritation to Hunter, as he might have expected, the sound was strangely comforting.

Once home, Penny settled the children in the nursery, with strict instructions to Hamish that he was to keep Maisie busy and not come out of the room until he was called. Hamish agreed, nodding his head and crossing his heart in a solemn gesture of obedience.

Then Hunter led the way to the study. He entered and went to stand by the window. The same window he'd thrown a bottle of whiskey from. He could still remember exactly which corner of the barn he'd seen Wyatt's shadowy form hovering about. If only he'd known it then that he wasn't hallucinating, he would have been able to confront Wyatt and figure out what game he was playing.

He heard Penny close the door softly behind her. Then he spun round to face her, leaning his hands on the windowsill and crossing one boot over the other.

"So, what did the old coyote have to say for himself, then?" he demanded hotly, the bubbling anger rising to the surface once more.

"It was nothing, Hunter. He simply introduced himself."

She was hiding something, he felt sure of it.

"I've known Wyatt since we were both knee high to a jackrabbit. Nothing is ever simple with that man."

"Yes, he mentioned you two went back a long way." She looked uncomfortable, and it irked him, made him even more suspicious.

"So, he didn't simply introduce himself." Hunter crossed his arms over his chest.

"Well, that was part of the introduction." She was scowling slightly.

"What else did he say?"

"Nothing, Hunter, nothing at all." Her unease was growing, and with it grew Hunter's distrust.

"Did he threaten you?" His words were angry, angrier than he wanted them to be. He wasn't sure who he was angry at. Wyatt, Penny, or himself. Perhaps all three.

"No! No, he didn't," Penny said, a little too quickly, Hunter thought.

"But he said something you don't want to tell me."

Penny adjusted her spectacles. "Hunter, why can't you just leave it be?"

He regarded her silently for a while before he replied. He had to choose his words carefully. "Because I don't trust Wyatt Blackwell as far as I can throw him." He paused. "And I swear it feels like you're hiding something from me."

Penny fiddled with the narrow frill on the end of her sleeve. She shifted her weight from one foot to the other. Hunter held his gaze steady on her face.

"Well," she began hesitantly. "He does unsettle me a bit, I suppose. But then, he was betrothed to Amy for a while, and he noticed her likeness in Maisie. I find it hard to believe anyone is entirely without feeling. Even a man like Wyatt Blackwell."

So, there it was. He had gotten to her. He'd tried those tricks with Amy, too. Tried to put guilt on her for breaking off the engagement, told her he would die if she didn't marry him, and it would weigh on her conscience forever. Thankfully Amy had told Hunter everything, and he'd been able to break the man's hold on her mind.

"You'd better believe Wyatt Blackwell ain't got a feeling of a day old. That silver-tongued sidewinder's got a heart like flint. You stay away from him, Penny, I'm warning you."

She still faced him, but her gaze darting this way and that, as if she were afraid to look him in the eye.

That settled it for Hunter. "Matter of fact, maybe I'll just go ahead and warn him to stay away from you myself, before he gets his lying hooks into y'all."

Penny looked startled. "I don't think that's a good idea, Hunter."

"Why in heck not? I don't want him near you."

"I just think it's a little rash, that's all. He wasn't causing any trouble." Penny said, looking alarmed. "I told you, he didn't even threaten me."

Hunter opened his mouth to retort and then shut it again. Perhaps it was a little rash. Perhaps he was being unreasonable. But he couldn't shake the feeling that Wyatt was up to something. Why would he be sneaking around the Blakely ranch? Peeking through the window at the Blakely wedding? And why did Penny still look so uneasy, almost guilty? What was she not telling him?

"You sure there's nothing else he said that I ought to know?" Hunter made one last ditch effort.

"I'm sure," Penny said, her mouth set in a determined line.

Hunter regarded her thoughtfully for a moment. He'd managed to get a handle on his anger, but the suspicion still niggled at him. She might have had a hard life, but she was still young, not yet twenty and still susceptible to the likes of Wyatt.

"All right, then," Hunter said with a sigh, standing up straight again and marching to the door. "I reckon we both need us a good night's rest, and then we'll talk again in the morning." He paused and turned to look at her. "I still think I ought to let him know he better keep his distance."

Penny nodded, but the look in her eye told him she didn't feel comfortable with that idea at all. Stubborn woman. He turned on his heel and headed for the front door. "I'm going to check on the ranch," he flung over his shoulder. He needed to think, and he did that best on the back of a horse.

***

That night Hunter still wasn't done thinking. He lay on his back, staring up at the ceiling while he tried to order his thoughts and feelings. He'd moved past that crushing cycle of always expecting Amy to come back home, as if she'd been away on a long trip all this time, only to have his heart ripped out of his chest every time he was faced with the reality that he wasn't ever going to see her on this side of the grave again.

What he couldn't quite get a handle on was the sense that Amy was gone because of him. Because she had lived with him on his ranch out in the middle of nowhere. He couldn't shake the belief that the few miles' difference of living in town might have saved her life.

If she'd been Wyatt's wife, living in his stately house just a mile away from the general store, maybe she'd still have been alive. He wondered if he would have preferred that.

On the one hand, he did. Even if he couldn't have her, at least knowing she was on the earth, pouring all her joy and beauty on those around her, would have been enough for him. On the other hand, he knew that Amy herself would have been deeply unhappy, married to Wyatt. Even if she had been able to hide it from others, Hunter would have known, and it would have been just as bad as her being dead. No. It would have been worse.

His thoughts made him feel heavy and restless, so he tried to think of other things and inadvertently went back to remembering his talk with Penny.

It was the same thing, really. Penny was in danger because of him. The simple fact that she lived under his roof was the very thing that was placing her in jeopardy. And not only her. This time there was a child involved. Hunter's chest blazed with anger as he thought of Wyatt harming Hamish.

But did Hunter really think his arch enemy would do that? Harm an innocent child? He didn't know. That was the worst thing about it. If he could see into the man's head and know where he was liable to draw the line, he would have felt more secure, more prepared. As it was, Wyatt was a loose cannon.

At last Hunter fell into an uneasy sleep, filled with confusing dreams of Wyatt slipping around the ranch like a ghost, impossible to catch and yet constantly materializing in the strangest places. All the while Hunter tried unsuccessfully to hide Penny and Hamish in the cellar, the attic, the broom cupboard under the stairs, even under his bed.

At one point the ghost grabbed hold of his shirt and began shaking him, shouting, "Aunt Penny! Aunt Penny!" in a child's voice.

Hunter woke with a start and grabbed at the sleeve of his nightshirt. The hand was still there, but it was the small, bony hand of a child. The child screamed. Hunter came fully awake and realized he was looking into the pale, frightened face of Hamish.

"Uncle Hunter! It's Aunt Penny! I think she's dying!"

Hunter's heart constricted painfully. No! She couldn't! He wouldn't let her!

In three strides he was out of the room, Hamish running along behind him. He burst into Penny's bedchamber and found her sprawled across the bed. It sounded like she was gasping for air.

Rushing across the room, Hunter sat down beside her and lifted her up. A jolt of shock ran through him. She was limp as a ragdoll.

Did the varmint poison her? The thought flashed through his mind. *How'd he manage that without poisoning the rest of us?*

"Fetch warm water and salt in a cup, Hamish! Heaps of salt!" he barked. The boy left the room immediately, sobbing loudly, but obeying without question.

Hunter drew Penny into his arms, hating the helplessness washing over him, but unable to shake it off.

"Just keep breathing," he ordered in a whisper. "Just you keep on sucking air, Penny Blakely."

He couldn't tell if she could hear him. Her eyelids were fluttering, and a mumbling sound came from her lips, but that was all. And he wasn't even sure if she'd started doing that before or after he'd picked up her unresponsive body.

Cradling her head against his shoulder he fought back tears. Was he cursed? Was every woman who ever came into his life going to die in his arms?

I cain't live like this, he thought despondently. *I got to put an end to it once and for all. I won't hold to no woman dyin' in my house again.*

He had no idea how he was going to stop it happening again, though. He couldn't leave the ranch—it was all he had left of his parents. He could take Penny and Hamish to Prescott. Nobody knew her there. She could pretend to be a widow. There were plenty of eligible bachelors in that area. Even some eligible widowers. He'd find someone to take care of her and her nephew.

The thought of her leaving bothered him more than he anticipated. It was a crazy idea anyway. The rambling thoughts of a desperate man. Sooner or later, someone would find out who she really was, and she'd never live it down. Besides, she wasn't the kind to lie. He knew that much about her.

Penny had begun to twitch, her mumbling sounding slightly more coherent, her breathing slightly less belabored. Hunter rocked her back and forth, crooning and consoling her.

"There, now, rest easy," he said. "We'll get this out of you and then we'll get you away and safe soon as you're fit to travel."

Hamish came in with the water and salt. Hunter took the cup and tried to drip the saline liquid between Penny's lips. All at once she gasped and then exploded into a fit of coughing. Lurching forward, she spat out the salt water and raked in great lungsful of air, as if she couldn't get enough.

Hunter let the tears flow, then. He couldn't remember when last he had been so happy to see someone alive, or when last he'd felt so determined to keep them that way.

Chapter Eighteen

Penny found herself drifting through the empty ranch house. There was no furniture in the rooms, as if the house were either newly built or had been evacuated. The light coming in at the windows seemed hazy and opaque, swirling and sighing as if it were a live presence. Penny felt weightless, her feet barely making any sound on the floorboards that were bleached white, from what, Penny didn't know.

The sound of voices drew her to the parlor, from which an even brighter light spilled, shimmering and animated. Penny paused. Could it be? Were those Evie and Sarah's voices? With a stomach full of butterflies, she moved quickly toward the room and burst in.

At first the light blinded her, and she could only make out figures in dresses. As her eyes adjusted to the brightness, her sisters' faces crystalized into view before her.

"Oh! Evie! Sarah!" she cried out and ran sobbing into their open arms. "I've missed you so terribly. And I'm so sorry for what happened. Please, please forgive me. It should have been me, not you. Hamish needs his mama ..." she trailed off, suddenly wondering where Hamish was, and pulled back.

"It's not your fault, Penny," Evie said gently. "Anyway, we're happy where we are now, and I'm sure you're being the best mama to Hamish that he could ever hope for."

Tears were rolling down Penny's face, but she didn't try to hold them back.

"No, Evie, no. You should both be here with us at the ranch. I'll fetch Hamish—he'd love to see you. I just don't know where he is right now."

"I think he went that way," Sarah said, her dimples playing about her cheeks.

Penny's eyes followed the direction her sister was pointing in. All at once the outer wall of the parlor began to crumble and fall away, the rock and plaster disintegrating into thin air. Beyond it the blue Arizona sky stretched away over the Black Hills and ended in a mass of dark, roiling thunderheads.

An icy wind picked up, whipping at Penny's face and clutching at her clothing. "Hamish? Hamish?" Penny cried out, but no sound came from her lips.

The next instant the clouds were overhead and, stepping down from them as if they were a mountain, came Mr. Blackwell. His boots were polished to a dazzling shine and his suit was immaculately tailored. He was slapping his cane across one hand and looking like the cat who had got the cream.

"Just the ladies I was looking for," he said, landing on the parlor rug in a wide-legged stance. "What do you think you're doing here? Get back where you belong and take her with you!"

Penny realized with a shock that he was speaking to her sisters and pointing at her. He began beating Evie and Sarah with his cane, driving them away from Penny. She tried to scream, to tell them to head the other way, but still she was mute. The hills were shaking and heaving as a huge chasm opened up where the rolling semi-desert used to be.

Penny lunged forward, desperate to stop her sisters' headlong flight into the chasm, but she found herself going nowhere. Her feet were stuck to the floor, seeming to have grown roots that reached down through the floorboards and right into the earth.

No! No! This way, Evie! This way, Sarah! her mouth formed the words over and over, but her lips were cloaked in thick silence, even though her throat ached as if she were screaming like a banshee. She felt weak and powerless under the black clouds that seemed to be pressing down on her shoulders, a heavy, melancholy weight.

Mr. Blackwell seemed to have disappeared, but her sisters were still fleeing. They reached the edge of the precipice and then disappeared from sight, too. Penny collapsed on the floor, sobbing silently, unable to move a muscle, scarcely able to breathe for the heaviness pressing down on her chest.

Then, strong, gentle arms surrounded her, lifted her up, cradled her carefully in the whirling darkness. A voice hushed her, crooning encouraging words, but she couldn't see anyone. Slowly, the life began to return to her limbs. Her breathing eased. Warmth seeped into her from the unseen, unknown being who held her.

She felt something warm against her lips. The acrid, metallic taste of salt filled her mouth. She drew in a breath to protest and choked. Spitting out the warm, salty liquid she fell forward, coughing and spluttering.

Small hands patted her rapidly on her back.

"Oh, dear, Aunt Penny, are you all right? Aunt Penny, please say something!"

"Hamish!" she managed to croak out in a hoarse whisper, realizing that she was waking from a nightmare.

"Oh, thank God," Hunter's deep bass tones rumbled through her.

"What happened?" Penny asked, rubbing her temples. Her head hurt, and her teeth ached, as if she'd been chewing through leather.

"You weren't moving, Aunt Penny, and you couldn't breathe," Hamish said.

"First thing I thought was that you'd been poisoned," Hunter said.

Only then did Penny realize he was sitting beside her on the bed. Had it been his arms that held her? Filled her with life and warmth? An involuntary thrill ran through her, and her cheeks tingled with heat.

"Oh, dear, no, not poison. I think it was a nightmare," she said, wiping the perspiration from her brow and trying not to touch him.

"Do you get nightmares often?" Hunter asked, his voice a strange mixture of concern and pragmatism.

"I don't know," Penny said hesitantly. "I've only had a few since, well, since Evie and Sarah left us. I don't remember having such bad night terrors before that happened."

"Nothing a little chamomile tea won't fix," Hunter said briskly, rising to his feet and lighting the kerosene lamp beside her bed. "What do you say we all go down to the kitchen and boil a pot. I could do with some myself, if I'm honest."

"Yes, I think that'll do just fine," Penny agreed. She tried to stand, but her body still felt weak.

"Here, lean on my arm."

Penny reached out and took the arm Hunter offered and let him help her to her feet. Hamish scurried around to her other side and placed her hand on his shoulder.

"You can lean on me, too, Aunt Penny," he assured her.

Together they made their slow way down to the kitchen and Penny's menfolk helped her into a chair.

She sat watching Hunter set about making the tea with Hamish eagerly helping. Her head felt fuzzy and thick, her limbs heavy, but watching them gave her a sense of peace and normality after the unsettling confusion of her dream.

When Hunter set the cup of tea down in front of her, she inhaled the calming, herby fragrance gratefully. It really did help to clear the fogginess in her brain and ease the tightness in her jaw. She took a tentative sip, not wanting to scald her lips.

"Hamish, why don't you go check on Maisie? I'll take care of your Aunt Penny," Hunter said.

"Sure thing, Uncle Hunter," Hamish said with the briskness of a soldier at arms. The next moment he was gone.

Hunter took a sip of tea and looked intently at Penny. She smiled wanly.

"Thank you for waking me from that awful dream," she said.

"I surely thought you'd been poisoned," Hunter said, his eyes searching hers as if he wanted to make sure that wasn't actually the case.

"Well, I'm grateful I wasn't, though night terrors are not my favorite thing, either."

"My ma always had me talk about my night terrors. She said that would make them seem smaller and less scary, if I spoke about them, told them out loud to someone else."

Penny returned his gaze thoughtfully. It made sense. And if she wasn't mistaken, him telling her that sounded uncannily like an invitation.

"I dreamed of Evie and Sarah. They were here, in the parlor, but the house had no furniture and Mr. Blackwell came in a big storm and whipped them with his cane. Chased them into a great big chasm in the earth that just opened up like the mouth of some hungry monster."

She shivered.

"That sure sounds nasty," Hunter said. "Reminds me of night terrors I used to have after Amy passed."

Penny took a few more sips of her tea, feeling the warmth fill her belly and radiate through her tired limbs.

"I've had me a notion that maybe dreams are our heart's way of figuring out things that don't make sense to our brains," Hunter went on, his eyes looking past her, at what, Penny could not know.

"What makes you say that?"

"Well," Hunter gave a little cough and his eyes locked onto hers momentarily before flickering away again. "In my night terrors there's always something stopping me from saving Amy. Leastways, there was, the last time I had one. It's been a while, now."

Penny wanted to ask him a question, but she wasn't sure if she dared. Not so soon. And yet, he seemed to be opening his heart to her more than ever before.

"Do you think there was anything you could have done to save her? In real life, I mean?" The words forced their way out of her mouth.

Hunter gave her a haunted look, then he took a gulp of tea and set the cup down, staring into its depths.

"At the moment the fever took her? I reckon not. But there's a whole heap I could have done different, long before she even delivered Maisie."

Penny sat silent, wanting to comfort him, but not knowing how.

"And after she was gone, I couldn't look at Maisie without feeling like some devil was sticking a red-hot poker through my chest. How d'you think a father feels not being able to pick up his little girl 'cause he's scared his heart'll break?"

If Penny was struck dumb before, she'd completely lost her command of speech now.

"The only thing that could stop the terrors and the memories from ripping me apart was that dang Old Farm Pure Rye. Reckon that doesn't make me much of a man now, does it?"

He looked up again, holding her gaze. His hazel eyes were transparent, the wall of guardedness gone. Penny reached out and took his hand. She wasn't looking for words anymore. There weren't any that could say any more than her comprehending silence could. Instead, she returned the favor he'd bestowed on her, opening her heart for him to see inside.

"I miss my sisters terribly," she said softly. "Evie and Sarah were my whole world. I never knew our ma and pa, but my sisters were both father and mother to me. And then they were gone in the blink of an eye and the bottom fell out of my world. I was left standing on nothing, feeling like I was drowning and no land in sight."

She could tell by the look in his eyes that Hunter needed no further explanation. He'd walked that road, floundered in that ocean. It was good to know that someone understood. That he understood.

"There's not a day goes by that I don't wish they could be here with us, with Hamish and I, but somehow being here, taking care of you and Hamish and Maisie, makes it easier. I suppose it gives me purpose, keeps my mind occupied." She shrugged, feeling suddenly embarrassed.

"Yeah, purpose," Hunter said distractedly, his eyes travelling to some far-off place again.

Penny felt a little tug of longing at her heart. It was wrong, so wrong, to feel that way, but she felt certain he was thinking of Amy, and she couldn't help wishing he would think of her, instead.

Faded echoes of the townsfolks' remarks drifted through her mind.

I was sure he'd grieve himself right into his grave, poor feller.

Never was a man so devoted to a lady. It was something ta see, I tell ya.

I figured he'd never get over Amy's passing, but it sure looks like I was wrong.

Penny drank the last of her tea and held out her cup for Hunter to fill again.

No, ma'am, you weren't wrong, she thought. *He never will get over losing her, and it's nobody's place to try to make him move past it. Least of all mine.*

Chapter Nineteen

The morning felt different to Hunter as he washed and dressed, despite the familiarity of the dawn chorus's cheerful cacophony flooding in at the window. For a few moments he couldn't put his finger on what could possibly be making him feel that peculiar, long-lost sense of expectation.

Taking care of you and Hamish and Maisie makes it easier. Gives me purpose, somehow.

Hunter stopped in mid shave. Purpose. Yeah. That was it. He felt more of a sense of purpose, too, now that he had Penny to take care of. And take care of her, he would.

He walked down to breakfast feeling lighter than he ever had. Once she was packed off to Prescott, he'd be able to breathe completely freely.

Penny would be safe, and he wouldn't have to worry about being the reason harm came to her or Hamish. The thought of Maisie not living under his roof was a little tougher to deal with. Still, he'd be able to visit her in town at least once a week.

When he stepped into the kitchen, it was a hive of activity. Penny was spooning flapjack dough into a pan. Hamish was clattering about, setting the table, his mouth going nineteen to the dozen as usual. The already strained milk stood cooling by the window. Maisie sat in her highchair, banging a spoon against the wood of the table and matching Hamish word for word, even though nothing she said was entirely intelligible.

"Well, it sure is a good morning today, ain't it?" he said, feeling a sort of peaceful contentment settle over him.

Penny looked up from the pan and flashed him a smile. "Good morning, Hunter. Breakfast's almost ready if you've a mind to take a seat so long."

"Howdy do, Uncle Hunter," Hamish said, setting a pot of preserves on the table and sticking his thumb in his belt.

Hunter laughed and sat down. Watching Penny dish up the hot flapjacks with Hamish clapping his hands in anticipation, he felt his resolve wavering. It was hard to believe they'd only been there a couple of short weeks. Now that he thought about sending them away, he could hardly imagine the ranch without them anymore.

Penny sat down opposite him and gave him a slight nod, as if to indicate that he could take over the breakfast proceedings. Looking into her soft brown eyes, his mind drifted back to their conversation at that same table the night before.

Now there was something else that was hard to believe. Had he really shared so much of his heart with her? Had she really responded with so much honesty and openness of her own? Or had he dreamed it all?

"Would you like me to say grace this morning?" Penny said, startling him back to the present moment. Her eyes shone with a gentle light that drew him in and set his heart galloping.

"Ah, no," he began and then realized he wasn't in the frame of mind for saying a coherent grace. He glanced at Hamish. The boy was watching him expectantly. "How about we give Hamish a turn?" Hunter said, grasping at a straw. "I reckon a feller ain't ever too young to learn how to pray."

Hamish's eyes grew wide. "Oh! Yes, I'd love that!" he said happily and promptly screwed his eyes shut, clasping his hands tightly in front of his chest. “Dear Father God,” he said, his voice animated and strong.

Hunter looked at Penny and they exchanged a smile before both bowing their heads and imitating Hamish’s body language.

“Thank You for always giving us enough to eat, and thank you for Aunt Penny and Uncle Hunter and Maisie. Thank you that we can be a family and please bless Mama and Aunt Sarah, wherever they are. And tell them we love them. Amen.”

He looked up, his face flushed, his eyes dancing with joy as he looked expectantly at Hunter. With a start, Hunter realized the child was waiting for him to appraise his prayer. As if he were qualified to do anything of the sort. He wanted to tell Hamish so, but something stopped him. How could he crush the boy’s spirit like that? All he needed was encouragement. That was the least Hunter could give.

“A finer prayer was never said before any breakfast I’ve ever had,” he declared, keeping his features grave and his voice factual.

Hamish beamed like the sun just beginning to stream in at the window.

Hunter spent the entire meal wondering what he was going to do about keeping them safe. It felt like a fool’s errand. They weren’t safe with him. Nobody was. And he couldn’t bear to think of them being harmed in any way.

When he stood in the doorway, ready to go out and start his day’s work, he paused.

“Penny,” Hunter said.

She dumped dishes into the washbasin and lifted searching eyes to his.

"About last night ..."

"Yes, about last night, there's something I didn't say that I should have," she interrupted before he could go any further. "I've noticed how you've been resisting the drink. And I think that says more about you as a man than the fact that you drowned your sorrow for a few months. In my book, the most masculine thing any man can do is admitting he has a problem. It's an admirable testament of character. Evie always told me that."

Her cheeks were as red as her full, sensitive lips. The desire to take her in his arms and kiss her overcame Hunter like a flash flood.

"Ah, thank you, Penny," he stammered. "That sure means a lot." His heart thudded against his ribs and breathing became difficult. Goldarnit, she was making things hard. For a timeless moment their eyes locked, and he knew in that instant that he would go to the ends of the earth, lay down his life, if need be, just to keep her safe.

He coughed and turned abruptly away, staggering down the stone steps of the back porch like a blind man. Taken by an impulse, he headed not out to the stables, but up the hill behind the house, to the grove of aspen that his father had planted. The grove where he'd laid his beloved Amy to rest.

He wasn't sure why he was headed there, just that he had a driving need to look at her headstone.

As he came close, he wavered. How long had it been? Had he even been there once since they'd lowered the spruce casket into the ground and covered it with the sandy, rocky earth?

He couldn't remember that, but the stone looked the same as he remembered it. A large, flat-topped boulder into which he had painstakingly etched her name and the span of the days of her life. There was the inscription, too. Two simple words: *Remember Me.*

His heart ached looking down on it. He didn't know he'd taken off his hat until it was in his hands. He didn't know he was weeping until two fat droplets splattered on the sandstone between the deeply etched words. He sat down on the stone and brushed away the dust and leaf particles that had fallen into the grooves of the lettering.

All at once a rustling in the aspens alerted him. He looked up, but his sight was blurry with tears. The white trunks of the aspen warped and wobbled. Hunter drew his sleeve across his eyes and looked again. The tall figure of a man dressed in black appeared, carrying a cane.

Hunter stood to his feet. "Get off my land, Blackwell!" he growled, his hands immediately clenched into fists.

Wyatt acted as if he hadn't heard him, striding nonchalantly closer.

"Are you deaf as well as brazen?" Hunter snapped, his hand hovering near the Colt in its holster, slung snugly against his hip. He kept it there in case he needed to shoot a rattler or a wolf, but he'd never thought of ever using it on a human being. Not until that moment. "I said get off my land!"

"Not before you've heard me out, Blakely," Wyatt replied with infuriating calm.

"There ain't a thing you can say that I want to hear, now get ..."

"You might want to reconsider, especially when it has to do with young Penny down there."

Hunter felt his nails digging into his palms. "Touch a hair on her head and I'll have you hanged!" Hunter snapped.

"Now, now, cowboy, there'll be no need for that," Wyatt said, leaning rakishly on his cane. "As long as you both do what I say."

"Why should any of us here do what you say, Blackwell? You've no quarrel with Penny, nor with me. Leave us alone." Hunter eyed his lifelong adversary, wondering if he had a derringer hidden somewhere in his immaculate three-piece woolen suit.

"Oh, I have a quarrel with you all right. Or have you forgotten that you stole my fiancé?"

Hunter laughed in sheer exasperation. "We've been over this a million times, Blackwell! Amy had her own mind, and she made her own choices. It's high time you quit flogging that horse! It's dead in the traces!"

"Not until you've paid for what you did. She was my reason for living, and you took her away from me. You, the one with the happy family, the one with all the breaks. You took the only thing on earth that made me feel like I had a hope in life."

"Oh, come on, Wyatt! Let it go, man!"

Wyatt stepped closer, his eyes flinty and sparking venom. "You think you can just get yourself another girl and pick up where you left off on your happy life with your ready-made family, do you? While I suffer every day from the blow you dealt me? You've got another think coming, cowboy."

"It's all in your head, Wyatt. You can stop suffering any time you choose." Hunter released his fists, the initial burst of anger replaced with a weary irritation. He turned to walk away, tired of the old argument that always ended up going around in circles.

Wyatt took another step closer and slapped his cane across Hunter's chest, stopping him in mid stride.

"Remember all the bad luck old Captain Smith had when he went against my father's wishes?" Wyatt said ominously.

Hunter gave a short, humorless laugh. "What, are you going to burn my stables down and poison my horses so I cain't pay rent and you can evict me?" He glared pointedly at Wyatt who didn't respond, his lips set in a tight line. "Oh, of course, here I am forgetting that I own this land. Cain't nobody evict me for nothing!"

He shoved Wyatt's cane away and tried to leave a second time.

"There's other ways I can hurt you, Blakely," Wyatt's voice hit Hunter's ears like ice daggers. In that moment his eye caught a movement down below and he stopped dead in his tracks.

Penny was outside, hanging out laundry to dry. Hamish was playing with Maisie, making mud pies near the hand pump. A man dressed in denim trousers and a gray sack coat walked up to Penny and began speaking to her. Penny turned and listened, then began to gesture. Hunter went cold all over, as if he'd just fallen through the ice of a frozen pond.

"You and I both know that money can't make a fellow happy. It's the love of a woman, the legacy of children, something to live for, someone to care for, that makes it all worthwhile, ain't it? My pa, rest his soul, he rejected all of those things, for the love of money, and I saw him turning bitter and twisted, day by miserable day. Folks hated him, and so they hated me. I hated him for that, you know. He made my life a living hell, just like he made his tenants' lives hell."

Hunter hardly heard him. His eyes were riveted to the scene below, his hand ready over the butt of his revolver. It was a stretch whether he was within range of hitting anything, but that wouldn't stop him trying if the man down below threatened his wife in any way.

"Amy was a breath of fresh air, I'm sure I don't have to tell you. She was my way out of the life my father had lined up for me. With her I would have had a fighting chance to be happy. She brought sunshine into the darkness of being a rich landowner's son. And then you took her away."

The man below bowed his head briefly in what looked like a gesture of thanks and then walked away. Hunter followed his progress around the side of the house and into the yard where his horse must be standing.

"Yeah, take a good look, Blakely," Wyatt concluded. "Don't forget how easy it'll be for me to have your happiness taken away in the blink of an eye."

"What do you want from me?" Hunter said, still watching his homestead below, his eye roving to Hamish and Maisie, then to Penny, then to the direction he'd seen the man go.

"Send her away, and I'll let her live. Her and the boy. And don't you even think of calling in the sheriff. You've got three days."

Hunter bristled. Who did he think he was, giving orders like that, telling Hunter what to do with his life?

"Penny ain't going nowhere. You know as well as I do, it'll ruin her. She's my wife, and she's staying right here. I'm warning you, Blackwell, keep away from my family, or, so help me, I'll make you pay, sheriff or no sheriff."

There was no response, and Hunter swung round, ready to pierce his opponent with a withering glare, but all he saw was the flash of black coattails disappearing amongst the white trunks of the aspens.

Hunter started to walk after him, but as he passed Amy's grave, he stopped. That would be foolish. The man was deranged. Who knew what might be waiting for Hunter among the trees. Instead, he stared down at his late wife's headstone.

I swear this will be the last woman I bury, he vowed silently as the overwhelming desire to protect Penny and Hamish from any and all harm washed over him stronger than ever before. *Come hell or high water, I won't let it happen again, not ever in my life.*

Chapter Twenty

Penny watched the man go, wondering how he could have missed such an obvious turning to the Mitchell ranch. Then again, when one was in an unfamiliar environment, it was never easy to notice anything except the newness of the place. She shrugged to herself and reached down into the laundry basket for another bedsheet.

Her mind drifted back to Hunter in the kitchen that morning. The look on his face, the way their eyes had locked when she'd told him that she thought him admirable for resisting the urge to drink. She couldn't remember a man ever looking at her like that before. It had made her feel warm and giddy and unspeakably happy.

A smile danced on her lips just thinking about it and she frowned, vigorously shaking out the sheet in her hands, as if that would shake loose the tendrils of attraction that were growing stronger and tighter around her heart. The frown was soon gone, though, and Penny began to hum an old tune she'd heard played by a band of travelling musicians in Central Park when she and Hamish were on one of their walks. She could only remember one line from the song.

Ida Red, Ida Blue, I got stuck on Ida, too.

A giggle escaped her as she imagined replacing *Ida* with *Hunter*, but quickly pulled herself up short. Firmly and decisively, she jammed the wooden pegs over the crisp, damp cotton, pinning it to the clothesline.

No. She'd made herself a vow not to want romance from him, and she'd better keep it. That wasn't getting any easier with Hunter talking about warning Mr. Blackwell to keep away from them. Surely that wouldn't have mattered to him, if he wasn't also feeling the tingles she was starting to feel just by looking at him, just by knowing he was near.

The laundry basket was empty, so Penny hoisted it onto her hip and walked around the flapping, billowing sheets. Her eye fell on Maisie at the hand pump, covered in mud.

"Oh, Hamish!" she exclaimed laughingly. "However do you let her get so grimy?"

There was no response. Hamish was nowhere to be seen.

"Hamish? Where are you?" Penny called out, certain he was playing one of his impromptu games of hide-and-go-seek. She went to stand by Maisie and set the basket down, her eyes roaming the courtyard and the vegetable garden beyond. Seconds ticked by. Maisie gurgled. Cicadas chirped.

"Hamish? Come on out, now. This isn't funny anymore."

Her heart began to thump in her throat.

"Hamish! Come out this instant."

The silence taunted her, throwing her mind into a tumult of imagined horrors, telling her that her worst fear was coming true.

Penny picked up Maisie and put her in the basket, still clutching her mud pies, then carried her into the house and set her down in the kitchen. The pounding of her heart was reaching to her temples making her head ache.

"Hamish? Hamish!" she called running from room to room, frantic, fearful. At last, she ran outside. Had he wandered over to the stables? He knew not to leave Maisie alone, not to go off by himself, especially to the horse corrals.

"Hamish! Where are you?"

The sound of thundering hooves reached her ears at the same time she saw the large corral's gate hanging open, swinging gently back and forth on its hinges. A scream rent the air. Penny echoed it with her own.

Big Red was bearing down upon her at full gallop, his eyes rolling, nostrils flared, ears plastered back against his skull. Clinging to the horse's flying mane and screaming at the top of his lungs was Hamish. The horse had no saddle and no bridle, only a halter with the rope flying alongside the horse's body, slapping his flank as he went.

Penny stood rooted to the ground, even though every instinct told her to run for her life. A courage and a determination welled up in her that she had never before experienced.

"Stop! Big Red, stop!" she commanded the colossal animal in a voice she herself hardly recognized. She may as well have commanded an avalanche to stop. The horse kept on coming toward her. Penny ran for the gate. If she could close it in time, if she could grab the trailing halter rope ...

Big Red reached the gate at the same time she did. He snorted and shied, his massive shoulder just missing her. The heat of his breath and power washed over her, the cloying odor of dust and sweat mingling with that earthy scent so peculiar to horses.

"Hunter!" Penny screamed, grabbing at the rope and holding on for dear life. Immediately she was jerked off her feet. The rope burned her palm like a handful of flaming hot coals, and she released it, crashing into the rocky earth with a painful thud.

At once she lunged to her feet, barely able to stand, she was shaking so hard. She knew she was hurt, but somehow, she didn't feel any pain. Every fiber of her being was consumed with watching her precious, terrified Hamish being carried off into the wilderness beyond the homestead.

"Hunter! Hunter!" she screamed again, stumbling along helplessly in the galloping horse's dust cloud.

The next moment he was there, his arms strong about her waist just as she tripped over a rock. He held her up, his grasp firm yet tender, his presence a refuge.

"Hunter ... please ... Hamish ..." she gasped, her voice breaking off in a sob.

Hunter held her close to him and took a deep breath. Penny collapsed against his solid bulk as he began to whistle. Three short chirps and then a long warble, starting high, pitching a little higher and then dropping to a low, mellow timbre.

Penny stared at the haunches of the departing horse as the whistle echoed around them. Her heart constricted. He couldn't hear Hunter. He was too far away. She let out a little groan of despair. Hunter held her tighter and whistled again.

The sound reverberated and quivered like a live thing, reaching out to the fleeing horse. His head came up. His gait slowed. Hunter whistled a third time and a fourth. Big Red turned, his ears straining forward now as he headed toward them.

Hunter kept whistling, dropping the pitch with each repetition. It was a soothing, almost mesmerizing sound. Big Red's pace dropped as he came closer. By the time he reached them he was walking, and Hamish had stopped screaming. Instead, he buried his head in the horse's mane and sobbed.

Big Red reached his master and dropped his head, shaking it as if in contrition. His sides were heaving and his muscles twitching as he blew out a long sigh.

"Easy, old boy, easy now," Hunter said gently. Then, in the exact same tone, so that Penny couldn't tell the difference between him speaking to Big Red and him speaking to Hamish, he said, "You're safe, little buddy. Just you go ahead and let go that mane."

Penny realized that Hunter had left her side and was reaching up to steady Hamish. Her nephew lifted a tear-streaked face, his eyes locking immediately onto Hunter's. The faith and trust that she saw there took her already shaky breath away.

"Just lean over onto my shoulder and slide off, easy like," Hunter said, his voice still low and calming. Hamish obeyed and the next moment he was straddling Hunter's hip. The tall horseman carried his burden to where Penny stood and bent his knees so she could reach Hamish's tousled head.

"See, he's all right now. Just a little shook up, is all. He'll be right as rain in no time. I sure am proud of you, little feller. You stuck to him like a burr to a flannel petticoat. I bet those fingers of yours are aching and cramping like nobody's business right about now. But don't you fret, we'll get you all nicely cleaned up, lickety-split, no question, and it'll all just feel like a bad dream."

He kept up the soothing monotone while he shepherded Penny gently into the house, the sound of his voice drowning out the fear, the terror, the shock, until all she could feel was grateful relief.

It was only later, after her rope burned hand was swaddled in a poultice bandage and her cuts and scrapes cleaned and dressed with ointment that she felt strong enough to feel the anger that one or both of them had coming.

Hunter had settled them both in bed and was feeding a pale-faced Hamish some of the hot broth that Penny had put on the stove that morning before the accident. Maisie lay on her stomach on the floor, fiddling intently with the edge of the rug, her ragdoll discarded.

"Hamish," Penny said. "I need you to tell me what possessed you to go into the horse corral alone. And especially what possessed you to climb on Big Red's back when I expressly forbade it."

Hunter looked up, his eyebrows raised, shaking his head ever so slightly. Penny ignored him. She wanted to make sure Hamish would never do a foolhardy thing like that again. If he faced his actions while he was still smarting for them, perhaps it would make a deeper impression on him.

Hamish was staring at her with wide, teary eyes as he swallowed a mouthful of broth.

"But, Aunt Penny, I wasn't alone. I swear it. Cross my heart!"

The look of sympathy on Hunter's face changed to horror.

"What's your meaning, boy?" he said sharply. Then he softened. "How do you mean, you weren't alone, Hamish?" Concern was etched on his forehead and in his eyes.

"There was a man, a kind man, who asked to see the horses. I showed him all of them and I told him you've been teaching me to ride, Uncle Hunter."

Penny went cold. She locked eyes with Hunter as they listened to the rest of Hamish's story.

"He asked if I'd ever ridden Big Red, and I said no, 'cause Aunt Penny said I couldn't yet, and so did Uncle Hunter. The man said that was too bad. He asked me if I wanted to feel what it was like up on a big horse like that. Of course, I said yes. He said he'd help me, and I didn't have nothing to worry about."

Hamish paused. Hunter looked down at him. Penny bit her lip, trying to remember what the man had been wearing, the man who'd asked her if this was the Mitchell ranch.

"And he helped you up onto Big Red then, Hamish?" Hunter prompted.

Hamish nodded, looking guilty. "Yeah, he did. He told me to hang on to Big Red's mane. Said he'd lead me around the corral. I said we should shut the gate, but he said Big Red ain't going nowhere. And then he slapped him on his behind with a short switch. I don't know why he did that, Uncle Hunter." Hamish's lower lip began to quiver. "'Cause that gave Big Red an almighty big fright, and he just upped and ran ..."

Hunter put an arm around the boy and clucked reassuringly. "There, there, big feller. You're all in one piece and that's all that matters, ain't it?" He looked over at Penny, who was struggling to hold back her own tears and the thick lump of fear that was growing bigger and bigger in her chest, seeming to crowd out her lungs so she could barely breathe.

"Oh, I almost forgot," Hamish said, reaching into his pants pocket. The man gave me something before he slapped Big Red. He said to give it to you, Uncle Hunter. Said it was a nice surprise for you and Aunt Penny."

He pulled out a folded piece of paper and handed it over. Hunter took it, looking like he was reaching for a rattlesnake.

Slowly, he unfolded the paper and read. His face blanched. His lips and eyes hardened.

"What is it, Hunter? What does it say?" Penny demanded.

In reply, Hunter stood up. "You stay here and rest, Hamish. Your Aunt Penny and I need to talk."

Penny's heart lurched painfully. She got out of the bed, hardly aware of anything but the grim look in Hunter's eyes. She followed him to his study, ignoring the protestations of her battered body.

As she walked, a firm resolve began to take hold of her. Whatever that man had written in that note, she would stand by Hunter. They would stand against that threat together and fight as a unit. She knew in her heart of hearts that they could triumph, they would triumph. Together.

No matter what, she would not desert him. They had a common enemy now, and with it a common purpose. Wild horses would not drag her away from seeing it through with her man.

Chapter Twenty-One

Hunter let Penny walk past him into his study and closed the door behind him. He leaned back against it with a sigh and held out the note for her to read.

I wasn't joking. Three days. Don't forget.

Penny looked up at her husband. "What does this mean, Hunter? It doesn't make any sense. What's meant to happen in three days?"

Hunter sighed again and brushed past her, headed for his desk. Penny followed his progress, the note feeling like a lead weight in her hand. Hunter sat down heavily in his leather chair and held his head between his hands for a few moments, his elbows propped up on his desk. Penny's heart was racing. She'd never seen him like this.

"Hunter! Please tell me! What is it?"

He cleared his throat, looked up and motioned to Penny to sit down. She did, her eyes still fixed on his face.

"I reckon you could say our Mr. Blackwell's a sight more serious than I figured," he said, a dull resignation in his eyes. It scared Penny more than any flash of fiery anger might have done.

"More serious than you figured? Please tell me straight what's going on, Hunter." Penny's fingers hurt from gripping the note.

"He's threatened you and Hamish. Said I got to send y'all away," he motioned to the note in her lap, "in three days, or you won't be safe no more."

Penny caught her breath.

“Surely, he won’t dare do something serious? We could get the law in. There is a sheriff’s office near here, isn’t there?”

“Prescott. It’s a whole day’s ride from here.” His tone was flat.

“Well, let’s go get the sheriff,” Penny said, aware that her voice was rising in pitch. “We’ll be back with him before three days are up.”

Hunter shook his head and waved his hand, indicating that she should sit down. Penny sat, with a new understanding of what it meant to be chafing at the bit, as the saying went.

“We cain’t all go riding out to Prescott,” Hunter began.

“Hamish and Maisie could stay with Matt and Sally,” Penny said.

Hunter closed his eyes, then slowly opened them. He looked like a man weary of carrying a burden too large for his shoulders alone. “Sally’s about ready to have her own baby, I cain’t saddle them with two more young ‘uns now. Besides, Wyatt warned me not to call the sheriff. If we go riding off to Prescott, or anywhere, he’ll know what we’re up to.”

“We can’t just let him get away with this, Hunter. We can’t let him order us around, tell us what to do with our lives.” Penny could tell her words resonated with him, and yet he shook his head.

“I’m taking you and Hamish into Prescott tomorrow on the stage.”

Penny felt as if he’d punched her in the gut.

“I won’t go.”

Hunter eyed her, exasperation starting to show in his face and eyes. “He’ll kill you, Penny. And Hamish. Is that what you want?”

Penny gasped. “You said he wasn’t dangerous.”

“I thought he wasn’t dangerous,” Hunter corrected her. “That was before he pulled this little trick.” He clenched his teeth, the muscles in his jaw rippling as he gazed somewhere beyond her face. “He could have killed Hamish. Could have killed you.” His eyes flickered back to hers. “You’re getting on that stage tomorrow, so you’d best start packing.”

Penny felt weak. She sat limply in the chair, just staring at him. His jaw was set, his eyes resolute yet haunted, his mouth rigid. For a long while she simply sat there, willing him to relent, willing the whole nightmare to end. His face was unreadable, his eyes hooded. She didn’t dare ask him what her heart was clamoring to know, and yet she couldn’t stop her lips from speaking.

“Do you want me to go?” she asked softly.

“Penny! For the love of Mike!” Hunter stood abruptly and strode to the window. He stood with his back to her, looking out, his hands clasped behind him.

“You don’t want me to go, do you?” she prodded, feeling reckless. This was like one of her stories, her favorite part, when the danger sets the heroine’s heart to beating like a wild bird breaking out of its cage, and all caution is flung to the four winds for the sake of love.

Hunter’s knuckles turned white as he gripped his hands tighter together.

“We can’t let him win, Hunter,” Penny said, feeling more emboldened by the second. There was no doubt in her heart now. He loved her and he wanted her there as much as she wanted to be there. "We can beat him together, you and I. I know we can."

"Wyatt and his pa, they had tenants on their land. Strangest things always happened on those homesteads." Hunter's speech was slow and ruminative, as if he were talking to himself, brooding over something.

"Pigs and cows dying of what, nobody could tell. Barns burning down. Water dried up. Outlaw attacks out of the blue. Folk's falling off stuff, or down holes. Horses going loco. Folks always figured it was just bad luck, but not me. I figured something was out of fix. It was always folks that owed them rent or wouldn't do what they wanted."

"Do you mean you think they were responsible for those accidents?" Penny asked.

"I made noises like that up on the hill today. He didn't deny it. Didn't even flinch. I always figured I was just suspicious, but now I ain't so sure. After all they did to hurt folks, it'll only be a small step to …" he paused. "… killing somebody."

"Hunter, bullies only get their way because people let them. If we don't face up to him, he'll think he can always get whatever he wants just by threatening us, and we'll never be rid of him. We can make it stop right here and now. Please, let's fight this together. Don't send me away."

Hunter whirled round, his eyes red rimmed and glistening with tears. "Will you shut your darn mouth? Cain't you see it ain't no use? Sooner you and Hamish get to Prescott, the better. You can both stay there until Wyatt'll has no more cause to hurt ya."

"And how long will that be, Hunter?" Penny asked. "If Wyatt has held this grudge against you for so long, when exactly is he going to change his mind? Or are we just going to wait for him to die?"

Hunter looked perplexed and frustrated. "I don't know, Penny," he snapped. "All I know is he nearly killed Hamish. I cain't keep him away from you, but I can keep you away from him. That's all there is to it. Now get packing."

"I'm not going," Penny said, rising to her feet.

"Must you be so stubborn, woman? How's a man supposed to protect his family if they won't let him?" Hunter came toward her, his face a gamut of emotion. He gripped her shoulders.

Penny stood tall, lifting her face to his.

"I won't be the reason you're six feet under. I won't let that happen ever again, you hear me? Maybe it will just be better for everyone if I live on my own for the rest of my days."

"What about Maisie?"

The question hit him hard. Penny could see it in his eyes.

"She can live with Sally. I'll visit her as much as I can, and when she's old enough, she can come home again."

"Hunter, you can't possibly be serious. Every little girl needs her papa, just like every little boy does. Maisie needs you as much as Hamish needs you." Penny paused. Dare she say it?

"As much as I need you."

Something flashed in Hunter's eyes. Penny's heart was pounding. Hunter leaned in toward her, his soulful brown eyes locked on hers. There was a fire raging there in those eyes. Not one fueled by anger or hatred. It echoed the burning desire in Penny's heart. It fueled the terrifying exhilaration that roared through her veins.

He leaned even closer, still holding her gaze and she felt herself melting into him. Everything else faded away. Nothing mattered but the two of them. Penny lifted her hands and slid them up along his broad shoulder blades as she felt their bodies touch. His breath was warm on her face.

For a beautiful, breathtaking moment, time stood still. She knew she wanted to kiss him as much as she could tell he wanted to kiss her. It wasn't something she knew by looking or listening, it was something she just knew, without knowing how she knew it. He had called her and Hamish his family. He was so close to letting her in. So close.

"Consarnit," Hunter muttered angrily and pulled away.

Penny's hands fell limply to her sides, staring into the empty space he had just filled. Her lips were tingling, her heart trembling like a cherry blossom in a spring breeze. The slamming of his bedchamber door told her he was no longer in the room.

Penny stood rock still, letting the tears roll down her cheeks, but inside her that dogged determination was growing stronger, like tempered steel. The more it's plunged into the heat and the more it's hammered, the stronger it gets.

You're afraid of losing me, aren't you? she thought, and the thought was achingly sweet. *I won't let Wyatt come between us. I won't let him be the reason I lose you, Hunter. I know why you're afraid. I'm afraid too. But I can be strong for the both of us. I've done it before. I'll do it again.*

She didn't know what she was going to do, but somehow, she'd have to find a way to buy more time, so she could figure that part out.

***

Penny did as Hunter had asked. She packed her bags and Hamish's the next morning. The process was fairly awkward with her rope-burned hand still wrapped in a clumsy bandage and extremely sensitive to the touch, but she was taking her time, anyway.

"Where are we going, Aunt Penny?" Hamish asked standing beside her while she folded his clothes and laid them carefully into the trunk that Hunter had brought her.

Penny looked at him, wishing she could tell him the truth. "It's a surprise," she said, giving him a quick hug and what she hoped was a convincing smile.

"Are we going to the ocean?" Hamish asked.

"Now, Hamish, you know it's against the rules to ask questions about a surprise," she admonished him fondly, tapping her forefinger to his nose.

Hamish giggled. "Yeah, I know. I'd love to go to the ocean." He grew solemn. "But I won't stay there forever. I'll need to come back to the ranch to help Uncle Hunter. And I still want to ride Big Red properly one day."

Penny gaped at him. "Good heavens, Hamish! I thought you'd be scared stiff of riding that big brute after what happened yesterday."

"Oh, no, Aunt Penny," Hamish said, his eyes wide and deadly serious. "Big Red ain't a bad horse. He's a very good horse. It ain't his fault that bad man hit him with the switch and gave him a fright." He grinned. "And besides, didn't you see how he came back soon as Uncle Hunter whistled for him? That's one smart horse, that is."

"But weren't you terrified with him galloping so fast?" Penny was aghast.

"Yeah, I guess I was, but I held on, didn't I? And I didn't get hurt, did I? It was a good kind of scared. I reckon I really liked it, matter of fact, now that I think about it. I think he must have looked just like my wooden horse, the one Matt gave me. Did he look like that when he was galloping, Aunt Penny? Did he?"

Penny gave a nervous but relieved laugh. "Well, I'll be," she said, not knowing how to finish off the phrase.

She closed the lid of the trunk and straightened up. "I'm afraid I can't remember what Big Red looked like, my dear. All I was looking at was you, and praying you wouldn't fall off." She patted Hamish on the head. "I'm going to have a word with Uncle Hunter. Why don't you pack up your schooling things?"

"Yes, ma'am, Aunt Penny!" Hamish replied enthusiastically.

"There's a good chap." Penny made her way down the hallway. She found Hunter in his study, poring over his drawings again. He looked up as she entered and then looked right past her.

"Ready to go?" he asked, his voice flat.

"Almost," Penny said, taking a seat in the chair opposite. "I have a favor to ask."

Hunter's eyes flickered to her face and then away again. "Fire away."

"I'd like for us to spend some time with Sally and Matt before we go. I can't help feeling it would just be horribly rude not to say goodbye to them properly."

Hunter looked up, scrutinizing her face for a breathless moment. Penny held his gaze resolutely, even though her insides were turning to jelly again.

"I reckon that's a reasonable ask," he said stiffly.

"Thank you," Penny said, rising. "We'll be ready in a few minutes."

Hunter nodded, avoiding her eyes.

Penny left, her heart aching and yet hopeful. She hadn't spent as much time with Sally as she might have liked to, but one thing she knew instinctively. She had an ally in Sally. If anyone could help change Hunter's mind it was his cousin and adopted sister.

Dear Lord, let my plan work, she prayed inwardly as she walked down the hallway to her bedchamber. *And keep us safe from Wyatt Blackwell.*

Chapter Twenty-Two

Hunter drove without talking. Penny sat beside him, her hands folded in her lap while she surveyed the scenery. She seemed so self-contained, so certain of herself. Hunter wished he knew why, wished he could feel that same certainty.

"Uncle Hunter, when I come back, I still want to ride Big Red. I ain't afraid of him, you know," Hamish said.

Hunter flashed Penny an unhappy look. Hadn't she prepared him for what was to come? Hadn't she told him they were leaving the ranch with no idea of when or if they might be coming back? Was she leaving it to him to do?

Penny returned the look with no expression in her eyes. She simply pushed up her spectacles and then looked away again.

Hunter decided to play her game. "Well, well, well. You ain't afraid of him, you say? Sounds like you're shaping up to be a regular bronc buster, you are." He glanced at Penny. She kept her eyes focused on the track ahead of them.

"You really think so, Uncle Hunter?" Hamish's voice trembled with excitement.

"I reckon. After a ride like that, if a body still wants to ride, and ride the same horse, to boot, well, that's the mark of a born and bred bronc buster."

"Well, dogies!" Hamish exclaimed.

Hunter caught Penny's eye and saw the twinkle before she could hide it. He steeled himself. He had to believe he was doing the right thing. As long as they were safely away out of Wyatt's reach, he could figure out the next step. What it was he didn't know, but thinking about that too much would distract him from the task at hand. He had to deal with one thing at a time or go crazy.

Hamish was nattering on about how he was sure Hunter's riding lessons had helped him stay on while Big Red was galloping off with him. Hunter listened with one ear, making suitable noises to indicate that he was listening, while his mind battled his heart.

She'd known he was about to kiss her the night before. There was no point in pretending otherwise. His heart still leapt at the memory. But there was also no point in revisiting that moment. It would only make both of them want to finish what they'd started. He couldn't let that happen. For both their sakes.

He had no idea how things would go after Penny and Hamish were gone. He supposed Wyatt would leave him alone, satisfied that he'd ruined his life and got his revenge. Hunter could already feel the void his ready-made family would leave in his life and heart if they were forced to leave. If only there was another way. If there was, he couldn't see it.

Until he'd figured out what to do, he could go to Prescott to visit them. For Hamish's sake. And his own, if he was honest. He only wished he could be honest with Penny. If he could only tell her how he longed to hold her close to him, to kiss her lips, to spend every night of the rest of his life listening to her fantastic tales of adventure and mystery and wonder, perhaps that would make it easier for him. He wouldn't be suffering alone.

But that would be selfish. As long as he stuck to his guns, making her believe that he wasn't affected, that he would get by without her, she would be more likely to willingly go where she would be out of harm's way.

Four Horse came into view around the next bend. Minutes later he was helping Penny down from the buggy, and Sally was standing on the porch telling Matt to help them with their things.

Once inside, the pleasantries taken care of, Sally sat them down while Matt went to the kitchen to make a pot of tea.

"You're going to the Fall Barn Dance, ain't ya?" she said happily, glancing between Penny and Hunter. Hunter felt confused.

"There's a fall barn dance?" he asked, looking over at Penny. She shrugged.

"We hadn't planned on it," she said, her eyes fixed rigidly on Sally.

"Is that the surprise, Aunt Penny?" Hamish's face lit up. Hunter cringed. He knew what was coming, and he didn't know how to stop it.

"No, Hamish, that's not the surprise," he said, feeling like a heel when the joy in the boy's face was snuffed out like a candle at bedtime.

"Oh, dear, that won't do at all," Sally said, her spirits not in the least dampened. "It's tonight, you know. You may as well stay here until the morning, so you don't have to go home in the dark. We do have a spare bedchamber after all, and Hamish can sleep in the nursery."

"I cain't put that on you, Sally. Your little one could come any moment and you'll ..." Hunter began to protest.

"Oh, hush, brother. How long have you and Penny been married, and you've not yet been to a barn dance?"

"Well, it ain't all that long, couple weeks is all," Hunter defended himself, wondering why he even felt the need to.

"Besides, the Winters are hosting it," Sally went on, undaunted. "You wouldn't want to disappoint them by not attending with your new wife, would you? They told me they met Penny at Granville and Sons the other day. They'd be thrilled to have you there."

Hunter grunted. He was being painted into a corner, and he didn't like it.

Sally turned her attention to Penny. "The Winters cared for us when our ma and pa passed on. Hunter was only eighteen and I was a tender sixteen at the time. If not for them, Blakely Ranch might not be ours anymore."

"Oh, then I'd love to go!" Penny exclaimed. "They did seem like lovely people when I met them."

"You know we cain't go, Penny," Hunter said shortly, conscious that he'd better put a stop to this before it went too far, but already feeling like it was too little, too late.

"You cain't? Why ever not?" Matt said, walking in with the tea on a tray.

"Yeah, why not?" Sally added.

Hunter shoved his hands into his pockets and stepped over to the window that looked out on the street. An uneasy silence hovered behind him while he battled his thoughts.

"Perhaps we should tell them, Hunter," Penny said, startling him. He spun round and gave her a scowl.

"Tell us what?" Matt asked, pouring the tea.

"Hunter's taking me to Prescott," Penny said. "And Hamish, of course."

Hamish perked up. "Where's Prescott? Is it by the ocean?"

"No, not the ocean. Why don't we go pick some flowers for the dinner table, Hamish?" Penny said, rising to her feet. She gave Hunter a meaningful look. He wasn't sure whether to feel grateful or peeved as he watched her go, Hamish skipping happily beside her.

He stayed standing at the window, scarcely able to make eye contact with his sister and brother-in-law.

"Quit beating about the stump, Hunter. Out with it. What's going on?" Sally had lost none of her directness, bulging belly and all. Hunter vaguely noticed that she seemed uncomfortable, but his mind was too occupied with the answer to her question to pay it much mind.

"It's Wyatt."

Sally's eyes grew wide, and Hunter told her the whole story, still standing there with his hands in his pockets. When he was done, both members of his audience had an identical look of stubborn determination on their faces.

"You cain't let him push you around like that, Hunter," Matt said.

"It ain't just him," Hunter said, feeling the black hopelessness returning that had begun to lift a little more each day he'd had Penny and Hamish under his roof. "I reckon I ain't meant to have a family. Every time I love a woman, she ends up pushing up daisies. I ain't letting that happen this time."

Sally gave him a look of sudden comprehension. "You still think it's you, don't ya?" she said softly. "You still think it's all your fault."

Hunter didn't reply.

"Well, might be there's some wisdom in making him think they're gone, for a while at least," Matt said slowly.

"Yeah, might be," Sally agreed with her husband, laying her hand on his knee. "But I still say y'all should attend the dance. You'll both be safe there, with so many folks around. You do have three days, after all, don't ya?"

"Yeah, we do," Hunter said. "If we don't do anything to set Wyatt off."

"That's enough time to fetch the sheriff, ain't it?" Sally said. What was it with women and the sheriff?

"It sure is enough time, but Wyatt warned me not to fetch any sheriff, or there'd be trouble. If he sees me lighting out for Prescott, he'll know what I'm up to, and he'll be mad as heck. Like as not he'll go back on his three-day deal, and I cain't risk that."

"I could go," Matt offered.

Hunter shook his head. "With Sally ready to deliver any moment? I cain't let you do that, either, Matt. My sister needs you. Besides, Wyatt'll likely be watching us all, him and his gunmen. I don't aim to make you two a target, too."

"Matt could drum up someone else to send for the sheriff, couldn't you, Matt?" Sally was not letting things go easily.

A grudging gratitude began to well up in Hunter's heart. He was sure he'd found the safest, most surefire way to protect the woman he loved, even if it meant sending her away for a while. And yet he longed to hope for more. His heart and soul yearned for a better outcome than obeisance to a man who was little more than a thug in coattails. All that held him back from blatantly ignoring Wyatt's demands was the crippling fear that he might cause Penny's death.

"I sure could drum up a messenger for us," Matt agreed wholeheartedly. "Matter of fact, I think I know just the feller to ask."

Hunter didn't have the heart to stop them. They were laying their lives on the line for him and for Penny. It felt like too much to ask, and yet they were giving it so willingly, it felt wrong to refuse. He stepped over and sat down in an armchair, feeling suddenly tired.

"Right, then. It's settled," Sally said, her voice full of satisfaction and a little tiredness, too. "You'll take Penny to the dance, and Matt'll send someone to fetch the sheriff. That'll give us some time to figure out how we're going to do this."

Hunter gave his adopted sister a puzzled look. "Do what?"

"Get shed of Wyatt Blackwell for good is what," she retorted, as if he should have known.

"Ain't nothing short of lead poisoning'll stop that one," Hunter said, morosely.

"If that's what he chooses, then that's what it'll be." Sally reached out and patted his hand. "You don't need to figure this out on your own, Hunter. That's what family's for, remember?"

Yes, it was. He had forgotten. The dark days of grieving Amy's passing had left him feeling like a foreigner in his own home and community. Perhaps it was time to let himself be gathered back into the fold. Perhaps it was time to trust again, let folks in.

He sighed and lay back in the chair. It would be good to relax a little. But not too much. Wyatt was not to be trusted. He was still a loose cannon who could go off at any moment, and Hunter couldn't bear to imagine what kind of damage such an explosion would cause.

Chapter Twenty-Three

When Matt left to muster up his troop, he sent Penny and Hamish back inside. Hunter looked up as she entered. Her face was flushed and her eyes bright. Her self-containment seemed to be slipping, although it was not jitters he saw, but rather an inexplicable glow of happiness and expectation. It made her look even prettier.

Hunter lowered his eyes, feeling the heat creep into his own cheeks.

“Well, then? Are we going to the dance tonight?” Penny asked a little impishly as she removed her glasses and cleaned them on her skirt.

Hunter hesitated.

“Oh, come on, Hunter,” Sally said impatiently. Then she drew in her breath sharply and held it.

Penny was at her side in an instant. “Are you all right, Sally?”

Sally closed her eyes for a moment, then let all her air out. Her eyes fluttered open, and she smiled at Penny. “Yes, yes, I’m all right. I figure maybe it’s just indigestion. Nothing out of the ordinary, what with this little feller line dancing on my innards for the last nine months.” She laughed, rubbing her hands over her belly, but Hunter could see she was still a tad out of breath and slightly pale.

He turned away, only to have Sally’s voice stop him in his tracks.

“Well, Hunter? What about the dance?”

Hunter closed his eyes and sighed. There was no way around it. He was going to have to knuckle under and humor his sister. He turned back to face the two women, trying not to think about what it would feel like to rest his hand on Penny's slim waist and guide her around a dance floor.

"Okay. Okay. We'll go to the dance. Even if it's only to get you off my back," he said, avoiding Penny's eyes.

"Better watch out for this one, Penny," Sally said with a wink and a voice full of mischievous sarcasm. "He's nothing but an incurable romantic."

Hunter turned away again, but not before taking a peek at Penny's face. She was smiling. A melancholy smile. The sight wrenched at his heart, but he had to keep his focus. Her life was more important that his desire to wrap his arms around her and kiss her six ways from Sunday. If he gave in to his emotions, he wouldn't be able to think clearly. He couldn't let Wyatt outsmart him. It might cost Penny her life.

Hunter shuddered at the thought as he went to stand by the parlor window, looking out onto the street. What he was looking for, he didn't know. Instinctively he just wanted to keep watch, be alert and ready.

"What will you wear tonight, Penny?" Sally was saying behind him.

"Oh, well, I hadn't really thought about it," Penny said, her voice tinged with sadness.

"In that case I'm sure I have just the thing for you. I reckon you'll look just fetching in it. Though it might be a mite big in some places. Thank goodness we still have plenty time before the dance. A nip here and a tuck there, and it'll be nothing short of perfect!"

Sally's voice faded as she and Penny disappeared into the Morgans' bedchamber and shut the door behind them. Hunter stood staring out of the window, hardly seeing the road in front of him. He could still hear Sally and Penny's voices, though their words were muffled. Their tone sounded quite serious, although their conversation was punctuated with a laugh here and there.

A movement at his left caught Hunter's eye. He looked down to see Hamish standing there, his face grave, his thumbs hooked into his belt. Hamish looked up at him, his youthful eyes holding a look of almost comical solemnity.

"Uncle Hunter," he said, "I sure hope you'll teach me to whistle for horses one day. Just like you do."

Hunter's chest contracted. "Sure I will, son," he said, without thinking. A flash of unspeakable joy leapt into the boy's eyes.

"Uncle Hunter," he said again, and then faltered.

"Yeah, Hamish, I'm listening," Hunter said.

"I ain't ever had a pa, you know?"

Hunter fought back tears. "I know."

"I reckon if I had a pa, I'd want him to be like you." He stopped and looked away out the window, squaring his small, bony shoulders. "I know Aunt Penny ain't my real ma, but she's sort of taken my mama's place. And you married her, so does that mean I can call you 'Pa?' 'Cause you ain't really my uncle, like Aunt Penny is really my aunt."

Hunter knew where Hamish's thoughts were going as clear as if the boy had spelled it out to him. He was crying out for a father. It took Hunter back in a flash. He'd been eighteen when he found himself an orphan. He'd known the love of a father, but that feeling was the same.

A girl needs her papa, just like every little boy does, Penny's words came drifting back to him. Yes. He knew that feeling. But how could he give Hamish hope like that when everything still hung in the balance? When he didn't even know when he would see them again? When they'd be living in another town where he'd see them maybe once a week at most?

A fly buzzed in the window. The voices behind the bedchamber door became hushed. Hamish looked up at him, expectancy shining in his eyes.

Hunter took a deep breath, but before he could get a word out, a loud, guttural cry filled the house. He'd know that sound anywhere. It was Sally. In pain. Hunter jumped and spun toward the door. He bounded over to it and was about to grab the doorknob when the door was flung aside, and Penny stood before him, her face white as a sheet, but set in an expression of immovable determination and deadly earnest.

"Hunter. Fetch Mrs. Aylward. Sally's going to have her baby."

For a moment, Hunter froze. He stared at Penny, her words echoing in his mind.

"Hunter! Now!" Penny urged, a frown creasing her brow.

"Mrs. Aylward?" Hunter repeated. He wasn't sure he wanted her around. Not only was she the town gossip, but she made no bones about the fact that she disdained him.

"Sally asked for her, and I'm not much help anyway," Penny said, holding up her still bandaged hand and clearly trying to curb her irritation at his reticence.

A low groan emerged from the room behind Penny, and she closed the door, leaving Hunter staring at the wood and knowing he had little choice in the matter. He turned to Hamish who was standing gaping at him.

"Hamish, you be a good lad, and take care of Maisie for me, will you? I got to go fetch somebody."

"Is Aunt Sally going to be all right?" Hamish asked, his lip quivering.

"Yeah," Hunter said, and then paused before adding softly to himself. "I sure hope so."

He squeezed Hamish's shoulder reassuringly and steered him in the direction of Maisie's Moses basket. She was, thankfully, still sleeping. Hamish went to sit obediently at her side and Hunter headed for the door.

***

As he had expected, Mrs. Aylward gave him an icy look when she opened her front door to find him standing on her porch. She didn't greet him. Simply arched one eyebrow enquiringly.

"Mrs. Aylward," Hunter said, removing his hat, "my sister, Sally, well, it looks like her baby's coming. She asked for you."

"Tell her I'll be right there," Mrs. Aylward said and closed the door without another word. Hunter rode back to the Morgan residence in a jumble of thoughts. He didn't want to be there, and it wasn't only because of Mrs. Aylward's presence.

He could remember the night of Maisie's birth like it was yesterday. It had been such a joyous day, once he'd got past the nerve-wracking part, pacing up and down the hallway of his family home, wincing every time a scream or a groan reached his ears.

Over time, though, a dark shadow had come to hang over that day in his memory. It was the events of that day that had slowly led to Amy's death. How could he be sure it wouldn't be the same for Sally? Perhaps he should ride for a doctor now, before things got too far along. But would that even do any good? The child might be born before he had even reached the doctor's house.

When he arrived back at the Morgan home, he found Hamish still sitting faithfully with Maisie. She was awake, and he was feeding her applesauce that Penny must have brought along in a jar. "That's a good feller, Hamish," Hunter said.

Hamish simply nodded and smiled a smile as tense as Hunter's.

Another cry rent the air, and Hamish jumped, his eyes widening momentarily. If only Matt would come back. Hunter couldn't sit down. He crossed his arms over his chest and took to pacing. A few minutes later, Mrs. Aylward arrived, and Hunter showed her to the room where Sally was.

"Where's the husband?" Mrs. Aylward said shortly.

"He's, ah, running an errand," Hunter said.

"Well, then. You get us as many towels as you can find and a large pail of hot water. Put them outside the door and knock. I'll fetch them myself. I don't want any men in this room until this baby's delivered, you hear?"

"Yes, ma'am," Hunter said, keeping a determined handle on his temper. He headed for the kitchen and heard the door close behind Mrs. Aylward.

All the while heating the water and searching for towels, he tried to ignore the sounds coming from the bedchamber. They would stop sometimes for a while, then start up again. Waves of fear swept over him, making him feel nauseated.

Heaps of womenfolk give birth all the time, and they don't wind up dead, he tried to reason with his riotous emotions. But it made no difference. Somehow, he just couldn't get rid of the fear. Fear of losing Sally. Fear of losing Penny. Fear of losing Hamish. Fear of losing himself.

He paused as he set the towels and pail of hot water outside the door and knocked. At that moment, the front door swung open, and Matt stepped inside the house, stamping the dust off his boots and looking happy. He saw Hunter standing in the hallway and grinned.

"Well, brother, I told you I'd ..."

"Sally's having her baby," Hunter interrupted as loudly as he could without shouting at his brother-in-law. "Your baby, that is."

Matt's face blanched immediately. The door to the bedchamber opened, as if on cue, and Matt's eyes flew to the opening. The sound of groaning filled the hallway, accompanied by Penny's voice.

"Just hang onto my hand, Sally. It'll be over in a few minutes."

Hunter turned to see Mrs. Aylward in the doorway gathering the towels up in her arms. As she reached for the handle of the pail, Hunter felt Matt shove past him. Mrs. Aylward dropped the handle and held up a hand.

"No men in here!" she commanded, but she might as well have tried to stop a charging buffalo bull. Matt disappeared into the room behind her. Mrs. Aylward gave Hunter a baleful glare. He shrugged his shoulders, and she turned away, taking the towels and water with her.

***

In the six or seven hours before Hunter finally heard the distinctive wail of a newborn baby in the next room, he had not a moment's rest. Hamish was silent, playing with Maisie and giving her milk or applesauce when she needed it, with Hunter's help. But Hunter's mind swung wildly between the painful memories of the past and the precariousness of his current predicament.

Even when Hamish asked for food, and Hunter managed to find some bread and cheese and apples in the kitchen, he didn't partake in the simple meal.

Every now and then, Matt appeared with the pail, which he would refill with hot water and disappear into the bedchamber without giving Hunter more than a nervous grin. The afternoon waned away, with Sally's cries and groans reaching a crescendo when the shadows were growing long.

At last, after a particularly loud cry from Sally that had Hamish pressing his hands over his ears, the baby wailed lustily, and Hunter felt ready to collapse. Penny soon appeared, carrying the pail of water and a bundle of bloody towels.

"It's a boy, Hunter," she said, pausing on her way to the washroom. Her face was radiant, though tired. "Sally was right! A beautiful baby boy!"

Hunter smiled weakly and Penny continued on her journey to the washroom.

"Welcome to the world, Simon. I hope it treats you better than it did me," he whispered to himself as Hamish ran after

Penny, wanting to know if Aunt Sally was all right and if he could help with anything.

Maisie, who had been tottering about with Hamish, now waddled over and put her chubby hands on his knees, gazing up queryingly into his face.

"Come and see," Penny said, emerging from the washroom. "I'm sure Sally won't mind."

"I don't think Mrs. Aylward ..." Hunter began, but Penny waved off his concerns.

"Never mind her. It's not her baby, after all."

Hunter hoisted his daughter onto his hip and followed Penny into the bedchamber. The late afternoon light gave the room a warm, golden glow. Sally was propped up in bed, holding a tiny bundle. Matt sat on a chair at the bedside, looking like the cat who got the cream.

Hunter had to fight the urge to flee as flashes of memory shot through his brain. But he had to stay strong for Sally. He held himself together as everyone cooed over the infant newcomer, and he shook Matt's hand, offering heartfelt, if inwardly fearful, congratulations to the new father.

"Hunter," Sally said, her voice weak, but happy. "There's still time for you ta take Penny to the dance."

Hunter didn't know what to say. His mouth opened and closed a few times without words coming out.

"I think it'll be best if we go," Penny said, her voice and eyes full of pragmatism. "Sally and Matt will want some time alone with their new son, I'm sure."

Sally smiled in silent confirmation. Matt was still staring rapturously at his firstborn.

"I'll take care of your brood, if you don't have any objections to me doing so, Mr. Blakely," Mrs. Aylward said, her tone cool.

Hunter knew he was cornered, and secretly, it was just what he wanted. He desperately needed a few lungsful of fresh air. He nodded and followed Penny out of the room. As she went, she picked up a dress that was hanging over a chair.

While Penny dressed in the spare bedchamber, Hunter waited in the parlor, trying to sort out his thoughts and feelings. If only it could come to an end. If only he could just close his eyes and rest. A glass of Old Farm Pure Rye would go down real well just then.

He tried not to think of places where the Morgans might stash alcohol. Instead, he watched Mrs. Aylward take his precious child behind a room divider, commenting on what a mess her diaper was and it what a good thing it was that she, Mrs. Aylward, was around to take care of things.

At last, when both he and Penny were ready, he hitched up the horse and buggy again and helped Penny up onto the driver's seat.

"Penny," he said, as he did so. "Between you and Sally and Matt, you've gotten pretty far in twisting my arm about you leaving. But, just so you know, come morning, I'm still sending you and Hamish out to Prescott and that's it."

"I told you already, Hunter. I'm not going," Penny said flatly. "Besides, Sally needs me now."

Hunter was about to give her statement a hot retort when a movement caught his eye. Hamish came round the back of the buggy holding a handful of daisies and looking as if he were about to cry.

"Why don't you want to go to Prescott, Aunt Penny? Is it a bad place?"

Hunter sighed inwardly. This was the last thing he needed.

"It's not a bad place, Hamish," he said, trying to think of something to say that would calm the boy's fears. But, instead, what came out of his mouth was the simple truth. "There is a bad man who is trying to hurt you and your Aunt Penny. I'm taking you away because it's not safe for you here."

Hamish's face crumpled and big tears began rolling down his cheeks in the waning light of the setting sun.

"Is it because I let the nice man put me up on Big Red? I promise I won't listen to strange folks again," he sobbed. "Please let me stay here with you. Please, please, please!"

Hamish dropped the flowers and ran at Hunter, wrapping his arms around Hunter's knees and clinging to him.

"Please, Pa! Please don't send me away!"

Chapter Twenty-Four

Penny's heart was hammering in her chest and hot tears stung her eyes. She could hardly believe what she'd just heard. It was clear that Hunter could hardly believe it, either, and yet his eyes told her that Hamish's words had touched him deeply.

Hunter was reaching down, patting Hamish on the back in an apparent attempt to comfort him or calm him. Penny clambered down from the buggy and knelt beside her distraught nephew.

"There, now, pumpkin," she crooned softly. "I'll be with you, and we won't be there forever. When the bad man is gone, we can come back, and you can play with Maisie again and ride the horses." She hoped Hamish would have more faith in her words than she did.

He released Hunter's knees and turned a tear-streaked face to Penny. "You promise, Aunt Penny?" he said. Penny bit her lip, fighting back the words she wanted to say, not to Hamish, but to Hunter.

"*I* promise, Hamish," Hunter answered in Penny's stead, his voice a little quivery as he hunkered down beside them.

Penny looked at him sharply. He'd better know what he was doing, making a promise to a child. Especially Hamish, who already idolized him.

"I love our family," Hamish said, sniveling as he dragged his sleeve across his nose. "I love Maisie and Pa and Aunt Penny, and I want us all to be together, for always and always."

"We will be," Hunter said, his voice sounding stronger now. "I promise you, Hamish. I need you to be brave and take care of your Aunt Penny for me just like I've seen you take such good care of Maisie. Will you do that?"

Hamish squared his shoulders and nodded solemnly. "Yes, sir," he said. "I sure will."

Hunter's words and his manner seemed to convince the tearful five-year-old, but Penny's gut twisted with fear. How could he promise that? How could he be sure? What if he couldn't deliver on those promises? What would that do to Hamish?

"That's a good lad," Hunter was saying. "Now you run inside and see if you can help Mrs. Aylward with anything, okay? Aunt Penny and I will be back later tonight, after the dance."

Hamish gave Hunter a watery smile and threw his arms around the big man's neck, almost knocking him over. "I will, Pa!" he declared, then turned and ran off to the house. The daisies lay scattered on the ground.

Penny picked some of them up, not wanting to look Hunter in the face. She didn't trust herself to speak civilly to him. Not yet. She let him help her up onto the buggy once more and sat arranging the flowers in her hair while she waited for him to come around to the other side and climb up onto the driver's seat.

Hunter gathered up the reins, clucked to Billy, and the buggy began to roll. Penny kept quiet, watching the countryside rolling by them, the stark beauty of the semi-desert softened and gilded by the warm glow of the golden hour.

For a while they rode in silence. Then Hunter spoke.

"Don't reckon I've been to a town function since before, ah, before Amy died," he said quietly.

Penny didn't respond. The words still racing around in her head would not have been a good response to his unexpected vulnerability.

Hunter went on. "We never did go to dances much, truth be told. Not that we didn't like dancing, mind. It's just real hard for a body to enjoy yourself with a couple of eyeballs shooting darts at you the entire time."

Penny frowned. "You mean Wyatt?"

"Yeah. Him and his pa."

Penny fell silent again, trying to imagine the scenario. Then a thought dawned on her.

"You think he'll be there tonight?"

Hunter shrugged. "Hard ta say. That Mrs. Aylward, now, she's his cousin. I'd not put it past her to have made sure he found out that we're going ta be there."

"She's his cousin?" Penny asked, but not disbelievingly. The woman's manner had always struck her as intrinsically heartless and cold. A shiver of foreboding ran down her spine. "Could they be lying in wait for us?"

"I'll be danged if I know. He did give us three days. Still a body cain't be too sure."

A sense of helplessness and hopelessness washed over Penny. Why was there always something crouching in the shadows, ready to pounce on what little happiness she had?

"I wish with all my heart that Wyatt Blackwell had never come into our lives," she said hotly. "I wish he would just leave us alone so that we can be together in peace."

Hunter looked at her, then. His eyes blazing with more than the reflection of the setting sun. A little thrill ran through Penny. She didn't know much about sparking beaus, but she could sense the passion and desire in him. Then a cloud of something veiled the light in his eyes. He looked haunted. Distant.

"Yeah, well, that's the way life is. My ma always said, 'If wishes were horses, beggars would ride.'"

Penny felt frustrated. "What does that mean, anyway?" she asked, irritation scratching at her throat.

Hunter's features hardened. "Just what it says, I reckon. We cain't always get what we want in life, now can we?"

"I never figured you for a man who'd give up so easily," Penny snapped without meaning to.

Hunter kept his eyes stoically ahead and didn't respond, but the muscle in his jaw was twitching.

"I figured you for someone who'd fight for what he wanted. Like you fought for Amy when Wyatt wanted to force her into a marriage with him." She couldn't stop the words coming out. They seemed to have taken on a life of their own.

Hunter still didn't respond.

"I keep wondering why you won't fight for Hamish and me like you fought for Amy. But I suppose we aren't worth fighting for, are we? You didn't want us here to begin with, so why should you fight to keep us here, right?"

Hunter's voice was low and cool when he replied. "You're forgetting that I already buried one wife. I ain't fixing to bury you, too."

A sense of desperation filled Penny's heart and mind. She felt reckless, willing to do or say anything that could possibly shake him out of this lethargy, somehow. She knew beyond a shadow of a doubt that it was not the real Hunter speaking. It was a frightened Hunter, a cowed Hunter.

He was better than that, she was sure of it. If only she could convince him to believe what she believed. Something in Hamish's unfettered pleading had loosened the restraints on her heart. She wanted him to know what he was doing to her.

"You say you don't want to lose someone to the grave again. Well, what about what I want? I don't want to leave, Hunter. I want to stay with you. I want to be your woman and stand side by side with you and fight this Blackwell fellow and anyone or anything else that threatens to tear us apart. Why won't you let me do that? Is it so much to ask? And we don't have to do it alone. We can get the townsfolk to stand with us, too. We can ..."

"I won't get other folks involved in this," Hunter snapped, his shoulders tense, his eyes still riveted somewhere ahead on the trail. "I got enough on my conscience without involving innocent townsfolk in a feud that's between me and that consarned Blackwell. That's all there is to it, and that's the last time I'm going to pick this bone with you."

Penny fell into frustrated silence once more. The sun was sinking lower, just like her hopes. This wasn't how she'd dreamed her first dance would be. This wasn't how she'd imagined her marriage would be. She watched the light slipping slowly away from the earth and shivered, anticipating the darkness.

At last, she sighed. "You know, Hunter, you may as well be burying me. What do you suppose folks will think of a young woman living alone in Prescott with her nephew as her only companion, and some man coming to visit her on the odd occasion? Don't you care about your wife's reputation?"

Hunter drew the buggy to a standstill. He turned to face Penny, his face stony.

"You said it yourself. You'll only be there until Wyatt is taken care of. Now can we please lay this to rest?"

Penny couldn't do that. Not until she'd made him see sense. "And how long will that be, Hunter? Months? Years? Are we going to wait until he dies an old man? Why, if I stayed here, that would force him to play his hand. That would be the quickest way to get rid of him, wouldn't it?"

Hunter shook his head and stubbornly refused to answer her. He picked up the reins again and slapped them across Billy's rump. The buggy rattled onward.

"Why won't you trust me to fight alongside you, Hunter? Why won't you stand up against Wyatt?"

"I see you've forgotten how he almost got Hamish killed," Hunter said tiredly, a ring of sarcasm in his voice. "I sure wish you'd trust me for once, Penny."

Penny was quiet after that. Perhaps he was right. Perhaps she needed to trust him that he was doing the best he knew how in a situation fraught with uncertainty and danger. For a few moments she teetered on the brink of asking him to turn the buggy around and take her back to Matt and Sally's place. With the all-too-familiar darkness descending on her heart, she just couldn't feel joy at the prospect of spending her evening in a barn full of happy, curious, cheerful folk.

Instead, she gritted her teeth and made up her mind to stick it out. What better way to distract herself from her frustrations than singing and dancing? Besides, she didn't want to burden Sally, what with her new babe in arms and all. The dear lady would be at peace as long as she believed her cousin and his new wife were having the time of their lives at a dance. She deserved as much.

As the buggy rattled closer to their destination, Penny's mind drifted back over the argument she and Hunter had just had. She tried to remember how it had started. Was it when they'd started talking about Wyatt and his father always glaring across the dance floor at Hunter and Amy, when she was still alive.

All at once, Penny wished Wyatt Blackwell would be at the dance. She'd walk right up to that no-good bully and tell him what he could do with himself and his threats. She'd expose him and his devious ways; tricking a child into riding a galloping horse that could very well have caused that child's death. She'd call him out in front of everybody there and then see how self-contained and confident he would be then.

The thought had barely crossed her mind when she knew she wouldn't do it. Part of fighting alongside Hunter necessitated that she follow his lead. Otherwise, she'd just be fighting on her own, in her own way. She wanted to trust him. She did trust him. At least, she hoped she did.

Before Penny could make up her mind whether she trusted Hunter's methods as much as she trusted his intentions, the buggy had rolled between the pillars of the Winters' ranch, and Hunter was reining Billy in beside the other buggies. Hunter helped her down.

"Watch your step," he said, his face inscrutable in the darkness as he led her over toward the barn. Light streamed out the main doorway of the barn, which was bursting with the sounds of cheering, whooping and breathtakingly fast fiddle playing.

Penny's heart leapt in her chest. For these few hours she wanted to forget about Wyatt Blackwell and his vile threats. For these few hours she wanted it to be just the two of them, Hunter and her, lost in dancing and music and laughter.

She peeked up at him as they stepped into the light. His face was unreadable. Penny turned her attention back to the interior of the barn. The band—the energetic violinist, accompanied by a banjo player, a guitarist and someone playing a hammered dulcimer—stood on some kind of raised platform made of wood, stomping their feet as they played.

In the middle of the hard packed earthen floor, people stood in lines, stepping back and forth in unison, sometimes to the side. A loose-limbed, lanky man on one corner of the square formation of dancers, was shouting out cues.

"Old Jimmy always was the best caller Four Horse ever had," Hunter said reflectively.

"Caller?"

"The feller calling out the steps, so everyone does the same dance," Hunter pointed at the lanky fellow giving the cues. "When there's no caller, everybody does the dance the way they like it, and let's just say everybody don't like to the dances the same way."

Penny couldn't help giggling at the mental picture that rose up in her mind.

"Well, I'm happy he's here, then," she said, sensing the blackness start to leave her again. Even Hunter seemed a little less tense, as if the atmosphere of fun and laughter was driving away the clouds of foreboding from his mind, too.

As they walked into the barn, Penny glanced around anxiously, her eyes scanning the few people who stood or sat along the walls of the barn. There appeared to be no sign of Wyatt. If he was there, he was hiding. That was good. As long as she couldn't see him, as long as Hunter couldn't see him, perhaps she'd be able to enjoy her first barn dance.

Hunter led her over to a vacant bale of hay, which seemed to be the seating of choice at the dance, and she sat down, her eyes following the dancers, her foot tapping to the breathless, vibrant rhythm of the music. Skirts swirled and hands clapped, gents lifted their knees high and swung their arms, adding their own flair to the steps as the crowd moved in almost perfect unison.

"Welcome, Hunter! Welcome Penny!" a woman's voice cried out.

Penny dragged her eyes from the dancers to see Abbigail Winters heading toward her, a cup of some kind of drink in each hand. Jeremiah Winters followed close on her heels. They were both beaming.

"So good of you both to come," Mr. Winters said as his wife handed Hunter and Penny each a cup.

"Have some punch," Mrs. Winters added. "You missed the fun of setting it alight, but it'll still taste good, I'll bet."

"Thank you, Mrs. Winters," Penny said, taking the offered drink and trying a tiny sip. It was sweet and tangy, smelling of nutmeg, cinnamon and citrus fruits. She took a bigger gulp and gasped. There was something fiery in it that took her breath away.

"Steady on there, dear. That's not lemonade," Mrs. Winters said, laughing good-naturedly. "I hope you two will have a wonderful time. There are plenty of snacks over yonder near the bandstand, so do please help yourselves."

"Thank you, kindly, Mrs. Winters, Mr. Winters," Hunter said, still holding his drink, untouched, in his hand.

"I'm sure I will have a wonderful time, Mrs. Winters," Penny said, feeling a little lightheaded. "It's my first dance, you know."

"It is?" The disbelief on Mrs. Winters' face was genuinely horrified. "Well, you just come with me, I'll teach you everything you need to know."

Penny laughed and swallowed down the rest of the fiery but sweet liquid in her cup. She gave another gasp.

"What is that, Mrs. Winters? That punch. What's in it?" she asked, as her cheerful hostess swept her off to the dance floor.

"It's a recipe my grandma passed down to me. Very easy to make. Just orange and lemon juice, water, sugar, nutmeg, cinnamon and, of course, some good old rum and whiskey."

"Alcohol?" Penny gaped. It was her first taste.

She looked back over her shoulder at Hunter. He was talking to Mr. Winters and giving his cup of punch frequent longing glances.

"Give me a moment, please, Mrs. Winters, if you would," Penny said. "I'll join you presently." Then she went right back to Hunter's side. He looked at her quizzically as she came to stand in front of him. His eyes widened a little as she took the cup from his hand and proceeded to drain it.

Inclining her head, she smiled at him, set down the cup and then turned back to Mrs. Winters and the floor full of dancers who were just lining up for a new dance. Her feet seemed to be floating an inch or so above the floor when she joined her hostess's side.

"All right. I'm ready now," Penny said. Every worry and care that she'd carried into that jovial space dissipated like smoke in the wind. Let Wyatt Blackwell threaten all he liked. Let Hunter cower in fear. Penny was dancing on Prince Hamish the Kind's hammock full of pillows and nothing could stop her.

She followed Mrs. Winters' instructions as closely and quickly as she could, sometimes tripping over her own feet or bumping into someone when she mistakenly mixed up her left and right. More than once, she almost lost her glasses.

Every time that happened, she laughed from her belly, carefree on her cloud of happiness, surrounded by more laughing faces. Nobody seemed to mind that she stepped on their toes. Nobody seemed insulted that she was bumbling along.

It felt so freeing not to worry, not to care.

As the group of dancers stepped and pivoted round and around, she frequently found herself looking at Hunter. He was alone, still standing by the hay bale. At first, she didn't feel much. The alcohol had numbed her. But as the dance went on, the initial effects wore off slightly, and she realized how lonely he looked standing there, watching her with a look of yearning melancholy on his face.

In a flash of clarity, she saw his heart. How easy it would be to numb herself with an alcoholic drink whenever the black moods descended on her, blotting out any sunshine that might try to come her way. How tempting it would be to just stop taking risks. How easy it would be to try to fix all her broken parts by herself and shut out everybody, every soul she loved, for fear of suffering the greatest pain: losing them.

All at once she wanted nothing more than to fling her arms around Hunter and hold him close. The memory of that almost kiss in his study mere days before drove her nearly to distraction.

Oh, Hunter, won't you let me in? Won't you let me love you? If only you knew how desperately I want to.

Chapter Twenty-Five

The second dance had just ended when Penny saw Wyatt Blackwell walk into the barn. She was making her way over to where Hunter still sat, looking forlorn, and she happened to look up at the entrance. Wyatt stood there, regarding her with a malevolent stare that made the hair stand up on the back of her neck.

Pretending she hadn't seen him, Penny hurried over to Hunter's side and plopped down beside him on the hay. At first, she wondered if she should tell him what she had seen. Then she realized she had better prepare him.

"The magnanimous Mr. Blackwell has arrived at the dance," she whispered in Hunter's ear. He jerked his head away to look at her.

"You saw him?"

"Yes. He came in the door a moment ago."

Hunter turned to look toward the door. Thankfully Mr. and Mrs. Winters were still being impeccable hosts and had already accosted Hunter's arch enemy, shoving a drink in his hand and distracting him with questions and salutations.

"If you want, we can scatter dust out of here," Hunter said softly. Penny looked at him, torn between avoiding Wyatt and daring him to do anything to harm them in a barn full of people. The look in Hunter's eyes silenced every rational thought.

He loves me, Penny thought. *He would walk through fire for me. I can see it.* Her heart fluttered. *And I'll walk through fire for him, too.*

She smiled and lifted her chin, feeling that recklessness from before wash over her again, only this time it wasn't from frustration, it was from pure devotion to her man, her beau, her beloved husband.

"Let Wyatt Blackwell do what he likes. I think it's time we rubbed his nose in it a bit," Penny whispered.

Hunter looked startled, then he frowned. "I ain't fixing to raise sand here in the Winters' nice barn. Just 'cause trouble comes visiting don't mean I got to offer it a place to sit down."

"What's he going to do here, in a crowd of upstanding townsfolk?" Penny challenged him.

"Probably nothing," Hunter admitted, "but he could do a whole lot later on. Don't forget our friend Wyatt ain't a feller who can be accused of forgiving his neighbor."

Penny stood, about to drag Hunter to the dance floor when the sight of Wyatt approaching froze her to the spot.

"Well, hello. If it isn't the newly wedded Blakelys," Wyatt said, his face full of bitterness and scorn. "How is marital bliss treating you two love birds? Not too well, I guess, eh? I'm so sorry to hear that Penny has to leave so soon."

Hunter stood to his feet, his chest thrust out, his jaw twitching. "Well, you can quit being sorry. You heard wrong, Blackwell. Penny ain't going nowhere. She's staying right here with me, where she belongs."

Penny stared at him. Wyatt Blackwell hardly existed for her anymore. All she could see was Hunter, standing like a rock, immovable in the glare of Wyatt's hatred.

Wyatt held his gaze, trying to stare him down, or so it seemed to Penny. Hunter didn't give him an inch. The band of musicians struck up another cheerful tune, the joy in the music contrasting almost comically with the daggers being exchanged between the two men in front of her. Penny held her breath.

At last, Wyatt rolled his eyes and shrugged. "I reckon you'll just have to learn the hard way, won't you, Blakely?" he said ominously.

"You try anything, and everybody will know it's you, Wyatt. You won't get away with it. I swear it." Hunter slipped his arm protectively around Penny's shoulders, his warmth soaking into her and making her feel safe and protected.

Wyatt shrugged again, giving a short, mirthless laugh. "Maybe so, but I'll hurt you good, just like you deserve. Just like you hurt me."

Hunter didn't reply, just kept staring at Wyatt. If Wyatt's words unsettled him, he didn't show it.

"You enjoy the rest of your dance," the latter said backing away, his eyes narrowed. "I reckon it might just be your last one."

With that, Wyatt turned on his heel and walked away. The joyful dance music was still ringing out across the room. Partners were taking to the floor now, dancing a lively, skipping dance. Penny felt flushed, her heart soaring. Hunter looked at her, his brown eyes blazing.

"Dance with me," Penny said, feeling a little out of breath and vaguely surprised at her own defiant reaction to the danger. It was as if it made her feel even more alive to have the threat of Wyatt's wrath hanging over their heads.

"He'll be watching us," Hunter said gravely.

"Let him watch. I don't care."

Penny's heart was racing. She knew her cheeks were flushed, and she didn't care about that either. All she wanted was to dance with her husband.

Hunter's eyes softened. He dropped his arm to her waist and led her out onto the dance floor. "You ever danced the galop before?"

"No, never. But Evie did teach me to waltz."

"All right, just follow my lead, then."

As they came into the area where the other dancers were whirling and skipping by, Hunter reached over and took Penny's right hand in a firm grip and pulled her round to face him.

"Now, you just keep your arms held out, like you see the other womenfolk doing, and hold your skirts in your left hand."

Penny did as she was told, looking eagerly into his eyes.

"Yeah, that's it. I'll lead you with my left hand on your right hand and my arm around your waist."

His eyes flickered downward, and Penny blushed. The dress Sally had given her fitted snugly onto her figure, accentuating her gentle curves. It was clear Hunter appreciated them. He coughed and looked up quickly, slipping his arm around her waist again. For a moment, Hunter stood still. Penny could feel his body moving in rhythm with the music, looking for the beat.

When he found it, he stepped to the side, and she felt herself being carried along with him. Round and round they whirled, their feet flying over the earth.

Hunter's lead was clear and consistent, his hand and arm warm against her body, his eyes watching her with calm confidence and unbridled admiration. It amazed her how easy it was to follow him and respond to his subtle but precise cues.

She knew nothing of the galop, and yet, under his guidance, she almost instinctively knew which way to turn, when to step to the side, when to kick up her heels, when to whirl outward and take a few modest steps side by side, with their hands on each other's backs.

Penny's heart felt ready to burst right out of her chest. The smile on her face made her cheeks hurt, but she found it utterly impossible to stop. At one point she almost stumbled, but he lifted her up and they went spontaneously into a little jig. Hunter smiled, his eyes warm and tender.

So, this was what the fairytale princesses felt like in her stories. She'd always tried to imagine how it must feel to dance with the prince, but nothing her imagination dreamed up could ever hope to match the feelings rushing through her in that moment.

All too soon, the music ended with a dramatic flourish, and the dance was over. Penny almost cried. She could have danced the entire night away and never tired of it. Hunter kissed her hand.

"Wait here," he said, a twinkle in his eye.

Penny stood in place, wondering what he was up to. Standing alone on the dance floor for a moment, she looked around for Wyatt. Had he seen them? She wanted to be sure he knew that neither she nor Hunter would let him steal their happiness.

But Wyatt was nowhere to be seen. Penny didn't know whether to feel relieved or disappointed about that. A tap on her shoulder spun her around, and Hunter stood with his arms reaching out, ready to hold her once more. The musicians began to softly play a sweet, gentle waltz. A shiver tingled up Penny's spine.

"You asked them to play a waltz for us?" she asked breathlessly as he drew her close to his chest.

"You betcha I did," he said, his voice husky and his breath warm in her neck.

Penny knew what to do. She stood still, allowing her body to sway with his, and the next moment they were off, moving slowly, savoring each other's nearness. Penny closed her eyes. She didn't even need to look around her. She knew he would take her wherever she needed to be, without allowing her to stumble, or to collide with anything or anyone.

It was a place of perfect peace, unbridled joy, heart swelling love. Here was a man she would follow to the end of the earth and beyond. If only he would give her the chance.

I sure wish you'd trust me for once, Penny, his words echoed in her heart. Penny stepped in closer to Hunter. Their bodies were touching. Penny put her lips close to his ear.

"I want you to know that I do trust you, Hunter. I'm so sorry I ever doubted you."

Hunter stopped abruptly and pulled back from her, his eyes searching her face. The music went on playing, the skirts of the women dancers around them rustled softly, the men's shoes scraped the floor as they spun on the balls of their feet.

"We can do things your way. I won't fight you on that anymore, I promise."

Hunter pulled her close again and went on waltzing. Penny felt a tear drop on her shoulder. Instinctively she reached up and gently brushed his moist cheek with her thumb.

Hunter came to a quivering halt once again. His eyes looked almost wild, with a kind of starving desperation. Taking her by the hand, he drew her to the back of the barn, behind a stack of feed barrels where nobody could see them. He took her face in both hands, his eyes shining with tears.

"I ain't been honest with you, Penny," he said. "I know you think I don't want you around, but the truth is, I don't know how I ever lived without you and Hamish. I cain't tell you how long I've wanted to hold you like this. But I figured you'd never think much of me. Not after you found me all roostered up, sleeping it off in my barn. Not after I treated you so rough."

Penny drew a breath and began to speak, aching to tell him how wrong he was, but Hunter shifted his thumbs over her lips.

"Hush, now," he said, with a tearful, but happy, smile. "You talk too much, my little mouse. It's my turn, now."

Penny's heart turned to melted wax, her knees almost buckled under her.

"I ain't got no inclination to send you away. I just wanted to keep you and Hamish safe. That's all I could think of. Hoped I'd figure out the rest along the way, but I had no idea what I was going to do, truth be told. It took me a while to figure it out, but now I know. With you here, I got no reason to play a lone hand anymore. I guess what I'm trying ta say is …"

He leaned in closer, his forehead touching hers, his breath warm on her face.

"I love you, Penny Blakely."

"Oh, Hunter! I love you, too. More than you'll ever …"

She didn't finish her sentence. His lips were on hers, pressing, exploring, caressing, coaxing. Penny responded in kind, the euphoria that filled her far surpassing that which Abigail Winters' punch had induced. She slipped her arms around him and pressed herself against his firm, warm bulk.

Everything but the music seemed to fade away around her. All she knew was Hunter, his warmth, his closeness, his ardent passion rivalling hers. His fingers glided from her temples, up into her hair, pulling her spectacles off and loosening her carefully piled curls so that spectacles and hairpins fell to the straw covered floor.

He ran his fingers through her hair, and down her neck. And all the while they drank of each other like two parched travelers that had stumbled upon an oasis in an endless desert.

At last Hunter came up for air. He looked into Penny's eyes. All the guardedness was gone, all the haunted fear. In its place she saw nothing but adoration, and a deep, mellow joy. The kind of joy Penny had only seen in those who had known heartbreaking loss and yet learned to rejoice again.

"Why'd we wait so long to do that?" Hunter asked her teasingly as he bent down to retrieve her spectacles and hairpins.

"I suppose because you took so long to start us off," Penny retorted with mock accusation in her voice.

Replacing Penny's spectacles, Hunter kissed her once more fleetingly on the lips and laughed a toe curling, deep throated chuckle.

"I ain't got no argument against that," he said. "You feel ready for another dance?"

“If we can end it like this again, I surely am,” Penny said, giggling.

Hunter was about to respond, when the music in the barn came to an inharmonious, chaotic end.

“Hunter! Where you at, Hunter? Anybody know where Hunter Blakely is?” a voice shouted. “His stables done caught fire!”

Chapter Twenty-Six

Hunter's blood turned to ice in his veins. His stables on fire? He didn't have time to think about how that had happened. Instead, he gripped Penny's hand and ran into the middle of the barn.

"I'm here!" he called out.

"Everybody saddle up!" Mr. Winters shouted. "We'll save whatever we can!"

"There's a couple of folks already getting your horses out, Hunter," said Jed Murray, who lived on the next ranch to the Blakely spread. "I came soon as I saw it on my way home. Sent my boys out to get the horses out and Marie rode to fetch the Helms."

In that moment, Hunter realized it was Mr. Murray's voice he'd heard calling for him.

There wasn't anything more to say. Hunter helped Penny up and sprang onto the buggy beside her. Everywhere townsfolk were strapping their horses back into their traces again, or throwing saddles on horses' backs. Billy was ready, the tension in the air already having added a flare to his nostrils and a spring to his step.

Hunter urged the faithful old horse on, thankful that he was young enough to still have a good turn of speed left in him, but experienced enough to negotiate the trail safely in the pale moonlight. As he drove, he wondered how the fire had started.

Could it have been Wyatt? But he had been at the dance. Then again, he'd had help that time when Hamish had almost taken his last ride. And Hunter couldn't remember seeing him after their little altercation. Maybe he shouldn't have challenged Wyatt. Maybe he should have just pretended to still be going along with Wyatt's demands.

But Penny had looked so fetching in that forest green dress that hugged her figure and made her eyes look like twin forest pools full of mystery and allure. It had fired him up like nothing else on earth could. It made him want her so bad that a sense of wanton recklessness had filled him. And the way she had taken the cup of punch from his hand. Her eyes had told him everything. She was sparing him the temptation.

He had the distinct feeling she had known what it was doing to him, and she, an innocent young thing, who had clearly never had alcohol cross her lips, had saved him from having to expose his alcoholism, or insult his host. And that at the possible cost of her own social standing.

He was so lost in thought that he completely missed the turn into their driveway. It was only Billy's unerring reliability that took them through the gates and up toward the homestead.

As soon as they reached the yard, Hunter drew rein and sprang down from the buggy. He rushed over to the stable. Mr. Murray was already there.

"The horses are all out," Mr. Murray said. "We're just trying to save as much of the stables as we can."

The fire lit up the night, casting an eerie light across the yard. Flames leaped high into the air on one end of the stable, licking along the wood frame and curling out through the windows. Hunter could see his horses milling about in the big corral. Big Red was whinnying and snorting, compulsively rounding up his mares and herding them back and forth.

People swarmed around the stables, tossing water onto the flames from pails of that were passed to them by those who had formed a loose chain from the hand pump. They were passing along those pails of water as fast as they could fill them. A few of the helpers were tossing water on the nearby barn to hopefully prevent that from catching alight, too.

Hunter pulled his bandanna up over his nose and mouth, grabbed a passing pail of water and went to work himself. He had no idea where Penny was, but he felt sure she would be helping pass the water. He badly wanted to check on his horses, but the first pressing priority was to get that fire fully doused. Mr. Murray and his sons had good horse sense, they would have made sure all his beloved animals were well out of harm's way.

Hunter had put out stable fires before, and this one was no different. Stables were giant torches, full of ready fuel waiting for hungry fires to consume in a matter of minutes. Hunter himself had seen a stable burn down to the ground in less than half an hour. It was nothing short of providence that had taken Jed Murray past his ranch and led him to discover the fire.

The heat was almost unbearable. Smoke choked him and stung his eyes, and sparks swirled about in the hot air and stung his forehead, sometimes kindling on his clothes. For a while it felt as if they were making no headway. Hunter kept on swapping out empty pails for full ones, trying to aim each torrent of water in a place that needed it the most, though his lungs burned, and his vision was getting cloudy. He kept doggedly at it, feeling as if it would never end.

But then suddenly, without him knowing how or when, the fire began to recede. Swirls of gray smoke filled the air, still partly lighted by the dying flames.

"It's nearly out!" a triumphant voice cried out, galvanizing the weary firefighters into renewing their efforts. The loud hissing that had previously accompanied each pail full of water that he dumped, became a low and short fizzle.

At last Hunter set down the pail in his hand and straightened up, placing his hands on his hips as he stared at the smoking remnant of the proud stable his father had built. It was not just a stable, it was an heirloom. Better not to think of it now. It would only make him angry, and he was too tired to be angry.

The next moment there was the sound of someone clearing their throat beside him.

"Well, we managed to save half of it," Mr. Murray said. "I sure am sorry we couldn't do more."

Hunter turned to look at him in the moonlight. "You did all you could, Mr. Murray, and I'm more than grateful. Heck, if not for you and your boys, I reckon I would've lost half my horses, too."

The thought sent a shudder through him. He'd seen horses maimed and killed in fires. It was a stomach-turning, heart-breaking sight. Most folks didn't realize that horses wouldn't naturally flee from a fire. In their panic and confusion, most horses, even once rescued from a burning building, would turn right around and head for the place they had always felt the safest: their stables.

"Matter of fact, Mr. Murray," Hunter added, "I reckon I owe you and your boys one almighty big debt. I know how hard it is to get scared horses out of a burning stable."

"You would've done the same for me," Mr. Murray said sincerely. "Thing is, we didn't give 'em a proper look over, yet. How about we go do that now?"

“I’d appreciate that,” Hunter said.

As he and Jed Murray walked away from the wreckage, Hunter glanced over the rest of the people. Some were still sifting through the remains of the stable, making sure there were no hidden pockets of smoldering hay or a beam of wood that might rekindle in the slight breeze that was springing up. Others were cleaning up as best they could in the darkness. He noticed Penny tending to a helper’s burned hand as he sat on the grass in front of her.

She looked up as Hunter passed. He gave her a brave smile and the lines of concern in her face softened. The man she was tending to said something. She looked down at him and replied, then flashed Hunter a quick smile and turned toward the house, walking briskly across the yard.

Hunter wished he could take her in his arms right then and there. The memory of their kiss was making his lips tingle. Once again, he could feel the ardent pressure of her body against his, taste the sweet softness of her lips, smell the heady scent of lavender on her skin. He shook his head and opened the corral gate.

Big Red needed some reassurance. He was still tossing his head and moving restlessly about, his nostrils flared. He snorted as the pungent fumes of water-doused smoke drifted across to them.

“Steady on, old boy. You’re all right. All of you are all right.” Hunter spoke in low, soothing tones, and the horse calmed visibly. Then he and Mr. Murray went to work, checking each of the horses in turn. Mr. Murray’s two oldest sons, Andy and Mark, joined them, leading away the horses who had already been inspected into a separate corral.

By some miracle, there was little more than singed tails and superficial scratches. No severe burns that they could see, and no serious injuries.

Hunter elected to leave the horses outside. They would feel better in the open, where they could more easily get away if anything threatened them. He hoped nothing would, but a body never knew. As he and the Murrays left the corral and headed toward the house, a thought struck him.

"You fellers happen to notice anybody skulking about or lighting out when you got here?" he asked his companions.

Mr. Murray looked over at his sons. "Cain't say I did," he said. "You boys see anybody?"

"No, sir, Pa," Andy said.

"Me neither," Mark added. "Though I reckon I wouldn't likely have noticed anyone who didn't come stand plumb in my way. All I could think of was getting them horses out of that burning barn."

"You reckon somebody might have started this fire a-purpose, Mr. Blakely?" Andy asked.

"I sure hope not," Hunter said grimly. "But it could be somebody did."

"Well, if they did, I sure hope you find whoever it was," Mark said, his voice angry. "Cain't figure what kind of a person would set fire to a barn full of dumb, innocent creatures like that."

"Just as well you cain't, Mark," Hunter observed wryly. "I'll scout around in the morning, see if I can find any evidence. There ain't much a body can do now, being nighttime and all. You boys go on home and get a good night's rest. And thank you kindly, once again, for all you fellers done."

"Any time, Hunter," Jed Murray said, gripping his neighbor's hand in a firm shake. "We'll be over in the morning to see how we can lend a hand."

"Thank you and goodnight," Hunter said.

His legs felt heavy, his brain foggy. How long had this day been? He'd become an uncle, bared his heart to his true love after almost losing her and had his stable burned down, to boot. Surely that was more than enough excitement to fill up a month of Sundays, never mind one day. He badly needed sleep.

The townsfolk came to him one by one, commiserating on his loss and promising they'd help rebuild—all he needed to do was give them a shout. Hunter thanked them, shook hands and smiled tiredly.

He knew better than anybody, he had done very little to earn their help, considering how he'd shunned everybody after Amy's death. It was a good thing country folks weren't picky about who they helped. If you were in their community, you were their neighbor, and that was reason enough for them to lend a hand wherever and however they could. That was just the nature of the people. Most of them, anyhow.

As he waved off the last of the helpers, he looked around, wondering where Penny was at. There was a light burning in the entrance hall. He could see it through the window. She must have gone inside already. Perhaps she had wanted to get cleaned up.

He remembered their kiss again. Had that been real? He longed for her closeness, her softness, and yet it all felt like a beautiful dream that would melt away into nothing when the sun came up.

He went inside and took the lantern from the round table in the middle of the entrance hall. The big old house was as silent as the grave. Just as well Hamish and Maisie were still at Sally's place. Somebody was sure to have told her and Matt about the fire. They wouldn't be expecting Penny and him back there tonight.

Hunter walked through to the washroom and stripped down. He washed cursorily, just getting the worst of the soot and sweat off his face and body. It was refreshing, invigorating. He walked up the stairs and paused at the top for a moment.

Down at the end of the hall was Penny's chamber. Before he knew it, he was standing in front of her door, his hand on the doorknob. Inside was heaven. A place where he didn't need to keep his guard up anymore; a place where he could lay bare everything and where he was without fear; a place where he could pour out his whole self and know none of it would be thrown back in his face.

But she must be exhausted. If he felt the way he did, what must she feel like? One night wouldn't make a difference, would it? He could wait one night. After all, he'd held himself in check far longer than that. No. Better to let her sleep. She needed it as much as he did.

Dropping his hand silently back to his side, Hunter turned and walked back down the hallway to his bedchamber.

Sleep didn't come easily, his mind was so awhirl with the events of the day and the worry of what might still come. But he did manage to doze fitfully through the night until the first cock crow woke him.

It was still dark. Hunter lay still in his bed. He wasn't tired, though his body ached a little. His mind was clear as crystal and alert to any sound or scent. But there was nothing. Other than the monotonous chirp of crickets and cicadas. No aroma of coffee boiling or bacon frying. No disjointed humming floating through the house.

Hunter smiled at the thought. He hadn't realized how much he loved it when Penny hummed while she worked. All at once he wanted her with him. He fought down the urge in his heart. She needed rest. Just a couple more hours.

What if I just look at her face? the thought drifted through his mind. *I could just sneak into her bedchamber and look at her beautiful face. She don't even need to know I'm there.*

Hunter didn't need any more convincing. He dropped his feet to the floor, not even bothering to slip them into the soft moccasins he used for lounging about in the house. He lit the lantern by his bedside, keeping the flame small so it would send out a gentle glow, just enough for him to see by.

Moments later he was at her door again. He turned the knob slowly and let himself in. The room was quiet. Too quiet. The lace curtains wafted gently in the night breeze coming in at the open window. Hunter lifted up the lantern to head height and muted light spilled across the room. For a moment he froze, the lantern swinging in his hand, his eyes riveted to Penny's bed.

It was empty. In fact, it didn't look like anyone had slept in it at all that night.

Chapter Twenty-Seven

At the first sight of the fire, a sickening fear had clutched at Penny's insides and paralyzed her for a moment. But as soon as that moment was over, she leaped from the buggy, not even waiting for Hunter to help her down. Without another thought, she dashed to join the line of townsfolk passing pails of water from the hand pump to the stables.

There was little talk among the helpers, other than, "Here!" or, "Look out!" or, "Coming through!" Working rhythmically, they passed full pails toward the stables and empty ones back to those manning the hand pump.

Penny kept looking anxiously at the fire, knowing that Hunter was one of the men trying to douse it with the water they were passing along. Every now and then, someone would cry out, making Penny's heart jump into her throat, fearful that it might be Hunter who was injured. For a while it seemed like the fire would never go out and Penny began to despair. But all at once, the glow of heat faded, no longer lighting up the night. The angry hissing and spitting of water hitting the flames died down to a sputter.

Relief filled Penny as the men staggered, exhausted, from the wreckage, one by one. Their neighbor, Mr. Helm sat down on the grass, looking dejected. He had a pail in his hand and had dunked his other hand inside it.

Penny rushed to his side. "Are you all right, Mr. Helm?"

"Please, Mrs. Blakely, might you have something for these burns?" He lifted his arm out of the pail and held it out for her to see, though she couldn't see much in the pale light of the moon.

At that moment, Hunter walked by. She caught his eye and he smiled bravely. Her heart thudded in her chest as she remembered their kiss.

"Mrs. Blakely?" Mr. Helm broke in on her thoughts. "Perhaps a poultice or something?"

"I believe I have something in the house," Penny replied dragging her attention away from Hunter. "Why don't you keep your hand in the water for the moment? I'll fetch some ointment for you."

She hurried off to the house, giving Hunter one last glance. He had the Murray menfolk with him, and they seemed to be going to check on the horses. She lit the lantern in the entrance hall and fetched the ointment before returning to her patient. Applying the ointment gently to Mr. Helm's wounded hand, she looked around. There were more men with burn wounds. Perhaps it wouldn't be a bad idea to whip up a soothing poultice for them. She had the makings, fresh aloe leaves and wild honey. She had some basil growing in the garden, too.

"Pass this around to whoever needs it, will you please, Mr. Helm?" Penny said, handing him the pot of ointment. "I'll be in the house if anybody needs me urgently."

Mr. Helm nodded, and Penny hurried back to the house.

Leaving the lantern on the entrance hall table, she hurried to the kitchen and lit the lantern by the stove. A scraping sound alerted her, and she turned round, then reflexively clapped her hand over her mouth.

"Smart girl," Wyatt said, his eyes cold. "You dare raise a ruckus, and I'll shut you up for good." He waved a pistol in her direction. Penny felt as if all the blood had just drained out of her body.

"What do you want from us, Wyatt?" she said, her throat dry.

"Don't play stupid, honey," Wyatt said, his voice flat. "You know what I want. I want revenge."

"That's it?" Penny asked, stalling for time, trying to think of something she could do to alert the folks outside to Wyatt's presence. "All you want is revenge? And how do you suppose that will make you feel better?"

"Who said anything about feeling better?" Wyatt pulled a thick coil of rope from his coat pocket. "I'm past feeling better. All I want is for Hunter Blakely to feel worse."

"Well, Hunter is sending me away, you know. Like you said he should."

Wyatt gave a short laugh. "Do I look like I just hatched out under a turkey?"

"He's sending me to Prescott. You said we had three days. We went to visit Sally and Matt, so Hamish could say goodbye, and she said there was a dance. What Hunter said at the dance, he didn't really mean it. He just lost his temper. And his head. That's all." Penny was desperate for him to believe her.

"Oh, shut up, woman!" Wyatt snapped, his eyes glittering in the lamplight. "Your precious Hunter meant every dang word he said. That fool ain't never been fixing to send you away, nohow. He'd sooner cut off his own arm."

He shook out the rope in one hand, still holding the revolver with the barrel trained on Penny.

"But he was! My trunk is packed already! It's in ..."

"You think I ain't been watching you two love birds? I seen how he looks at you. The man's soft down on you like nobody's business. No point in me hanging about waiting for him to knuckle under. It's time he learned his lesson."

"What are you going to do?" Penny asked, her throat constricting.

"Now that would be telling, wouldn't it?" Wyatt said coldly. "I'll tell you what *you're* doing, though. You're coming with me. Now head for the back door and look sharp about it!"

"I'll scream," Penny warned, though still doing as he asked.

"You go right ahead, honey. I'm just itching to put a bullet in your back."

Even if Wyatt's tone hadn't told her he was in deadly earnest, Penny wouldn't have taken the risk of him delivering on that promise. She stepped toward the door, conscious that he was behind her and closing the gap between them quickly. She steeled herself, anticipating the iron grasp of impatient fingers on her arm.

It came, but right afterward came something she had not anticipated. A shadow crossed the wall in front of her. Too late she realized it was Wyatt's raised hand holding the pistol by the barrel. Before she could dodge, she heard the smack of wood on bone, and excruciating, blinding pain shot through her head.

She gasped, feeling as if the earth was heaving under her feet. Falling, she swung round to face Wyatt who was still holding her up by her arm.

"Sweet dreams, princess," he said, his eyes full of loathing.

And then all sight and sound ceased to exist.

***

The shock of cold water in her face jerked Penny awake. Coughing and spluttering, she raised her hands to her face, but there wasn't much she could do. Rough rope dug into the skin on her wrists. Her hands were tied together, palms inward. She struggled to sit up, wondering if the darkness was because her eyesight was damaged or because it was night.

"Sit up, we got to talk," Wyatt's voice commanded from somewhere behind her. Penny tried to move her legs, but her ankles were also tied together, although with a length of rope between them so she might be able to stand, or even shuffle along.

Coming into a lopsided sitting position she felt the rough solidarity of a boulder at her left shoulder. She leaned against it, feeling nauseated and dizzy. Her head ached.

"Where are we?" she asked groggily.

"Never you mind that," Wyatt snapped.

Penny held her peace and waited for him to speak again while she tried to think back over what had happened before she got there, wherever she was. All she could tell was that it seemed to be on a hill with a stand of aspen nearby, their ghostly white trunks looming up in the night.

"I've told Blakely where you are, so he ought to be here soon."

Penny was remembering now. The dance. Hunter defying Wyatt. The kiss. The stables burning.

"You set the fire, didn't you?"

Wyatt was sitting on the boulder beside her, smoking a pipe and looking around. "So what if I did?"

"It didn't bother you that you could have caused the excruciating deaths of innocent creatures?"

"Needs must," Wyatt muttered past the stem of his pipe.

"What needs?"

"You wouldn't understand. Now, when Blakely gets here, you better not try any shenanigans. You hear me?"

"What do you want with me, Wyatt?" Penny rasped in frustration.

"Tsk, tsk, you really ain't as smart as I figured you to be."

"Humor me," Penny said stubbornly. She wanted to keep him talking. Why that was, she wasn't sure herself. Perhaps it was just better than the silent waiting.

"All right, I'll spell it out for you again." Wyatt took a drag on his pipe, expansively puffing out the smoke before he continued. "Hunter Blakely stole my fiancé, *my* woman. All I'm doing is returning the favor. It's so simple a child could understand. Try to keep up, would ya?"

Penny thought how his voice sounded odd, as if he were a child himself. As if he weren't quite in his right mind. Perhaps it would be best for her to humor him.

"What was it you loved so about Amy?" she asked.

"What was it?" Wyatt echoed. "Why, you've seen her portrait, ain't that all you need to know?" He took another puff on the pipe. "Although, I reckon paper and pencil never could do her justice. She was an angel. Light followed her wherever she went. She was a right tomboy, a real rancher's girl, make no mistake, but oh, she carried herself with such poise and grace. I ain't seen a fairer face, and I've been all the way to San Francisco, you know."

"That's it?" Penny asked. "She was pretty and graceful?"

"No," Wyatt snapped. "That ain't it. She was also *mine.* Y'hear? Mine!"

"Yes, so you've said, but I was wondering, what about her mind did you like? Was she smart? Witty? Did she make you laugh? Was she kind-hearted? And what were her favorite things?"

"You talk too much, missy," Wyatt growled. Penny should have known to stop there, but she couldn't help herself.

"I just find it strange that anyone would look at another person in such a way, as if they were an ornament or a trophy, just to be put up on the mantelpiece, bragged about and ogled at whenever the fancy takes the owner."

"I loved her!" Wyatt insisted. "She was beautiful, and she was my fiancé!"

"You know what I love about Hunter?" Penny went on.

"Blakely? Who could love him? He's a closet drunkard and a coward!"

"He's also very strong willed, but in the best way I've ever seen. Nothing budges him once he's made up his mind about something. I'd say he's steadfast. That's an admirable trait in a man. But when his steadfastness is shown to be based on folly, he's humble enough to admit it, and—"

"Shut up!" Wyatt commanded. "Not another word out of your mouth, you hear me? I didn't bring you here ta sing Blakely's praises. Amy was supposed to marry *me. I* loved her. She was *mine* and he stole her, and then he killed her. And I'm the only one who's willing to make sure he suffers for it."

“I can’t help noticing that you don’t seem to care what Amy wanted. If she had been happy with you, surely, she would have stayed?” Penny asked.

“Blakely stole her!” Wyatt insisted through gritted teeth.

“But can a person really be stolen? A person with their own mind, their own will and desires? I don’t think so.”

“I don’t care what you think, woman,” Wyatt snarled.

“Well, I don’t believe you truly loved her. Any woman who is truly loved knows it, and she will stay put wherever that love is. It’s in a woman’s nature, I think.”

Wyatt let out a roar of frustration and pulled his pistol out of his pocket. He set the hammer and pointed the muzzle at Penny’s forehead.

“Another word out of you, and I’ll put one right between your eyes.”

Chapter Twenty-Eight

"Penny! Where are you? Penny!" Hunter's voice echoed back at him mockingly as he charged through the house, his pulse beating a frantic tattoo on his temples, fear taunting his skin with a million pins and needles.

"Dear God in Heaven, let her be okay. If he harms even one hair on her head, I swear I'll … I'll …" He didn't know what he would do, and that was partly what frightened him as he raced from room to room, hoping he would find her somewhere, perhaps having fallen asleep somewhere else and in the grip of one of her night terrors. At least then he would be able to comfort her, to save her out of it.

But if his worst fears were confirmed, and it turned out that Wyatt had done the unthinkable …

Hunter paused on the landing, certain that he'd searched every single room of the house and found nothing. Where to start looking next? Should he go get help, or would that cost Penny her life? If only they hadn't gone to the all-fired dance. If only he hadn't shot off his mouth.

Like horseshoes to a magnet, he felt himself drawn to Penny's bedchamber again. There was no reason to go back there, other than to think. Perhaps being in the room would give him some inspiration of where to look.

The light of the lantern, now turned up to full brightness, bathed the room in its yellowish glow. Nothing seemed out of place. There was Maisie's cradle and Hamish's cot, also neatly made up. Penny had put some flowers on the washstand. Hamish liked to bring her flowers. A book lay on the nightstand beside the bed. Hunter stepped closer.

Wuthering Heights.

Hunter paused. He recognized the book. It was one that Sally had bought out of sheer morbid curiosity, especially after the book, "had the oddest, most curious reviews you ever did see," as Sally had put it. "One critic called it, 'wild, confused, disjointed, and improbable,'" she had added with a grin.

"Sounds like our kind of reading," Hunter had chuckled.

"Yeah, like our old penny dreadfuls. Only better. I can't wait to read it!"

The memory faded, but the book lying there felt uncannily significant. All he could remember of the story was that almost everybody had wound up dead. Not a good omen. He picked up the book, wondering why Penny would have been reading such a dark novel. It didn't seem like anything she would enjoy. Perhaps that was why she had left it there.

As he lifted the book, a single sheet of paper wafted to the floor. Hunter stopped, looking down at the paper. It had writing on it, in large, obnoxious print. With his gut twisting, Hunter set the lamp down and picked up the paper.

AMY'S GRAVE.

ALONE.

I AIN'T JOKING.

All the blood rushed from Hunter's head. He steadied himself against the nightstand. There was no doubt in his mind that the note was from Wyatt. All at once, the dizziness left him. He dashed back to his bedchamber, pulling on pants and suspenders over his nightshirt with trembling hands. Grabbing his gun belt from the hook behind his door, he buckled it on.

For a breathless moment, he hesitated. He'd never used his gun on a man before. Killed a few rattlesnakes and put a horse or two with a broken leg out of its misery, but never had he even pointed a loaded revolver at a human being.

He almost hung the belt back on the wall, but for one sobering thought. It was almost a cinch that Wyatt would have a gun on him. Better to go prepared, even to do what he was most reluctant to even contemplate doing.

Hunter secured the buckle on the gun belt, checked the Colt's chamber to make sure it was fully loaded. It was. He took a deep breath, shot one final prayer heavenward and stepped out of the room.

***

The night was just beginning to fade to gray dawn as Hunter marched up the hill toward Amy's grave. Dew lay thick on the ground. The large boulder up ahead that served as Amy's headstone lay dark and brooding in the shadows. The aspen forest behind bowed, waved and whispered in the early morning wind. The birds were strangely silent. Even the roosters had ceased their dawn heralding.

As Hunter came closer, he scanned the trees up ahead and the surrounding hillside, but nothing stirred. There didn't seem to be anyone near Amy's grave, either. Hunter hesitated. Was he too late? Had Wyatt already ...

He couldn't finish his thought.

Then someone groaned. The sound seemed to be coming from behind the boulder that served as Amy's headstone. Penny? The groaning sound came again.

Hunter ran the last few yards, the uphill seeming to flatten out under the driving force of legs that had gained sudden superhuman power.

"Penny? Is that you?"

He rounded the boulder to find her lying there, her hair disheveled, her precious self wrapped in an old blanket and shivering. She looked dazed, as if she were trying to wake, but not really succeeding. Her spectacles were missing.

Hunter took a step closer and froze as the unmistakable, metallic ring of a hammer being drawn back on a revolver rang through the pristine pre-dawn air.

"You'll want ta keep your distance, Blakely."

Hunter held his hands away from his gun belt. "You wouldn't shoot a man who cain't see you, now would you, Wyatt?"

"Well, I don't know. What do you think?"

Hunter wanted to say he reckoned the no-account skunk was capable of anything at that point but decided against it.

"I'm sure hoping you won't want to do that to yourself," he said, instead.

"You're right flannel-mouthed when you need to be, ain't ya?" Wyatt stepped out from among the trees, the pistol pointed straight at, not Hunter, but Penny, who had begun to thrash about. She seemed to be trying to sit up, but somehow couldn't.

Wyatt walked over to her, the gun still pointed at her huddled form. He grabbed her arm and yanked her to her feet. She gave a little shriek of shock. It ripped through Hunter like a tornado through a settlement, wreaking devastation.

He took a step forward again.

"Uh-uh-uh," Wyatt warned pressing the revolver against Penny's temple as she came erect beside him. The blanket fell away and Hunter saw that her hands were tied. She was still wearing the dark green dress, but it was torn and dusty. Her face was smudged with dirt.

"What are you going to do, Wyatt? Kill us?" Hunter blurted out, his mind whirling.

Wyatt grunted. "You cotton on quicker than your missus, here, don't ya?"

"You won't get away with this, Blackwell," Hunter told him, fighting down panic. He wasn't even looking at Wyatt. All he could see was the man's finger lying almost casually on the trigger, the barrel pressed close, too close to Penny's terrified, but defiant eyes.

She was tired, he could tell, but something inside of her refused to be snuffed out. That stubborn, headstrong, outspoken streak of hers that had so irked him when he first met her, was exactly the thing that he found himself admiring in that moment. The very thing that might save them both.

"You got anything sensible to say for yourself, Blakely? You ready to take what you got coming to ya?" Wyatt taunted, arresting Hunter's attention once more.

"Well, now, that depends what I got coming to me," Hunter said, vaguely wondering if Matt's friend had managed to convince Prescott's sheriff to ride out to Four Horse to take care of a madman. It would be nice to have some back-up. The world around them was slowly becoming lighter, dark shadows beginning to take on their daytime shapes of trees, boulders, hillsides and gullies.

"I'm going to make you feel the pain of standing helplessly by while the thing you love most in the world is taken away from you," Wyatt said decisively.

Hunter saw Penny stiffen. He forced himself to stay calm. Any sudden movement could have Wyatt's finger tightening on that trigger, and there was no way in the world Hunter would be able to save her then.

"Take a look around you, Wyatt. You see this boulder lying here between us? I reckon you could say I already felt that pain. You going to let it go already?"

"Let it go? Why would I do a thing like that? You sure didn't take long to get yourself a new wife, a whole new family. Heck, Amy ain't even a year below snakes and you done forgotten her already. You never loved her. Not like I loved her." He spat into the ground at Hunter's feet.

"Well, Amy loved me, Wyatt. That's all that mattered, ain't it? It was her choice to make. It's time you wised up to that."

Wyatt's eyes were strangely fixed, unresponding, as if he wasn't hearing anything Hunter was saying.

"But I seen you around this pert little piece of calico. You really love her. It'll kill you if she dies and you cain't do a thing to stop it, won't it?" He looked at Hunter and his eyes told the whole story of what was going on in his mind. In that moment it became crystal clear that Wyatt fully intended to murder Hunter's wife, and no amount of reasoning would change his mind.

Hunter felt dizzy. Dark spots swirled in front of his eyes. His breath was ragged and rapid.

"Please, Wyatt, don't do it," he said, hating himself for resorting to begging, but completely at a loss what else to do.

Wyatt's trigger finger twitched, and his hand tightened on her arm. Penny's eyes grew wider as she caught her breath.

"Kill me, Wyatt!"

The words burst from Hunter's mouth before he even thought them.

"Kill me if you have ta kill someone. I'll take her place. Just leave her be. She ain't got no part in this. It's between you and me. Let's just settle it, like men. Right here, right now."

"Hunter! No!" Penny cried out. "You can't do that. I won't let you!"

Hunter went numb. He locked his gaze onto Penny's.

"I cain't let you pay for things you had no part in, Penny. If blood is what Wyatt wants, it'll be mine he gets, not yours. Hamish needs you. I know you'll be a good mama to Maisie, and Sally'll find you a good man to care for you after I'm gone."

"No, Hunter, no!" Big tears painted pale lines through the grime on Penny's face.

"Penny, it's better this way."

Wyatt looked confused, suddenly flustered. He swung the gun from Penny to Hunter and back again.

"What are you two up to?" he snapped. "Or did you both just go plumb loco?"

"Wyatt," Hunter said, calming himself and speaking in a low, even tone. "Let her go. You can kill me. Make me pay for stealing Amy. You were right. I deserve it. Just let her go."

Wyatt hesitated. Hunter could see the veins standing out on the man's gun hand. His eyes flickered. Then in one quick movement, Wyatt trained the barrel on Hunter. Hunter let out a sigh of relief. He felt strangely calm as though he wasn't staring death right in the face. It was as if, in that one moment, he had fulfilled everything it meant to be a man.

"No!" Penny screamed. She lifted her bound hands and reached for Wyatt's pistol, pulling it back and pressing it against her temple once more. "I won't let you kill my husband. Take me and let him live. I beg you, Wyatt! Don't kill him!"

"What in tarnation?" Wyatt yelled. "You folks sure are one brick short of a pile!"

He yanked the gun away from Penny's grip and angrily shoved her away from him.

Hunter took his chance and reached for his Colt.

Chapter Twenty-Nine

Penny screamed as she fell, trying to take a step to catch her balance, but coming up short against the ropes around her ankles. The ground rushed up to meet her, rocks and dirt and prickly bunch grasses. She couldn't see them clearly without her spectacles, but she felt them solidly enough.

As she hit the ground with a thud and a grunt, two gunshots rang out in the clear morning air. They were so close together they sounded almost like one.

Penny screamed again, but it came out as a ragged squeal. The fall had knocked her wind out, and her ears were ringing from the gunshots. She heard something heavy crash down hard nearby. Harder than she had. Somebody groaned and let out a long, raspy, rattling sigh. Then silence. Penny felt dazed.

"Hunter?" she murmured.

Footsteps crunched on the gravel. Someone was coming closer. She tried to get up, only to be reminded of the ropes around her wrists and ankles as they chafed against her flesh and frustrated her attempts to get away.

A deep terror filled her. What if it was Wyatt coming to finish her off, too? She whimpered, fighting the fog in her brain.

"Penny, Penny. Hush, Penny. It's me."

He didn't have to say his name. She'd know that voice anywhere. It washed over her like balm on a wound.

A gentle hand rolled her over onto her back. He was kneeling beside her on the ground.

"Are you all right?"

"I don't know."

He held her arm, and she could hear his knife biting through the ropes on her wrists. Feel the bonds going slack. Moments later she was free.

Hunter took her in his arms and her heart finally registered that she was safe. Something inside her cracked, and her body began to shake. She thrust her arms around him and clung to him like a drowning woman, burying her face in his shoulder, tears soaking his nightshirt, sobbing like an infant.

"Penny, Penny," Hunter crooned, his voice breaking. "My beautiful, brave, contrary Penny. I'm here. You're safe."

That only made her cry harder, but Hunter didn't seem to mind. He rocked her gently, just as he had when she'd had the night terror. Just as she knew she would always want him to, whenever she felt lonely or afraid or lost.

He began to sing. A lullaby that Penny liked to sing to Maisie. At first his voice was clear and steady. Then it began to crack and falter. Penny drew back and looked up into his face. Huge tears spilled from his hazel brown eyes, catching the light of the first tentative sunrays creeping over the horizon.

It was then she noticed the dark red blood glistening on his shirt. Penny sat up sharply.

"Hunter! You've been shot!"

He nodded and smoothed her hair back with one hand, his eyes full of tenderness.

"I know. It ain't a bad wound. Bullet went clean out on the other side. Looks worse than it is."

"And Wyatt?" Penny asked, suddenly fearful that he might still be lurking about, ready to try his luck a second time.

"Wyatt ain't going to bother us no more."

There was no gloating in his voice, no glee or satisfaction. It was a tired statement. With a shadow of regret.

The implications of that statement slowly filtered through to Penny. Hunter glanced back over his shoulder, and Penny followed the direction of that glance. Wyatt lay spread-eagled on the ground, his gun flung from his hand, his chest motionless, a crimson stain spreading across the front of his snow-white shirt.

Penny looked quickly back at Hunter.

"What happened?" she asked softly.

Hunter sighed, as if reliving the moment was a burden he would rather not bear, but he squared his jaw.

"When Wyatt pushed you down, I saw my chance. He wasn't focused, what with you confusing him and all, but I was pretty sure he was getting ready to put some lead in me. I drew my weapon, figuring if I could get him in the shoulder, his gun hand would be useless."

Hunter paused.

"Right after he pushed you, he swung that gun right at me and fired. It was so quick, my gun was still coming up 'cause I had to draw before I could aim proper. So, I just shot off a round at him, but I had no idea where it would hit him, 'cause we were both moving. All I knew is, you were out of the way, so I could let him have it. Next thing I felt the bullet rip through my arm. Then Wyatt dropped his six shooter and staggered back, pawing at his chest."

Hunter stopped. His features were dark and heavy.

Penny took his right hand, his gun hand. "You've never shot anyone before, have you?"

Hunter shook his head and sighed again.

Penny held his hand up to her face and kissed it, cradling it in hers and holding it against her cheek. She knew in that moment she would lay her life on the line a hundred times more for this man, and not think twice about it.

For a long time, they sat, just being, just letting their senses settle. Penny's head still hurt, but the dazed feeling was dissipating. Her mind began to take stock of the situation.

Hunter was injured, and Wyatt was dead. Whoever it was Matt had sent for the sheriff might well be returning that day or the next, with the law in tow.

"What now?" Penny asked.

"When the Prescott sheriff gets here, I'll have to tell 'em the truth. The truth that I shot him."

A stab of fear pierced Penny's heart. "What if they arrest you?"

"They won't. Might hold an enquiry if someone asks for it. But they won't lock me up. Not after what Wyatt did to you, not after he shot first. That's the way it works out here in the West." Hunter's voice was pragmatic.

Penny held his gaze, pondering his words.Even after what he'd said, the idea of an enquiry made her worry. "I was here. I saw he had his gun out before you could draw yours. I'll tell them. I won't let anyone call you a murderer," Penny said decisively. "Now let's get to the house so I can take care of that bullet wound in your arm."

"Penny Blakely, you are just way more woman than I could ever hope to deserve," Hunter said huskily. He slipped his hand behind her neck and pulled her close. For a heady moment they stared into each other's eyes, and Penny knew she didn't want to be anywhere else ever again, but at Hunter Blakely's side.

"You really do love me, don't ya?" he said, the corners of his mouth twitching, despite the tiredness evident in his whole body.

"You bet ya, I do," Penny replied, grinning coyly into his face.

Hunter chuckled that deep throated, toe-curling chuckle.

"Well, then, I reckon I must be the luckiest son of a gun alive."

And then his lips were on her lips once more, pouring his soul into her, drinking thirstily of her own. It was the kind of kiss Penny imagined could only happen if those who partook in it truly understood what a miracle it was to simply be alive.

***

Sheriff Sam Grosvenor arrived early that same afternoon. He nodded at the Murray boys who had been taking turns with their pa keeping the coyotes away all day. Then he went to stand over Wyatt's body and rested his chin on his hand, studying the lay of it, apparently.

Muttering to himself, the sheriff walked around a little, looking at the surrounding earth that had been scuffed up in the struggle. Penny showed him where she had lain, trussed up and shivering, seeking shelter against a gravestone through most of the night.

The sheriff took Hunter and Jerry Winters aside for a few moments, and they had a hushed conversation, then Sheriff Grosvenor turned to Penny.

"We've had a request for an enquiry into this here shooting, ma'am."

Penny's throat constricted.

"Your husband says you're willing to testify, before a judge, that he shot in self-defense and to save you from being shot." The sheriff's tone was grave and official. "Is that so, ma'am?"

"Yes. Yes, I would very much like to testify."

"I wouldn't sound so eager if I were you, ma'am," the sheriff said, not unkindly. "Some folks might be inclined to think you were biased. It's bad enough that you're the feller's wife."

"Oh," Penny said, taken aback. She hadn't even thought of that.

"Don't fret yourself, I'll be testifying too, and I've seen what I need to here." The sheriff waved a hand at the ground around Amy's gravesite. "I'll just rest a little easier if I know it won't be too taxing on you to talk about what happened here, ma'am. It cain't have been a cakewalk for ya."

Penny inclined her head in a show of respect and gratitude. "That's very kind of you, sheriff, but I'm sure I'll be just fine. Hunter is innocent, and he saved my life. It's the least I can do for my husband to testify on his behalf, regardless how it may impact my state of mind."

"Alrighty, then, that's settled." The sheriff seemed satisfied.

"I reckon we'll find a few more folks to testify to Blackwell's character, or lack of it," Mr. Winters said, matching the sheriff's grave intonation.

"We'll need to have some character witnesses for Mr. Blakely, too, then," Grosvenor pointed out.

"I'm sure we can arrange that, sheriff," Penny said, stepping closer to Hunter and slipping her hand into the crook of his arm. Hunter reached his other arm across and wrapped her fingers in his warm, rough hand.

"Well, like I've said, I've seen what I need to see here, Mr. Winters. Y'all can take care of the body and make sure the kin are notified. I'll see how soon I can get a circuit judge to come around this way."

The sheriff turned away and walked back to his horse. Mr. Winters doffed his hat to Hunter and Penny and followed in the lawman's wake.

Penny watched them go, feeling as if a heavy weight had just been lifted off of her shoulders. Hunter slipped his hand into hers, intertwining their fingers. Penny gave his hand a little squeeze and leaned against his shoulder. They walked back down to the house in silence.

***

Matt arrived a couple of hours later, with a pine coffin in the back of his wagon and a somber expression on his face. Penny guessed he must have made it. The wood looked fresh and raw.

"Sheriff Grosvenor sent me to fetch Wyatt's body," he said, jumping down from the wagon and leaning against the railing of the porch steps. "And Mr. Winters told me everything that happened. I'm sure am sorry you folks had to go through all that. Sally and I told Hamish you folks were having a little trouble."

He paused and shook his head at the memory, a fond smile softening his features. "Little feller was bound and determined to come out here and lend a hand. I told him he'd be helping the most if he stayed put and took care of his little sister. That boy sure loves y'all, but he loves that little Maisie like she was his blood kin."

"Thank you kindly, Matt," Penny said, blinking back bittersweet tears. "I truly appreciate all you and Sally have done for us."

Hunter put his arm around her and squeezed her shoulders. "Yeah, you folks sure have made everything a whole lot easier on us." He released her and joined his brother-in-law at the bottom of the stairs. "Let's you and me go take care of this, but you be sure and take some tea with us before you head back to town."

The men left for the hillside behind the house and Penny went inside to get the tea things ready. By the time they came back, she had rustled up a flapjack mix and was ladling the batter onto the hot, fat greased griddle, a plate full of the hot griddle cakes already piling up on the cabinet beside the stove.

"Well, I didn't expect you ta go to that much trouble," Matt said as he sat down at the table.

"It helps to keep busy," Penny replied as she flipped over a flapjack. "Keeps my mind off things I'd rather not be thinking about."

"Yeah," Hunter agreed with a sigh as he sat down in his usual chair at the head of the table. "One moment I'm grateful Wyatt's gone, happy to get on with my life. The next moment, I'm wishing things could have been different."

Penny flipped over the rest of the cakes on the griddle before she turned to look at Hunter.

"Was he always like ... that? The way he was at the dance, and after, when he ... kidnapped me?" She wanted to believe it was not so. She could never fathom how any person could be intentionally evil.

"No," Hunter said, leaning back in his chair and crossing his arms over his chest. "Wyatt always was a mite persnickety. Had strange little habits, always wanted things done just so or he couldn't sit still until they were set right to his liking."

Hunter paused. He smiled sadly, "But we had us some good times, that's for sure. His ma used to school all the kids in town, and Wyatt himself was right smart. Smarter than all the rest of us. Came up with all sorts of ideas for how we could make learning more fun. But when his ma died of the fever, it was like something died inside Wyatt, too. He weren't never quite the same again."

Matt nodded his agreement. "Working for his pa didn't help any," he added. "He just got meaner and ornerier until I couldn't tell a difference between Amos Blackwell and Wyatt Blackwell. I never figured he'd go this far, though."

"Me neither," Hunter said. "All I can figure is that it must've been a slow change we didn't hardly see. Add to that, we didn't see much of him for the last five years or so."

"It's just too bad, is what it is," Matt said, shaking his head sadly. "I thought for sure he was going to turn out the best of us all, seeing he was so much smarter than the rest of us."

"We all did."

Penny listened while she busied herself with serving the light meal and pouring the tea. She remembered something that Evie had often told her.

"We all have a choice about what we do with our hard times, Penny. They can make us bitter people without hope, or they can make us better people, full of hope. And the only way we can make sure they do the latter is to hold on to the faith that there is still good in the world, and that we have a good Father in Heaven, who won't let us be tempted with more than we can bear."

Dear God, help me hold onto that faith, Penny prayed silently. *And help Hunter, too.*

Chapter Thirty

Sheriff Grosvenor was true to his word. A circuit judge arrived in Four Horse a week after Penny and Hunter's night of terror. The inquisition was held in Ned's Lucky Horseshoe Saloon, simply because it was the biggest building in town, with the most available chairs.

Hunter sat next to Penny, gripping her hand tightly while the townsfolk dribbled in, slowly filling up the seats.

He looked pensively at his wife, wondering if she could sense what he was feeling, sitting in a saloon with the question of his innocence or guilt hanging in the balance, and a wall full of liquor to his left. The shelves full of bottles and kegs were hidden behind a sheet that Ned had tacked up for the inquiry, but everybody knew what was behind that poor camouflage.

Penny must have felt his eyes on her because she met his gaze with a questioning expression.

"Are you nervous?" he asked her.

"Not in the least," Penny said with a little toss of her head, her green eyes indomitable behind her spectacles. "I believe in you, no matter what anybody else says."

Hunter wished he could kiss her right there, but it didn't seem like a fitting time or place. He simply squeezed her hand and smiled, hoping she'd know how much her words meant to him.

The sound of a swishing robe and a man clearing his throat, arrested their attention and Hunter faced forward in time to see the judge sweep in behind the table that had been set up as the judge's podium. Another, smaller table and chair to the left of the judge, had been set up for the witnesses.

First to testify was Sheriff Grosvenor. He sat to attention as he gave his report and then answered the judge's questions about his investigation in a clear and concise manner, his strong, confident voice ringing through the saloon. If that was where it had ended, it would have been an open and shut case, Hunter thought.

Next on the stand was Jasper Knight, one of the late Wyatt's tenants. Sheriff Grosvenor was the one asking the questions now.

"Mr. Knight, could you tell us about your former landlord, the late Mr. Wyatt Blackwell?"

Mr. Knight nodded. He was a lean, wiry old farmer with thin, graying hair and scraggly whiskers, but he had a keen eye and a quick wit.

"That Blackwell, he liked things his way, he did," Mr. Knight began. "Spent a lot of time inspecting everything I did on the land he leased me. Told me how I should clear the land, how I should plow, how I should plant, how I should harvest. Wanted me to sell my cows one season, when I had a poor crop of melons and got behind on my rent. I told him not a chance, promised I'd pay him double soon as the next batch of calves was ready for market."

"Can you tell us how Mr. Blackwell reacted?" Sheriff Grosvenor cut in.

"Sure can," Mr. Knight replied. "He got almighty upset, nigh on pitched a fit right there in my own parlor. Next thing I know, my cows are getting ripped by wolves, one by one. Five nights in a row. Well, you can bet I sold 'em then, and old Blackwell, he was there the very next day, holding out his hand for his money. Funny thing was, though, I never told him I'd sold 'em, but it was like he knew already."

"Did you have trouble with wolves preying on your stock before then?" the sheriff asked.

"Naw, not like that, I didn't. Sure, I'd have a calf stolen here and there. Sometimes a yearling. I don't know how he did it. Maybe it weren't wolves, maybe it was dogs. I never saw 'em attacking, myself. Just saw what was left of my cows."

"Thank you, Mr. Knight. That'll be all."

Mr. Knight returned to his seat, avoiding Hunter's eyes. Hunter looked a Penny to gauge her reaction. She looked perplexed.

The next witness, another character witness, was also one of Wyatt's tenants. Mr. Jameson. He told the story of how his barn had mysteriously burned down after Wyatt had insisted that he tear it down and build a bigger one.

One by one the late Mr. Blackwell's tenants came forward, recounting stories of tongue lashings from their landlord, cattle and sheep being poisoned, crops being burned down overnight, the family dog disappearing and later found drowned.

Hunter listened, wondering why nobody had stepped up sooner, why nobody had spoken up sooner. Why had they let Wyatt ride roughshod over them? Surely, they had known they would have help from the other townsfolk?

The next to testify was Penny. Hunter watched her walk to the stand, wishing he could spare her the ordeal and yet filled with a sense of admiration for the way she carried her petite frame so regally, so purposefully to the witness table.

Sheriff Grosvenor asked her about the first time she had met Wyatt, what her impression had been of him and what had happened at the dance. She answered every question truthfully and concisely, keeping her eyes fixed on the sheriff. Not once did her gaze flicker in Hunter's direction as she listened carefully before answering.

The sheriff was the perfect gentleman throughout, clearly sensitive to the terror she must have endured. He kept the pivotal question for last.

"Mrs. Blakely, were you able to see who shot first? Mr. Blackwell, or your husband, Mr. Blakely."

Penny shook her head. "I'm afraid not, Sheriff Grosvenor," she replied. "Mr. Blackwell had just pushed me aside when they both shot at almost exactly the same time. I was falling, trying not to land in a cactus."

A smattering of whispers greeted that tongue-in-cheek response. How Penny could still entertain a sense of humor in that situation amazed Hunter, and he loved her for it.

"But I did see that Mr. Blackwell had his gun out long before Hunter, that is, my husband, had even drawn his. Or, at least, I knew it, since Mr. Blackwell's gun was pressed against my temple, out of my line of sight," Penny continued. "I am convinced that, especially considering that my husband sustained a bullet wound to his shoulder, Mr. Blackwell aimed to kill him and that my husband shot Mr. Blackwell in an attempt to save his own life. And mine."

Sheriff Grosvenor thanked Penny and dismissed her from the witness table. Penny walked back to her seat the same way she had left it, looking outwardly unruffled and stoic, but when she sat down and Hunter took her hand, he could feel that she was trembling.

"I'd like to call Mrs. Ida Louise Aylward to the witness stand," Sheriff Grosvenor said, before Hunter could congratulate or comfort his wife.

Penny caught his eye. *Mrs. Aylward?* she mouthed, her eyes wide with surprise and foreboding.

Hunter pursed his lips together. He'd had an inkling that might happen. The lady was Wyatt's cousin, after all. She and her son might well be his only living relatives, if Hunter wasn't mistaken. It was only to be expected that she would be called to the stand. It wouldn't surprise him if she had been the one to call for an enquiry.

"Mrs. Aylward, what was your relationship to the deceased, Mr. Wyatt Montgomery Blackwell?" Sheriff Grosvenor opened his questioning.

"He is, was, my cousin on my mother's side," Mrs. Aylward said her face expressionless, her narrow shoulders pulled back at the top of a ramrod straight spine, her hands clasped tightly in her lap.

"And would you care to tell us what your personal relationship with your cousin Wyatt was like?"

Mrs. Aylward looked over at Hunter, her eyes cold. He felt his heart grow heavy. He wished he could spare her the pain of having to answer, but when she began to speak, her eyes still fixed on him, he began to wonder if she would have taken a way out even if it had been offered.

"My cousin was a hard man, sheriff," she said. "Took after his pa, he did. Didn't have time for mollycoddling and soft-soaping folks. First time I met him, I was sixteen and was his nurse for a while, when his mama took ill just after he was born. After she got well again, I went back to my folks in San Francisco. Five years later I met my husband, Earle Aylward, and we had us a little boy of our own."

“That’s your son, Peter, ain’t it?” the sheriff enquired.

“Yes. Peter James Aylward. He’s the one stands to inherit all of Wyatt’s property.”

“I see, and how soon after that did you see your cousin again?”

“Fifteen years,” Mrs. Aylward said. “My husband passed on and I was left alone with my boy. Wyatt’s pa, Amos, he had me come to Four Horse, gave us a house in town. Had me doing his books for him, since Milly was with the angels by then.”

“Did Mr. Blackwell’s father treat you well?”

“He never raised his hand to me, if that’s what you mean,” Mrs. Aylward said. “I never gave him the chance. But he scared me.”

“Scared you? Why?”

“He could get terrible mean, that Amos. A temper like the devil. You got out of his way when he walked into a room in a black mood, no question. I’m sorry to say, Wyatt got the worst of it. He didn’t have anywhere he could run to.”

Hunter wondered how he’d missed all of this. A body thought you knew people, but it was beginning to dawn on him that probably everybody had two lives in some sense. The life everybody else saw, and the life they really lived. Sometimes those were very nearly the same, like Sally and Matt’s, and sometimes they were worlds apart. Like Wyatt’s, and Penny’s. Like his own.

“What happened when Mr. Blackwell’s father passed on?”

Hunter couldn’t help noticing the sheriff’s voice was softer, gentler than before. He sounded more like a father speaking to an injured child than a sheriff holding an inquiry.

"Well, Wyatt took over. He picked up right where his pa left off."

"And did he treat you better than his father?"

Mrs. Aylward paused. "No. I was scared of him, too, truth be told. He wanted Peter to come work for him, but I wasn't having any of that. I sent Peter off to boarding school. I had money Wyatt and his pa didn't know about. Money that Earle left for Peter and me. I was laying it by for my boy's college education." She shrugged. "He never did get that college education his pa dreamed about."

"I have two more questions, Mrs. Aylward, if you'll bear with me," Sheriff Grosvenor said.

Mrs. Aylward nodded.

"Do you know anything about your late cousin's relationship to Mr. Hunter Blakely?"

Mrs. Aylward turned her hard eyes on Hunter again. "Sure, I do. Wyatt didn't keep that a secret from anyone. He hated Mr. Blakely. Especially after Wyatt's fiancé, Amy, ran off with Mr. Blakely. Wyatt was ranting one day, yelling and screaming about how his oldest friend had stolen his only love and how he was going to make him pay."

"Did you think he would do it? Make him pay, that is?"

"No. I figured it was all blusteration. And he laid off talking about revenge after young Amy died of the childbed fever, although he blamed Mr. Blakely for her death. Said it was blind justice or something like that. Said Mr. Blakely deserved to suffer. But when Mr. Blakely got married again, well, Wyatt went back at it. Ranting and raving for hours."

"Thank you, Mrs. Aylward. I know this cain't be easy for you to talk about, but I have one last question for you. Do you think your cousin, Mr. Wyatt Blackwell, was capable of attacking Mr. Blakely and trying to kill him?"

Mrs. Aylward paused a moment, looking right into Hunter's eyes. "Yes, I do. Mr. Blakely never hurt a fly. Wyatt, now, he was crazy enough to do a thing like that. There ain't a doubt in my mind."

"Thank you, Mrs. Aylward, you may return to your seat."

Hunter's ears began to buzz after that. He hardly heard the rest of Sheriff Grosvenor's presentation to the judge. Penny was gripping his hand, squeezing it over and over. He could feel her joy pulsating through him. His legs felt shaky.

At last, the judge cleared his throat. Hunter focused on him as best he could.

"From what I've heard today, and thanks to Sheriff Grosvenor's most commendable and thorough investigation, I find no evidence to suggest that Mr. Hunter Blakely shot Mr. Wyatt Blackwell for any reason other than the preservation of his own life, and the life of his wife. I therefore rule self-defense in this case. This enquiry is hereby concluded."

The room began to buzz with voices. The judge nodded at Hunter, giving him the shadow of a smile. Then he pulled out a gleaming fountain pen, signed a document in front of him with a flourish, and held it out for the sheriff.

The sheriff took the document, signed it himself and then blew on the ink while he carried the document across to where Hunter sat.

"In case anybody tries to lynch you," he said with a wink and handed the paper to Hunter.

"Thank you, sir," Hunter heard his voice say as if it came from somewhere outside of himself.

As soon as the judge and the sheriff were out of the door, Penny flung her arms around his neck and the townsfolk clamored around him.

"We never did cotton to that Wyatt Blackwell," someone said.

"Just never could prove he'd done anything," another voice added.

"We're sure grateful you and your missus stood up to that bully," someone else chimed in.

Hands slapped him on the back, grabbed his hand and shook it, patted his shoulder and tousled his hair. He wanted to be alone with Penny. He wanted to go home and sleep until he couldn't sleep any longer, huddled up against his wife's warm, soft body. In silence.

As the well-wishers began to drift away, still talking excitedly about the events that had shaken their sleepy town, Hunter noticed Mrs. Aylward standing a few feet away, her hands clasped in front of her. She had a strange look on her face.

"Mrs. Aylward," Hunter began, wanting to say something to her, but not really knowing what, or how.

"Hush, Mr. Blakely," she said, stepping closer. "It's me who needs to say something to you."

Hunter nodded and stood to his feet. It felt wrong to sit while a lady was standing in front of him. Penny linked her arm through his and stood up, too.

"Mr. Blakely, Mrs. Blakely," Mrs. Aylward said stiffly. "I ain't been fair to the both of you. I'll be honest, I knew about your drinking, Mr. Blakely. I can see it a mile away. You see, my husband was a drunkard, and he beat me something awful. Died of drink, he did. But he was smart, too. Knew how to make money without working hard. Anyhow, I figured you were the same, just a no-account drunkard. I reckon I thought about as much of you as Wyatt did, if not less."

Hunter looked down at his shoes. He should have known. He wondered how many others knew.

"But I see now I was wrong about you, Mr. Blakely, and I reckon it's nothing less than my duty to apologize to you both. That's one reason I requested the enquiry. I wanted to be sure folks knew who you really are. And who Wyatt really was. I hope y'all can find it in your hearts to forgive me."

"Oh, dear, no, Mrs. Aylward, there's no need to apologize. I sure was a no-account drunk until Penny here—"

Mrs. Aylward held up her hand. "I ain't done, yet, Mr. Blakely," she said stiffly. "I reckon I owe you the whole truth if I'm going to tell you the truth at all. Like the good book says, the truth will set you free."

Hunter nodded, wondering what was coming next.

"It was me who told Wyatt that you two were at the dance. He didn't think you'd go, but after I helped deliver the Morgan baby, I went to him and told him. I figured if I didn't, and he found out, he'd take it out on me later. I really ought to have warned the whole town against him a lot sooner. I knew a long time ago that boy was capable of vile things."

"Oh, Mrs. Aylward," Penny blurted out, stepping forward and taking the woman's hand. "We don't hold that against you. Wyatt was a dangerous man. You were powerless against him. Besides," she glanced back at Hunter before she continued, "I'll own I'm rather glad everything came to a head quickly. I don't think I could have stood that situation dragging out for months on end."

Mrs. Aylward held her head high, her hand unresponsive in Penny's eager grasp. "Truth be told, I figured that cousin of mine was headed for an early end. Just didn't know when it would be or who'd go down with him." Her eyes were veiled and hard, but they glistened with unshed tears.

Hunter stepped forward, his heart breaking for the woman who had been so mistreated, so misunderstood.

"Mrs. Aylward, let's let bygones be bygones. I sure hope you'll come on down to the ranch sometime for a pot of tea."

"Thank you, kindly, Mr. Blakely, I reckon I will." She broke off then, nodded what appeared to be a choked-up goodbye and abruptly left, her shoulders twitching.

Penny slipped her arm around Hunter's waist as they watched her go.

"I think we just made ourselves the most unlikely friend, Hunter," she said, her voice full of tremulous, vibrant hope.

***

A few days later, with his family safely home and his shoulder healing well, Hunter found himself with a sketch pad and some pencils, sitting under the old oak tree that shaded the small corral. It was late afternoon and the townsfolk, who had been helping him and Matt rebuild the burned down stables, had all gone home for the day.

Hamish came running over from the house, his eyes bright. Penny was following slowly behind him, watching Maisie chase insects in the warm afternoon air.

"What are you doing, Pa?" he asked eagerly.

"I figured I'd do some drawing again," Hunter said. "Helps me forget the bad things."

Hamish's eyes widened. "Can you draw something for me, Pa?"

"Sure, I can. Name it!" Hunter said with a chuckle.

"Draw me a picture of Big Red, running like the wind," Hamish said.

Hunter smiled and began to draw. But he didn't just draw Big Red, he drew a boy. A boy who looked just like Hamish, riding the horse bareback, his hands gripping Big Red's mane, his feet flung out in carefree abandon, his head thrown back and his mouth wide with laughter.

Hamish stared, transfixed, as the image took shape before his eyes. Penny stepped closer, with Maisie on her hip, the little girl chattering away in her baby gibberish.

"Look, Aunt Penny!" Hamish said in an overawed whisper as she came to stand over them, peering at the object of Hamish's interest.

"Oh, my! That *is* beautiful, Hunter! Utterly beautiful!"

Hunter smiled up at her. A look of dawning realization spread across Penny's face.

"If I wrote a story, would you draw the pictures for me, Hunter?" she asked, her eyes dancing with anticipation.

"Of course, my love. I'll do anything for you," he said, his heart overflowing with joy and contentment.

"I don't doubt that for a moment," Penny said. Then she leaned over and kissed him on the mouth.

Epilogue

A high-pitched squeal rent the midsummer air, followed by a torrent of shrieking laughter. Penny looked up from the book in her lap. The bright sunshine made her squint.

"Hamish! Don't let your sister trip and fall, now, you hear?"

"Yes, Mama!" Hamish flung over his shoulder as he chased down the almost three-year-old who had recently begun to move with astonishing speed for her age. Penny smiled. She loved it that Hamish was calling her Mama too, now.

She remembered when he had just turned seven years old a few months back. He'd been in the middle of reading a story when his head popped up and he looked at Penny with consternation written all over his face.

"You know, Aunt Penny," he had said. "Now that Maisie's learning to say so many words, and she's calling you Mama, and you and Pa are telling her I'm her brother, well, I figure it just might confuse her too much if I keep calling you Aunt Penny."

Penny had kept her face grave, even though she longed to set free the smile that was tugging at the corners of her mouth. She didn't want him to think she was laughing at him.

"I suppose that could be true, Hamish. What do you suggest we should do about that?"

Hamish had sat up at that point, abandoning his customary position of lying on his stomach while he read, and regarded her with a deep crease forming between his eyes.

"Well, I was wondering, would it bother you a heap if I called you Mama?"

Tears had leapt into Penny's eyes at that point.

"I'd love for you to call me Mama," she had said. "But only if that's what you really want to call me."

Hamish had nodded slowly, his eyes still thoughtful. "I reckon my other Mama won't mind, since she's in Heaven with Jesus and the angels, and you're married to my Pa."

"I'm sure she'll be happy as long as you're happy, dear Hamish."

The frown on Hamish's face had smoothed into a smile. "Yeah, I reckon you're right, Aunt ... I mean, Mama." Then he'd grinned and run into her arms, giving her the biggest, tightest hug she could ever remember.

Watching him now, Penny knew she would never forget that moment, as long as she lived. She leaned back against the sturdy trunk of the oak tree and caressed the large bump below her bodice, letting the book fall to the quilt she sat on.

Hunter emerged from the house, carrying a tray with a pitcher and tumblers. He walked over to where Penny sat, his eyes full of adoration.

"Are you comfortable, my love?" he asked as he kneeled and set down the tray on the low table that stood in the shade beside the quilt.

"A pillow would help. Won't you be a dear and pass me one?" Penny said.

"I'll do you one better," Hunter said with a wink. He picked up one of the pillows lying on the quilt and carried it to where Penny lay against the tree trunk. "Here," he said, kneeling down beside her and offering his hand. When she took hold of it, he pulled her upright. Then he held the pillow in place behind her back and eased her back down.

"You weren't kidding," Penny said, lifting her face to his. He kissed her gently.

The sound of horse's hooves accompanied by the jingle and rattle of a buggy made them both look in the direction of the yard. Happy voices cried out in greeting as the horse drawn vehicle came into sight and headed for the stables.

"Sally! Matt!" Penny cried out, waving vigorously. Hamish scooped up a squealing Maisie and staggered over to the quilt where Penny sat. He plopped the little girl beside her adoptive mother.

"Hello, Hunter! Hello, Penny, dear!" Sally's voice rang out as Matt helped her down. "I hope you folks don't mind—we brought Mrs. Aylward along with us, and the Winters said they'd like to join in, too! They should be arriving in the next few minutes. Oh, my hat! Isn't this all just so exciting? You're a real published author, Penny! I'm pretty sure you're the first published author Four Horse has ever had. I declare, we should have a monument set up."

Sally was tripping across the grass as she spoke, carrying a large square basket with a tea towel draped over the top. She stepped right up to where Penny sat, smiling and feeling a little flustered. She wasn't used to being the center of attention.

"I hardly think I deserve a monument. It's just a children's book, and I couldn't have done it without my talented illustrator," she said, blushing and giving Hunter a coy glance. "And I'm very glad you brought Mrs. Aylward and the Winters along."

The lady in question was helping two-year-old Simon Peter Morgan off the buggy and holding his hand as he tottered along toward the quilt, jabbering away with excitement.

"Look!" Hamish said. "Simon's happy to see all of us!"

"Yes, he is," Hunter said, striding over to the buggy so he could help Matt unhitch the Morgans' horse. "I'll bet he's happiest to see you and Maisie, though."

"Good morning, Mrs. Aylward," Penny said.

Mrs. Aylward nodded curtly. "A good morning to you, as well. Are you well?" Her eyes drifted toward Penny's stomach.

Penny smiled. She was glad Mrs. Aylward had quietly agreed to be the newest Blakely's godmother but wished the woman could be more comfortable around them. It seemed she still felt guilty for not warning the town about Wyatt's worsening mental condition.

Penny smiled at her and was rewarded with the ghost of a smile in return. But if she was not mistaken, there was a consistent pattern of improvement in the widow's demeanor. She seemed a little more relaxed, more at peace, each time Penny saw her. All she needed was time. Time and patience and heaps of kindness.

Between herself and Hunter, Sally and Matt, and even the Winters, there was enough kindness to go around and then some to spare. Penny lay back on her pillow again and savored the deep sense of fulfilment that settled over her. She had only one regret. She wished Evie and Sarah could be celebrating with her.

The Winters arrived moments later, and there was a flurry of activity while ladies bustled around getting the picnic fare all set out and the drinks poured, while still protecting their sumptuous luncheon from overly eager toddler's fingers.

At last, everyone was settled, grace was said, and the repast thoroughly enjoyed by all present. Fried chicken, cured ham, pickles, fresh greens, and a generous, delicious potato salad made from a recipe that had been handed down through generations by Jerry Winters' German forebears, as Mrs. Winters proudly reminded her companions.

The conversation was lively and spirited. The women talking about recipes and gardening, moving on to their children and the shenanigans they got up to. The men lounged about, earnestly debating the virtues and vices of the Dawes Act. Penny listened with half an ear, wishing she could join in, but not having the energy.

The meal was rounded off with a delicious lemon meringue pie that Mrs. Aylward had brought along.

"What's those calf slobbers on the top?" Hunter asked, tongue in cheek.

"Why, you know as well as I do that's meringue," Penny chided him laughingly.

"Had to at least take a shot at turning you ladies off it," Hunter teased. "Looks plumb good enough to eat all by myself!"

"I don't mind eating calf slobbers, either, Pa," Hamish said, giggling hysterically. "I'll help you put that away, for sure!"

The pie washed down beautifully with some vanilla milk Penny had made that morning and the company began to settle down, even the children's eyelids drooping contentedly under the weight of their full bellies and satisfied palates.

The wind whispered and birds tittered amongst the leaves of the large, spreading oak tree. The summer grasses beyond the homestead waved and rippled in the sunlight. In the far corral the horses grazed peacefully, every now and then lying down to take a luxurious roll in the dirt.

Penny closed her eyes and began to doze.

“Tell us a story, please, Mama,” Hamish said, plopping down beside her and laying his head on her lap.

“Story!” Maisie agreed from her perch on Hunter’s shoulders. She clapped her hands and squealed happily.

“Oh, I don’t think so, dears,” Penny said. “Not now. I’ll tell you both a story tonight at bedtime.”

“But I also want to hear a story,” Mrs. Winters said. “I’ve heard so much about the fabled tales that Penny Blakely weaves out of thin air, or so it’s been described to me.”

Penny laughed.

“Yes, why don’t you tell us all a story, Penny?” Sally urged her. “The whole reason we’re here is to celebrate your book being published, after all, and I reckon I’m in the mood for some harmless entertainment myself, anyhow.”

Penny shook her head, still laughing. “I don’t know what it is, but the longer I am with child, the less I seem able to focus on anything for more than half a minute.”

“You could read us one of the stories in your book,” Matt said. “That’ll be a treat, and no need for you to think up something new.”

“Yeah, ain’t nobody can give a story its due like the author can. We’ll pretend we’re at some fancy library in the big city, and you can pretend to be Charles Dickens, reading your own book to a captivated audience,” Hunter suggested with a grin.

“Oh, well, that wouldn’t be too much of a stretch,” Penny said, raising one eyebrow. “After all, my *nom de plume* is

Pendleton Blake, and I am most certainly not a man, so pretense is already well established in my limited collection of skills."

Hunter laughed, as did the rest of the company.

"Read us your favorite one, Penny," Sally said, caressing Simon's baby curls where he lay dozing in her lap.

"Oh, well that would have to be the story about Prince Hamish the Kind," Penny said, giving Hamish a wink. His eyes grew wide as he stared up at her.

"You put Prince Hamish's story in your book?" he said, aghast.

"As your pa would say, 'You bet ya I did, scuttlebug!'"

Hamish sat up straight. "So, children all over the world will hear it?"

Penny laughed. "Well, I'm not so sure about all over the world, but certainly there will be many children in our nation who will hear all about Prince Hamish the Kind."

"Well, then, what are we waiting for?" Mrs. Aylward said, making herself comfortable in one of the low wooden outdoor chairs that Matt had made for sitting under the old oak.

Penny smiled, picked up the book still lying by her side and first caressed the cover, printed with gold embossed writing. *Once Upon a Rainbow – A Collection of Children's Stories, by Pendleton Blake, Illustrations by Hunter Blakely.* She found herself marveling, for the umpteenth time, at the knowledge that her dream had come true. A dream that was one of many, most of which she had hardly dared to dream. She had everything her heart had ever wished for, secret desires of her soul woven into all of her stories.

A loving, doting husband for herself; a father for Hamish; a delightful, adopted daughter whom she loved like her own child; a supportive extended family in Sally and Matt and even Mrs. Aylward; a community she knew she was loved and accepted in.

Then there were the things she hadn't even imagined could be hers. The beautiful horses that had helped her conquer her fear of large animals. Add to that, the fact that she had learned to ride, winging across the hills, the wind tugging playfully at her hair. The wild, rugged Black Hills themselves and the Arizona monsoons that had given her a broader view of the awesome greatness of her Creator.

But the greatest miracle of all, her own tiny babe, growing inside of her, the precious culmination of her and Hunter's love for each other. She stroked her growing belly and then opened the book, riffling through the pages until she found the right place.

She cleared her throat and began to read.

"Once upon a time, in a land far, far from here, there lived a prince named Hamish the Kind. Prince Hamish lived in a palace, as you might imagine any prince would, dear children, but the palace Prince Hamish lived in was not any kind of palace you've ever seen, or, I dare say, even heard of."

A contented, indulgent grin plastered itself across Hamish's face. His big, ocean blue eyes stared up into the waving branches of the oak tree above. Penny knew he was seeing that palace already, imagining the stars twinkling in the night sky beyond the palm trees. Imagining his Mama Evie and Aunt Sarah dancing to an orchestra of forest animals, beneath the huge hammock full of pillows.

Two bittersweet tears collected at the corners of Penny's eyes, and a lump in her throat threatened to silence her altogether, but she took a deep breath and continued on, telling the fantastic adventures of the kindhearted Prince Hamish.

If only her precious nephew knew how truly the character in the story reflected the character of the boy who had inspired his creation. But then, perhaps it was better he didn't. The kindness that is not aware that it is being kind, but simply responds with compassion and empathy, is the truest kindness.

At last, the story came to an end, with all the characters living happily ever after in their decidedly unusual palace, with the addition of a handsome prince for Princess Penelope, of course. The adults nodded and smiled, congratulating Penny on a remarkable, imaginative and original story. The children had all fallen asleep. That is, all except Hamish.

"I think I'd like to write stories one day, Mama," he said, his eyes dreamy. "I'll write stories about horses like Big Red and Black Bess and make up exciting adventures for them. I think I'd like that."

"And I think you'll write the most wonderful, stories, Hamish," Penny said, ruffling his brown curls. Her heart still felt heavy, but she didn't want to break the happy, contented mood of the picnic. As Sally had pointed out, it was meant to be a celebration.

All at once, she wanted to be alone with Hunter. She put the book down and sat up straight.

"I think I'd like to go for a walk, if nobody minds," she said, looking at Hunter, silently begging his support.

"I'm so sleepy from that wonderful meal and that story, I reckon a nice doze will be just the ticket for me," Sally said, throwing Matt a meaningful look. Matt simply grunted, pulled his hat over his eyes and lay back on a pillow.

"Could do with forty winks myself," he muttered.

"I'll watch the children for you," Mrs. Aylward said, her eyes almost tender.

"Jerry and I don't mind at all, Penny," Mrs. Winters said, as she pulled some crochet work out of the small craft bag she often carried with her on picnics.

Hunter stood up and helped Penny to her feet. "Mind if I tag along, love?"

"Of course not," Penny said, linking her arm into his.

They left the shade of the oak and wandered off in no specific direction. The most scorching heat of the day was past, and a cool breeze had sprung up. Penny sighed, filling her lungs to their very depths and exhaling until there was nothing left in them.

"Better not sigh too many of those," Hunter said impishly. "Where that sigh fell, ain't no grass ever going to grow again."

Penny laughed softly and laid her head against his shoulder while they walked, still headed for the hillside behind the ranch house.

"I really am happy, Hunter. So many dreams have come true for me. I've been blessed beyond what I ever thought possible. I've found hope and a reason to rise each day with the new sun."

She paused. Hunter didn't say a word.

"I just wish Evie and Sarah could have been here to see all of this. To see how Hamish adores you and looks up to you. To see how happy and fulfilled I am. To see my book being published."

Hunter gave a soft grunt, one which made her feel like he understood exactly what she meant.

"They would have been so proud of me. They always believed in me, and I believe that the faith they had in me is partly the reason I wrote a book at all, in the first place."

Penny sighed again.

"Easy there. I'll want to keep some grazing for my horses," Hunter said, kissing her on the top of her head.

"Oh, you're incorrigible!" Penny laughed, nudging her husband in the ribs. Then she looked up at him with pleading eyes. "I'm sure you wish Amy could be here to see how Maisie's growing up, to see what a happy, energetic little girl she is."

"Yeah," Hunter conceded. "Already showing the signs of turning into a right little Cattle Kate, that one. Just like her mama. Rode and roped like any cowboy worth his salt, Amy did, and I'll wager Maisie's going ta follow right in her mama's footsteps."

Then he stopped and took Penny's chin in his hand, turning her face so she had to look at him.

Penny's heart fluttered at the look in his eyes. They were deeply earnest. No, passionate. No, filled with a fire she couldn't put words to.

"If they were here, though, Amy and Evie and Sarah, I ain't so sure we'd be here, you and me, together like this. I ain't so sure this little peanut would be here either." His hand dropped to her belly, caressing it gently. "And I ain't sure I rightly know what I'd rather choose."

Penny gazed into his eyes, a sense of awe filling her. The man she had thought was a useless drunk when she first met him, was in fact a pillar of strength, wisdom and courage. She felt giddy and euphoric, as if she were falling in love with him all over again.

"If there's one thing these last three years have taught me, it's that I ain't in charge, and just as well, 'cause I would've got the wrong pig by the tail every decision I made, if I were. We can ask why we lose folks we love. We can ask why things don't pan out how we hoped, but that'll get us nowhere fast. All that matters is right now. What we got right now. Where we're at right now. Who we're loving. Right now."

He had come to stand in front of her and taken her face in his hands, just like that night in the Winters' barn, when he kissed her for the very first time. Penny's hands slipped around his waist and up his back as she stepped closer to him. That jolt of joy never failed to fill her when their bodies touched, and this time she could feel their child between them, surrounded, protected, hedged in by their closeness.

His face was so close to hers, it filled her entire vision, his eyes burning into hers. Everything he had just said sounded so simple, almost too simple, and yet Penny knew it was true.

All through her gloomy days of melancholy, she'd either been looking back at a past she couldn't change or looking forward to a future conjured up by her darkest fears. And all the time, she'd missed where she was in each moment, what she had in each moment, who she loved in each moment.

She would never forget her sisters, she knew that, and Hunter would never forget Amy. And that was good and right. But what the two of them had together in the glorious present, was equally precious and equally deserving of her full attention. The sense of heaviness began to lift off of her, and the painful ache of loss softened into tender remembrance.

"Did I ever tell you you're the best thing that ever happened to me, Hunter Blakely?"

He smiled and drew her head closer, kissing her deeply.

"I'm pretty sure you have, Penny Blakely, but I reckon I can stand hearing it a few million more times."

THE END

Also by Ava Winters

Thank you for reading "**Learning to Love Her Fearful Rancher**"!

I hope you enjoyed it! If you did, here are some of my other books!

My latest Best-Selling Books

#1 An Uninvited Bride on his Doorstep

#2 Once upon an Unlikely Marriage of Convenience

#3 Their Unlikely Marriage of Convenience

#4 An Orphaned Bride to Love Him Unconditionally

#5 An Unexpected Bride for the Lonely Cowboy

Also, if you liked this book, you can also check out **my full Amazon Book Catalogue at: https://go.avawinters.com/bc-authorpage**

Thank you for allowing me to keep doing what I love! ❤

Printed in Great Britain
by Amazon